In the Belly
of the
SPHINX

In the Belly
of the
SPHINX

a novel

GRANT BUDAY

BRINDLE
AND GLASS

Edited by Claire Philipson
Copy edited by Senica Maltese
Cover design by Jazmin Welch
Interior design by Sara Loos

CATALOGUING DATA AVAILABLE FROM LIBRARY AND ARCHIVES CANADA
ISBN 9781990071157 (softcover)
ISBN 9781990071164 (electronic)

TouchWood Editions acknowledges that the land on which we live and work is within the traditional territories of the Lkwungen (Esquimalt and Songhees), Malahat, Pacheedaht, Scia'new, T'Sou-ke and WSÁNEĆ (Pauquachin, Tsartlip, Tsawout, Tseycum) peoples.

We acknowledge the financial support of the Government of Canada through the Canada Book Fund and the Canada Council for the Arts, and of the Province of British Columbia through the British Columbia Arts Council and the Book Publishing Tax Credit.

This book is a work of fiction. Names, characters, places, and incidents are either products of the author's imagination or are used fictitiously. Any resemblance to actual events or locales or persons, living or dead, is entirely coincidental.

This book was printed using FSC®-certified, acid-free papers, processed chlorine free, and printed with soya-based inks.

Printed in Canada

27 26 25 24 23 1 2 3 4 5

And where, I ask you, can a man escape to,
when he hasn't enough madness left inside him? —Céline

1874

FLORENCE FOUND A SEAT IN the third-class coach of the New York to Chicago train amid shouting men, screaming children, and exhausted women. The air was thick with the smells of bodies and smoke and beer. She cradled her satchel and avoided eye contact. Were people looking at her? Certainly, the men stared; the women in turn glared at their men. She tried to sleep, but each time she closed her eyes she saw the man and woman lying on the floor, skulls caved. She felt the weight of the rolling pin in her hand, then heard the thud as it dropped. After stuffing the satchel with fob watches and wrist watches and jewellery, she'd started walking, not running but walking, her face neutral though her gaze skating side to side and her ears alert. She'd boarded a train and the next morning crossed the St. Lawrence on a steamer, endured the interminable wait in line through immigration and then the official with the badge on his coat groping her torso with his slow and probing gaze. After that another train, and then the station in New York City, a chaos of kids and dogs and porters and anxious adults criss-crossing and crashing into each other.

Amid all of this she'd seen a man, a soldier, a hussar, in a pompous red uniform, standing on the platform as though posing for a photograph. One black-booted foot propped on his steamer trunk, he'd appeared supremely amused by all he saw; she'd envied and hated him. As she'd walked past, he'd offered to carry her bag; she'd declined. He'd asked her to join him in the dining car; she'd declined that as well, at which his moustache rode his smile like a cresting wave, making her hate him all the more.

Now she jerked awake. All around her silhouettes snored and moaned and whimpered. She wiped the tears from her cheeks. Hungry and yet sick to her stomach, she got to her feet and, hugging her satchel tight to her chest, waded through the sleeping bodies to the end of the coach and slid the door open, feeling the train's click-clack and sway, click-clack and sway, and smelling the smoke and beyond it the fresh fields. They passed a slough and she saw stars in the water and was tempted to jump.

At an early morning stop she descended to the platform. Black men passed back and forth with copper urns strapped to their backs. There he was, the soldier, the hussar, no longer in his full garb, chatting with a vendor ever so affably in his English accent. When he saw Florence, he immediately bought her a coffee and she, shivering, not thinking, dropped her satchel which hit the platform like a sack of sand, grabbed the cup and gulped the whole thing. Handing it back, she burped and thanked him, stooped for her bag, then strode off through the crowd as if she had an urgent appointment.

In Chicago, Pinkertons boarded—grim, officious men with badges on their lapels. Florence was young and tall and stood out. Trying not to panic, she moved through the coaches, satchel under her arm, seeking some nook or corner. She saw grubby faces, sleepy faces, bored faces, hungry faces looking at her and then gazing off. She peered out the window and studied the platform. More Pinkertons. The whistle blew. Soon they would be rolling. Pushing her way past passengers as they stowed their bags, she went out the far door and gripped the handle of the next car, the sleeping coach, but the door wouldn't open. She squinted through the window and saw only a few people in a staid atmosphere; a private parlour of calm and security. Florence looked back at the other coach and thought of a zoo cage full of dogs and monkeys. Without being too obvious, she gave the sleeping car door another try—locked.

"Miss?"

A porter. Cap at a jaunty angle, he looked about forty, with deep creases cutting across his forehead, watching her and no doubt reaching conclusions. How many hundreds of faces he saw every day, scads of confused people, anxious people, excited people, reunions and partings, tears joyful and tears painful.

A door slid open and a voice said, with just a hint of impatience as though Florence was forever late, "There you are."

The hussar signalled with his eyes for her to come up. She did. He reached inside his coat and tossed the porter a half dollar. The fellow snatched it mid-air, nodded his thanks, and touched his brow with the coin. A moment later Florence was in the hussar's berth and he was sliding the door shut and pulling down the blind.

"Excuse me." Leaning past her he looked both ways out the window to the platform, then drew those blinds down as well.

The twilit compartment smelled of wool and gin. Before either he or Florence could speak there was a gathering in the corridor, talk, doors opening and doors slamming, and all of it growing closer. He nodded toward a corner.

There was a sharp rap and a voice enquired, "Greyland-Smith?"

He winked at Florence, who withdrew behind a curtain, then he lifted the latch and opened up. Three faces, a Pinkerton and two clerks, one of whom consulted a clipboard and read his name out again.

"That's correct. How can I help?"

"Just you in the compartment, sir?"

3

"See for yourself." He gestured widely with one arm though did not move to allow anyone in.

The Pinkerton's right eyelid hung half closed, giving him a calculating appearance. He scanned the room.

"Something up?"

"Fugitive. Woman. Young. Tall."

"Tall? Shouldn't be too hard to spot then, eh." Greyland-Smith smiled.

"Sing out if you see her."

"What did she do?"

The Pinkerton regarded Greyland-Smith. "Bludgeoned her employer to death. Husband and wife. Robbed them of everything they had. Up in Canada." The Pinkerton spoke with some satisfaction, laying special emphasis on the word *bludgeoned*.

"Well then, I won't offer her a job, will I."

Again the Pinkerton scanned the room.

Again Greyland-Smith smiled.

"May I ask where you're bound?" The Pinkerton studied his uniform. "Major?"

"Lieutenant-colonel. India."

"Porter says he saw you talking to a tall woman."

"Porter?"

The Pinkerton said something to one of the clerks who went off down the corridor. "India?"

"Yes. Ever been?"

The Pinkerton winced at the absurdity and again his gaze combed the room. The clerk returned with the porter. "This the man?"

The porter made a show of eyeing Greyland-Smith up and down. "No, sir."

"No?"

"No."

"You're sure."

"Definitely."

4

"You said he was in uniform."

"Not that uniform."

The Pinkerton glared. "You see a lot of faces in a given day," he reminded him. "Look again."

He looked again, his gaze travelling up and then down. "No, sir."

The cop waved him away just this side of disgusted. Then he cleared his throat weightily, touched the brim of his bowler, and wished the smiling Englishman a good journey.

For the next five days Florence and Edward Greyland-Smith were never apart. They felt the rhythm of the train and they watched the spread of the land and they knew the draw of the long evening sunlight pulling them west, away from the past and toward the future. One evening, at a fuelling stop in Utah, they lay side by side in the long grass that glowed in the alpine light. He sang "Wild Rover" and she sang "Molly Malone." Together they sang "Red is the Rose." His hand brushed against hers—the only physical contact they'd had so far. Lying there on his back in the grass, a jewel beetle landed on his brow. He crossed his eyes, squinting up to see it. Florence laughed for the first time in months and it felt as if her face were cracking. He lifted the beetle with his forefinger and they studied it: iridescent copper with fine striations as if cut by a jeweller. He lay it upon the back of her ring finger and then recited:

> *There once was a lady on a train*
> *Who rode to escape the pain,*
> *When she arrived at the station*
> *Having crossed the nation*
> *She discovered that she must embark again.*

In San Francisco they spent a week in a hotel in Chinatown. She was often sick, which worried him. Returning to the room with candied ginger one morning, he found her burning her passport in the basin. They made enquiries and were directed to a printer who at first pretended not to understand but whose comprehension improved with each silver dollar laid on the counter. A few days later, they boarded a paddlewheeler to Victoria. Off the coast of Oregon, he was the one who was sick and so Florence procured ginger tea from the galley and helped him drink.

"However did you survive the Atlantic?" she asked.

He groaned as if the very recollection made him feel even worse. "Not much better."

"And you intend to venture across the Pacific, twice as wide?"

"Madness, yes?"

"Study the horizon," she advised.

"Ah, the horizon," he said, as if at a familiar but forever distant acquaintance.

In Victoria they disembarked together and, unused to solid ground, walked the streets as rubber kneed as drunks. In Chinatown they took separate rooms. He said it was a waste of money and she said she had plenty of money and hopefully a future here in Victoria. The next day he appeared in his full uniform and insisted that they have their photograph taken. Two prints were made.

"One for each of us," he said. "You must keep it. In this way I will be able to look into your eyes and you into mine." He slotted the photo of her into his journal, which, she noted, was empty apart from a few dried and crumbling rose petals.

What was he saying? What was he implying? She said, "The photo will go the way of those rose petals. Dust."

"What a glum beast you are," he said with that frown-smile of his.

"Did you not hear the Pinkerton? Do you not understand that I am a murderer? How many times do I have to tell you: I killed and robbed two people. Took everything they had."

He regarded her with bemusement. "I've lost count of how many I've done."

"Do you not wish to know why I did it?"

"All in good time, all in good time."

What a strange notion he had of time given that he was due to sail in a week; she wasn't sure if she was miserable or relieved. She was certainly confused. Holding his photograph, she said, "I don't want to look into the eyes of a dead man."

"Then come with me and keep me safe. Clearly you know how to defend yourself, why not defend me? What is there here for you? It's the edge of the world."

What was this madness? They had walked up and over Beacon Hill and down to the shore and were sitting on a sun-bleached log. Here, she hoped, was a life. She had no desire to traipse about deserts and mountains and jungles. "You've been more than gracious and gentlemanly," she said, "and I will always be grateful. It's been a fairy-tale idyll, but now it is done."

How round his eyes got.

Was he mocking her? She thought him a lout. It occurred to her to fetch him a good sharp rap on the nose. "I don't want to keep running," she added.

He grew uncharacteristically grave. "Then you will need a disguise. You will have to become someone else." He took her right hand and pressed it like a flower between his palms. "Can you do that?"

"I've already done it. More than once. You've seen as much."

He nodded, acknowledging this.

For a moment she wondered why, if he was sincere and not merely passing the time, he couldn't simply resign his commission and stay right here. What was all this business of Empire anyway? Why must men meddle in the affairs of others? Why could the British not simply stay home? They had been the ruin of Ireland, the sepoys in India had mutinied, there had been uprisings and rebellions in Jamaica, and the Native Americans who had not been slaughtered had been imprisoned on reserves.

When would it end? She voiced none of this. Instead, she asked him if he had dreamed of being a cavalry officer as a boy.

"Well, it was that or the coal pit. Don't let the braid mislead you."

"What, you're an imposter?"

He grinned, showing the gap where two teeth were missing. "Well, not as such."

"Then what, as such?"

"In some ways having no options is best. The road is clear. You go and don't look back."

She did not know that she agreed, for she found herself forever looking back. "And here you are gadding about the globe."

He became subdued. "Yes, well, I don't know that *gadding* is the exact word. I was injured."

The thought stabbed her. She looked away, out over the grey-blue water, which seemed low and still and waiting. On the far side stood the mountains of Washington. Just down the shore some Songhees ladies and their children were clamming, the kids yipping and splashing and the women going stolidly about their business in their woven capes and conical caps. At that moment theirs seemed an enviably stable existence. "I don't know what you're saying. Just ... trot along behind the army?" It was well known that armies had long trains of hangers-on, from cooks to washerwomen to procurers to whores. None of those roles much attracted her. What she wanted was peace, not cannon fire.

"Marry me."

He may as well have slapped her. She recoiled. "Don't be daft."

"Why not?" he asked calmly, his gaze steady and tone solemn. "What has Victoria to offer? It's a campsite full of mugs and thugs and chancers."

"And India? China? Afghanistan? What do they have to

offer? Besides fever and snakes and people who frankly wish you'd all pack up and go home?"

He regarded her and for an instant she feared she'd insulted him and he'd be angry. "Why, it has me to offer." And he grinned, his moustache rising and teeth showing, or the teeth he had remaining.

"You *are* mad."

"I'm alive."

"At the moment."

They'd known each other less than a month, and here he was nattering on about marriage. She wondered if his injury had been to his skull and he truly was more than a bit daft. She studied his head for a dent or scar.

"What is the phrase?" he asked, frowning to recall. "Ah, *carpe diem.*"

"Seize the day," she said.

"And," he added, "the night."

"Yes," she said. "I'm sure you are expert at that."

He barked a laugh then thrust his hand up and snatched something out of the air, though when he opened it his palm was empty. He laughed some more as if it was all a great lark. When he saw that she was not laughing along with him he caught her hand and held it tight. Levelling his gaze at her like a man taking aim at a moving target, he vowed: "Let us make the most of the night."

"I believe I've had enough of the night."

"And the stars in the sea?" he enquired.

She did not follow. Yes, a head injury. Perhaps he was not going to India at all. Perhaps he was just going around and around the globe and it had made him dizzy. "Why are you going west to the east? Wouldn't it have been shorter the other way? Wouldn't it have made more sense?"

"But then I wouldn't have met you."

Was he stupid or sublime? "Anyway," she said, "how will

you find me in the night?"

"Easily," he said. "You have a glow." And he framed her aura with both of his hands.

Chapter One

Victoria, British Columbia

WHEN PEARL WAS A CHILD she wanted to join her father on the other side of the glass. She stood on a chair to get as close to him as possible, but the glass over his face was as hard as the wall on which his picture hung, and unlike Alice she could not simply step on through. He was a hussar, an officer. She put her palm to the cool glass and then worried when she saw her fingerprints, for her mother disapproved of fingerprints on windows and mirrors and cleaned them with newsprint and vinegar. Pearl's father gazed at her from wherever he was, which was both near and yet somehow far.

When Pearl got older she understood the difference between photographs and real people. Nine years old and tall for her age, she no longer needed to stand on a chair to study her father. She scratched at her upper lip because the sight of his moustache and whiskers made her itchy. Even the word *whiskers* was itchy. His red uniform was a complex affair, all braids, buttons, and epaulets, with two decorative gold cords that angled from his right shoulder and under his left arm; a third cord ended in two braided acorns. He wore white gloves and his left hand gripped his sword. How calm he seemed, how noble. But she was troubled by his fur hat topped with that white plume. Would it not fall off during a cavalry charge? Pearl had seen men racing horses on Beacon Hill and they often lost their hats. It seemed to her that a pith helmet with a chin strap would be more appropriate, for it would not only protect one's head from the sun but from rocks thrown by enemies. Pith helmets resembled enormous eggs. What sort of bird would lay an egg so large? Ostrich and emu came to mind. She'd seen them in *Birds of the World*. Snakes also laid eggs. How terrible to be a snake and have no arms or legs. Of course, it was a punishment related to that business in the Garden of Eden. Were all snakes, even non-poisonous ones, related to Satan and therefore being punished? And what of worms? These thoughts ran through her mind as she stood on her tiptoes and peered into the photograph until her father's eyes were just bits of grey, like charcoal or graphite.

"He kissed you here and here and here," said her mother, touching Pearl's brow, nose, and chin—one, two, three. "And he sent letters. *Lots of love to my darling Pearl.*"

Eventually Pearl saw these letters. Her mother had kept them in a teak cigar box. *La Cubana*, it said in scrolled copper letters on black wood. "Your daddy's cigars," she said. "Can you smell the tobacco?"

Pearl thought so, unless it was only the wood and the paper. She could conjure the scent of cigar smoke at will, just as she could hear the hooves of his horse as he galloped into battle, even feel their vibration as they beat the ground. She often envisioned her splendid father here at home, striking a Lucifer and puffing profoundly before the fire, his booted feet crossed at the ankles and propped on the embroidered footstool. Did he wear spurs? Not indoors, of course. He'd take them off before coming inside so as not to cut up the furniture.

The first letter began,

My Dearest Darling Daughter Pearl,
The fighting has been fierce. The sun is hot, the
enemy wicked, the terrain difficult. But we slog
on. With evening the cool mountain air is a
relief and I am taking the opportunity to write
to you, whom I miss more than anything any-
where any time on earth. How I look forward
to seeing you again! I am going to bring you
many presents. What would you like? A silk
gown? Burma rubies? By now you are growing
up and I am sure behaving very well indeed
and making your mother and I proud. How
about a peacock? Would you like a peacock?
They are handsome but apt to be noisy. In
Calcutta I saw elephants. I would bring you one
but they are rather large.

Well, my dear, dear daughter, my candle is
burning down and I must rest.

I love you I love you I love you,
Your Father

Laying the letter aside, Pearl asked, "Did Papa win medals?"

"Three. But they were lost. Or stolen. No one knows. Afghanistan is a long way off."

Pearl frowned as if gazing at something inside her and at the same time in the distance. She had no memory of her father.

"Afghanistan . . ." she said, tentatively.

"Yes."

"Was he victorious?"

"Of course."

Pearl had a heavy brow, small chestnut eyes, a pug nose, and a wide chin. Her mother hoped that she would grow into her features, or out of them. She also hoped that Pearl's body would not grow as large as hers. Florence Greyland-Smith stood five foot ten and weighed fourteen stone. She was not fat; she was substantial, with a long neck and a pale oval face given distinction by eyebrows that were darker than her wavy auburn hair. She resembled a madonna by Rossetti, with sculpted lips and nose, vast eyes. In a rare moment of whimsy, she judged that if she were an angel, she would require wings with a twelve-foot span. She had the habit of narrowing her eyes and shifting her jaw to one side as if biting down on a particularly troubling remark or concept. She often adopted this expression when considering her daughter, who was forever posing outlandish questions: What does the soul smell like? How fast is sunlight? If God is everywhere, is He in the very air itself and do we therefore breathe Him in and breathe Him out? And what about farts?

"But why did he have to go to Afghanistan?" asked Pearl. "Did they do something very wicked? Father said the enemy was wicked."

Florence considered her answer carefully. The Great Game. Keep the Russians out of India by controlling Afghanistan. Sher Ali refusing a British ambassador while accepting a Russian one. How was Britain to reign supreme if it permitted such insolence? Florence doubted that the Afghans were any more wicked than the British, the French, or the Spanish, all of whom breezed about the globe blithely planting flags and laying claim to the homelands of others, but Florence kept such notions to herself. Pearl was far too young and their status in Victoria all too fragile for Florence to adopt *attitudes*, so she said something to the effect that politics were complex, which caused Pearl to frown more deeply.

"Is it like God?"

"Yes, exactly."

"There seem to be a lot of gods. Allah, Vishnu, Buddha, and many others. What is our God called? Not Jesus. Jesus is God's son."

Flummoxed, Florence said, "Why, He is simply called God."

"But what is His name? The others have names. And which one runs the show?"

"As I say, it is complex."

Florence often entered the parlour to discover Pearl before the photo, hands clasped behind her back, head tipped to one side or the other. Occasionally she heard Pearl murmuring to it, father and daughter apparently engaged in a private chat. This was only natural, she supposed, though Florence recalled no conversations with her own father, admittedly a furtive man who would absent himself for weeks at a time, return home in the night, and be gone before dawn. Curious as to the nature of Pearl's conversations with the picture, one evening in front of the parlour fire Florence mentioned, with elaborate casualness, that she herself had been talking to the picture that very afternoon.

Pearl was reading *Frankenstein: The Modern Prometheus*. She lay the book down. "And did he answer?"

Her mother feigned easy laughter. "Well, not as such. And what about you? Do you talk to his picture?"

Pearl was suspicious. Her mother knew perfectly well that she talked to the picture, for she had spotted her mother's reflection in the glass over the photo. "Yes. Why not?"

"No reason at all.... What do you talk about?"

Pearl grew mischievous. "You."

Nine years old and a formidable foe already. "Ah." She nodded and smiled as if to say she'd have expected nothing else.

If Pearl was evasive, it was only because she had learned the art from her mother. Whenever Pearl had too many queries about her father or indeed her mother herself, the answers somehow always slid past the question.

"What is your maiden name?"

"Jones."

"Jones is Welsh, is it not?"

"Not necessarily."

"Where are we from?"

"Britain."

"Yes, but where in Britain?"

"We moved about; it is the nature of army life. Why do you ask so many questions?"

"I'm interested in our past."

"You should think about your future."

"This book is very slow," Pearl said of *Frankenstein*. "I'm still waiting to meet the monster. It was the same with *Moby Dick*. Pages and pages of this and that and the other about whaling before you finally got to the chase."

"People were more patient back then," said her mother. "Think of it, in Mrs. Shelley's time they'd scarcely discovered electricity, there was no photography, no telegraph, few steam engines or steamships."

Pearl tried to imagine it. "What did they do on a winter evening?"

"Why, they sang to each other."

"And if you could not sing?"

"You played."

And if you could not play? she wondered, thinking how dreadful life must have been. Life back then seemed to have been taken up by plagues and poxes and agues and, without steam or rail, slow dull journeys from one dreary spot to another. Not that life in little Victoria was fast paced or sophisticated; it was no Chicago or London, with buildings serviced by elevators, *lifts* as her mother termed them. How had her father passed his evenings on campaign in Afghanistan? Pearl had overheard soldiers here in Victoria chanting ribald limericks. *There once was a Lady from Lahore* . . . Not her father, though. He would have played chess or read the classics or sung hymns. She looked at the photograph and imagined him leading a cavalry charge and wondered about his horse. Had it died as well? She would like a horse. "Can we afford a horse?"

"No."

"Are we poor?"

"Whyever would you ask?"

"Because we have no horse."

"Many people have no horse."

"Well, are we?"

"By no means."

"Then why can we not afford a horse and why do we have no maid?"

Florence was indignant. If Pearl but knew how diligent her mother had been in parlaying her modest cache to give them a decent life. She reminded her that she was, at that very moment, interviewing candidates for the position of maid. For weeks Florence had been talking to women young and old who had answered her advertisement in the *Colonist*. She had hoped to hire some austere, dignified, obedient figure who was noble yet humble, asked no questions and told no tales. Yet apparently this sort was rare, and Florence was beginning to suspect that the few who were appropriate rated her too low for their services and expected a salary beyond her means, which was how they ended up with Carpy.

Carpy was squat, with no neck and a small, sharp nose contrasting a big head of wild amber hair and clear eyes of a hard and unblinking blue. She put Pearl in mind of an owl. She was Roman Catholic, meaning that she was medieval and superstitious and irrational and idolatrous and popish. Pearl asked her about snakes, which Saint Patrick had driven from Ireland.

Carpy said she'd seen a white python in a circus in St. Louis. "Their eyes," she said, "they shine in the dark. It's not right."

"Wasn't everything made by God and therefore right," said Pearl, "including snakes?"

Carpy saw she was up against a smart arse. "So were rats, the pox, and the plague," she answered, putting the girl in her place.

Carpy was from Limerick though she had lived in London and Boston. She'd crossed the continent by train, lived in San Francisco, and then come north to Cumberland on Vancouver Island where her husband, *her man*, had died in a coal mine. "We should've gone to Pittsburgh," she said. "There were plenty of coal mines there to die in. He weren't strong. He tried barbering, but his feet hurt and his hands went numb. He thought he might be a cowboy but hurt his spine. He tried whaling but got the vomits."

Pearl pictured this man with bad feet, numb hands, and an injured spine who was prone to seasickness. The image that came to mind was not glorious. What sort of man would marry Carpy? She envisioned a runtish fellow with a beer keg chest, short fingers, small eyes, a blunt nose, low forehead, and a big messy beard with bits of stew stuck in it.

The day Carpy moved in, Pearl watched her arrange her possessions in her room off the pantry. There were dried roots that looked like naked gents, their todgers standing smart. The only todgers Pearl had seen were on horses and dogs. Carpy put some herbs in a porcelain bowl and set them alight. The smell was bitter and she waved her hands to spread the smoke.

"Runs the ghosts off," she explained. Turning in a circle she spat.

"What is wrong with ghosts?" asked Pearl.

"They haunt you."

"What about good ghosts?"

"If they're good they go direct to Heaven by way of the Bardo."

Pearl had never heard of the Bardo.

"A tram stop. Sort of like Purgatory, but better lighting."

Pearl pointed to some jars on the ledge. "And what are those?"

"Spirit bottles. Trap the ghost inside and put in the plug."

"Then what?"

"Release them in the sea and they become mermaids."

Pearl could not tell if Carpy was sincere or having her on. "I don't believe you."

Carpy shrugged then burped.

"Are there ghosts in any of these bottles?"

Carpy said no, they were vacant.

This was disappointing. "Were there ever?"

"Ever and never," chanted Carpy as if about to recite a poem.

Pearl frowned. Adults never took you seriously. "What about seances?"

"What about them?" Carpy dialled her bottles this way and that on the window ledge as if they were magnifying glasses and she was focusing the sunlight.

Pearl saw little rainbows suspended in them as if each contained the soul of a bird. "What about souls that don't want to be mermaids? What about men? What about your husband? Did you not save his soul in a bottle?"

Carpy's face tightened. "I wasn't there. You have to be there ready and waiting, all set up with your gear."

"Are you a witch?"

Looking at Pearl, Carpy's gaze seemed to withdraw and her eyelids lowered. "Do you have cats?"

"Cats make Mother sneeze."

"Sneezing's dangerous."

"Because you can lose your soul if you don't say bless me," stated Pearl knowledgably.

"That and you can get a nosebleed," said Carpy.

Pearl described her father the hussar and asked if Carpy could contact him, and Carpy said that that was a tricky business for the dead are like silt.

This was confusing. Was silt not the smooth, soft dirt found in riverbeds?

"Disturb them and they roil up like smoke," said Carpy. "You might raise things you'd best leave be. You should speak with your mother before meddling in such things."

Pearl asked her mother if they could hold a seance and speak to the soul of her father. The yearning hopefulness in Pearl's eyes was crushing. Would it be such a bad thing even if it was malarkey? thought Florence. Then again, it would encourage ridiculous whims of which her daughter had enough already.

"Do you believe that the eyes are the window onto the soul?" Pearl asked her mother.

"I suppose, in a manner of speaking. Why?"

"And if they are," pursued Pearl, "what about the eyes in a photograph?"

"You've got some strange notion by the tail, Pearl."

"I am just thinking of Alice. Could one not pass through the eye into the soul in the same manner as she stepped through the looking glass?"

"That is an interesting conceit. Have you tried?"

"I have tried to dream my way into Father's mind, but I always fall asleep." Pearl stated this with some defiance, lest her mother mock, not that she was inclined to mockery. If anything, she was the epitome of propriety and decorum. When her mother declined the notion of a seance, Pearl suggested tea leaves, tarot cards, and yarrow stalks. Florence was well aware that Carpy was not the sole source of all this, mysticism being *à la mode*. If the gazettes were to be trusted, the Great Ladies and Important Gentlemen of London, Boston, New York, Montreal, and Chicago were convening for seances most every night of the week. Then again, their positions were unassailable; they could indulge any whim they so chose.

That was the real reason they attended St. Stephen's church every Sunday. It had less to do with the state of their souls than with their tenuous state in society. There were only a few thousand English in Victoria, and of them only a few hundred of any consequence. If Florence was to give Pearl any chance of a decent marriage, respectability was essential.

After church, they often walked up and down the aisles, reading the memorial plaques to soldiers fallen in the service of Empire. One morning Pearl asked why there was no plaque for her father.

This caught Florence off her guard, and she promised that she would look into it. But the following week when it turned out that her mother had not looked into it, Pearl took it upon herself to confront Bishop Hills on the church steps where he was offering good wishes to departing parishioners. He was an amiable old man with alarming amounts of grey hair tufting from his nostrils and ears. Hard of hearing, he turned one of those furry appendages toward Pearl who voiced her concern regarding the absence of a plaque.

"Dates," he wheezed once he'd grasped what she was on about. "Brigade. Death certificate. We need the official bumph, and then, child, then you shall have your plaque." He settled his hand, which resembled a starfish, mottled and purple and swollen, upon Pearl's shoulder and, leaning close, his face split wide in what he intended to be a reassuring smile but which in reality revealed a shocking cavern of stalactites from whose depths, God knew, bats might fly. Eager to get the bishop what he needed so that her father, a neglected hero, a noble son of Empire, should have his plaque, Pearl reported all of this to her mother.

Florence praised Pearl's initiative.

"I only wish what is right," Pearl said, humble and selfless.

"He would be proud of your pluck," she said. "I will look into it." Some weeks passed and when Pearl asked how things were proceeding, she was told that it was proving complex, for letters must be written. "It will take some time," said her mother. Time seemed a very slow thing. Her mother advised her to divert herself and in this way time would speed up and appear to fly past like starlings in the evening. Starlings put Pearl in mind of small angels, which were another ongoing concern. She decided to consult the bishop about them.

"September 29 is the feast of Saint Michael and all the angels," said Hills as proudly as if he'd arranged it himself.

This was not exactly what Pearl was after. She needed detail: how tall were angels, what was their wingspan and eye colour, were they born or did a virtuous person achieve angelhood via good works? "Are there new angels?"

"There are saints. Individuals of exemplary service."

Pearl detected ambiguity. "Yet saints are not angels," she said, frowning.

"Well," said Hills, trying to jolly her. "They do not have wings, if that is what you mean."

Her frown deepened for he was not taking her seriously. "And demons?"

"Ah, my young dear, what an admirably enquiring mind. The concept of demons must needs be understood in a broader context. The demon of doubt. The demon of despair. The demon of atheism."

"And dragons? What about Saint George?"

He placed his palms together and rolled his eyes up as if to pray. "The dragon is a symbol."

Growing frustrated, Pearl asked about the Bardo.

Bishop Hills had never heard of the Bardo. Pearl quoted Carpy: "A tram stop en route to Paradise, like Purgatory. But better lighting."

Bishop Hills scrutinized this girl who would insist upon battering and bedevilling him with such questions. "Purgatory." He stared at the sky, searching his memory for Article 22 of the 39 Articles of Faith. "A fond thing, vainly invented, and grounded upon no warranty of Scripture, but rather repugnant to the Word of God."

"Repugnant," repeated Pearl when she and her mother got home. "Repugnant." What heft the word had, what a sopping blanket of a word it was. "Bishop Hills is repugnant."

"Pearl!"

"Well, he is... *Re-pug-nant.*"

"You had best learn to keep such views to yourself."

Pearl began to laugh. "I think Bishop Hills is repugnant to the eyes of God. And Carpy is re*pig*nant."

"Hush!" But even Florence smiled.

"She is. She has wrinkly little pig eyes, while the bishop has pug dog eyes."

"Your father would not approve of such talk. Go wash for lunch."

When Pearl had left the parlour, Florence wondered how to divert her daughter from this obsession with the plaque. She went to the photograph and peered into the eyes of the hussar and wondered which was worse: to be imprisoned in glass or locked like a memory in the mind. What would you do? she asked. Did he smile? Did the corners of his mouth curl upward?

Chapter Two

FLORENCE AND PEARL LIVED IN a middling neighbourhood of small but well-maintained houses. None had indoor toilets, but most had lush vegetable gardens full of potatoes, Jerusalem artichokes, carrots, and onions—but no garlic—and flowerbeds featuring daffodils, daisies, crocuses, and roses. Sea Street sloped gently away from Beacon Hill and was paved in blocks of Garry oak set in beds of sand. It was lively with the clamour of children and dogs and the occasional pop from across the lane where Mr. Livingstone's ale bottles were wont to explode. There were also the Stricklands. Mr. S. was an actuarial engineer who in his spare time was attempting to manufacture a line of chewing gum. "The challenge," he explained to Florence across the laurel hedge, "is whether to design a treat you swallow or one you expectorate." On the other side were the Sneads, glass blowers with a shop on Burns Lane who had an ancient dog called Medusa. Grandfather Snead had a white eye from having been splashed with hot glass. His eyeball looked like the wart on Desmond Terence Padraich Orlovski-with-an-*i*'s right foot. Desmond had become Pearl's friend. In fact, it turned out that he was more than a mere friend. Pearl, newly turned eleven years old, announced to her mother that she was getting married.

"And who is this young swain who has so won your heart?" enquired Florence.

"His name," said Pearl with great pride, "is Desmond Terence Padraich Orlovski-with-an-*i*."

"An impressive title indeed."

"His mother is an Irish queen and his father a Polish prince."

"Is that so."

"It is."

"And do you plan on living in a very big house?"

"Oh Mother, who can say, for Padraich has warts on his foot."

"That must be painful indeed."

"It is, but he can jump very high."

"He must have strong legs."

"And he has a big muscle here." Pearl flexed her bicep.

"Does he live nearby? I do not recognize the name."

"His mother sells frogs in the market."

"Is that why he has warts and jumps?"

"Oh Mother, really, that is absurd." But secretly Pearl wondered.

"A queen who sells frogs," said Florence with admiration.

"It is like something from a fairy tale," agreed Pearl.

"It is. And where is the father, this Prince Orlovski?" She resisted speculating that he was off fighting a dragon.

"I believe he is passed."

"Desmond must be sad."

"He does not talk about it."

Florence nodded as if to say that this was only proper.

Desmond was two years older than Pearl, and while not possessed of a gleaming intellect, he was considerate and he picked salmonberries and bear berries and huckleberries that he presented to Pearl in a cone cleverly fashioned from a menu card he'd pinched from the Tipperary Tea Room to which he'd been delivering coal. It was while delivering coal to the Greyland-Smith's house that he first beheld Pearl.

"I'll not always deliver coal," he said, frowning into the brilliance of his future and picking salmonberry seeds from his teeth with a stalk of field grass.

"Someday you will own more coal mines than Mr. Dunsmuir," said Pearl proudly. She had not told him the distinguished lineage she had invented for him for the benefit of her mother.

Owning coal mines had not occurred to Desmond, who had been thinking more along the lines of saving his money and buying Ronald Bench's old bow saw, which was rusty and dull and had no handle, but with a bit of work could be renewed, and with it he would go out on his own to cut cordwood. "It's cleaner," he explained. "You don't get the soot. There's pitch," he admitted, "but it smells fresh."

Before bringing Desmond home to meet her mother, Pearl confided to her that Desmond's royal lineage was secret and must not be discussed. Florence assured her that she understood and made a zipping-the-lips gesture. She did not know what she'd expected but was concerned to discover that young Desmond had hairs on his upper lip and smelled of soot and brine, needed a good scrub and a haircut as well as a decent set of clothes. They had roast pork and apple sauce that Desmond ate with gusto then, as eager and ingenuous as a young dog, he picked up his plate with both hands and licked it clean, smiled, and wiped his mouth with his sleeve.

Florence was grateful that Desmond had driven the business of the memorial plaque from Pearl's mind but decided that it was now time for a diversion from Desmond; she resolved to enroll Pearl in an academy. But which one? The best were expensive. Most of the local children, if they went to school at all, attended Bigg's Road Technical College where they learned the fundamentals of reading and writing and loyalty to Empire. Envisioning something more elevated, Florence wrote letters to various institutions enquiring about curriculum and tuition, and that autumn Pearl started at Lady Tweedsmuir Academy and found that she no longer had time for Desmond Terence Padraich Orlovski-with-an-*i*. To Florence's great relief, Pearl was so captivated by her new life and friends that she neither missed nor mourned Desmond. He, however, missed and mourned Pearl, and took to standing in the roses that grew outside her bedroom window.

"Oh, Desmond, I shall always cherish what once we had," cried Pearl. And then she lowered the window and pulled her curtains shut.

"Mother," she said over her eggs the next morning, "I have broken Desmond's heart."

Florence regarded her daughter. "In the fullness of time he will survive."

Carpy poured the Darjeeling, the milk wagon clopped past out front, and one of Mr. Livingstone's ale bottles exploded out back.

"Will you ever remarry?" Pearl suddenly asked.

To Florence's indignation the question was directed not at her but Carpy.

"I just might. Who can say? I'm not past it yet. Not quite."

"Just how old are you, Carpy?"

"Thirty-seven."

Pearl tried imagining such a fantastic age. What glories she would have known when she herself was thirty-seven, what heights she would have achieved and galas she would grace. Poor Carpy. Not only was she an over-the-hill Irish drudge but deluded to boot.

Florence thought, Carpy remarry but not her? Was she so plain, so ugly, so undesirable? She was twenty-seven years old.

Pearl asked Carpy if she had any particular gentleman in mind, imagining she had set her sights on some butler or drayman.

"Maybe I have and maybe I haven't."

"You are prying," Florence cautioned.

"I thirst for knowledge," stated Pearl.

At school she was proving an eager student and the first three years sped past. Thanks to her mother's tutoring, Pearl was well ahead in literature, French, and geography. Now her world expanded in other ways. She came home with tales of Miranda Robinson's epic rudeness to Meara the school cook, mimicked Glynda Bell's Scottish accent, spoke of Jo-Ellen Belvedere's insistence on singing instead of speaking, said that Clarice Lawrence had been born in Darjeeling, and described Moira York's left hand, which looked like a right foot. And then there was Beryl Morley who could recite her family lineage to Queen Anne and beyond. Her schoolmates were the offspring of aldermen, barristers, officers, and the elite of the Royal Engineering Corps. There was even one of James Douglas's granddaughters' cousins, who was masterful with the yo-yo.

Every evening Carpy bleached and mended Pearl's school dress, brushed her black skirt, cleaned her shoes, and rinsed her grey stockings, for it was imperative that she be impeccable. The school dress code allowed a narrow range of personal expression. No rings, earrings, brooches, bracelets, or cosmetics; hair bunned, lips and cheeks free of rouge. Her mother helped with her assignments.

"We are studying current events," explained Pearl, as if such wonders were beyond the ken of her doddering old *mama*. Unfolding the *Colonist* on the table, she found Harry Hearne's latest column and read it aloud.

> *London has now had five bombings and the*
> *year is not over. In each case it is the Fenians.*
> *Count them: Gower Street Station, the House*
> *of Commons, Westminster Hall, the Tower of*
> *London, and Harrow Road.*
> *Far be it from me to wish any man ill, but*
> *there be those amongst us whose absence would*

*only improve the state of the world. I speak
not only of murderers and grave robbers and
highway men, of thugs, louts, and layabouts,
but of men who foment revolution. Charles
Stewart Parnell is such a man. He is called
the Uncrowned King of Ireland. He is rallying
point and firebrand, arch deceiver and master
agitator, manipulating and misguiding the
gullible and ignorant. A malignant man and
no mistake. And now in the hung parliament
at Westminster he holds the decisive vote in the
balance of power between Mr. Gladstone's Liber-
als and Lord Salisbury's Conservatives.*

*And yet even if Mr. Parnell were put back in
Kilmainham Gaol, where he so surely belongs,
it would not address the root of the problem.
For he is but the topmost fruit of a tainted tree.
Even now the next Parnell buds, raw and green.
The only way to save the tree is to lop the of-
fending limb and graft on healthier stock. Per-
mitting Ireland to return to its native savagery,
to run amok, wild and uncultivated, would be
a foolish neglect of no benefit to Great Britain or
the Irish themselves.*

*Now of all times a United Empire is para-
mount. A forest stands strong whereas lone trees
are prey to the wind. Dear Reader, make no
mistake that the winds of ill are blowing.*

"Miranda Robinson says that Mr. Parnell is very handsome,"
said Pearl.

Florence agreed but thought it best to say nothing.

"What do they want, these bombers?"

Her mother cleared her throat. "An independent Ireland."

"Is England not good enough for them?"

"I suspect it is rather more than that."

"Miranda Robinson says the Irish are irredeemably Roman Catholic and that the Queen should set the dogs on them."

"It seems that your friend Miranda Robinson has many opinions."

Pearl smoothed the paper and went on to a report on the progress of the Louis Riel trial. It seemed that Ontario wanted him hung and Quebec wanted him pardoned while Sir John A. Macdonald was waffling. She then moved on to the Canadian Pacific Railway, which was nearing completion, then to a British victory over Boer forces in Bechuanaland. The story that moved her, however, the story that captured her heart, was of the train wreck in Ontario that killed P. T. Barnum's famed elephant Jumbo and broke Tom Thumb's leg.

"Is that ironic?" she asked. "Miss Granger said we must know the varieties of irony."

"I think not," said Florence, "though certainly it is odd. Perhaps it's an example of the comic grotesque, though it is not quite tragic, for neither Dumbo nor Tom Thumb are heroes in the Classical sense. Still, without doubt it is sad."

Pearl stared at her mother, not sure whether to be irritated or impressed. "What school did you attend, Mother?"

"I am an autodidact."

"What?"

"I am largely self-taught. Many women are. Now, do read on."

Pearl cleared her throat in a way that she thought was significant and proceeded to read an update on the dancer Penny O'Dell and her roller skating Gibraltar ape, Ulysses. Miss O'Dell and Ulysses had performed all up and down the coast. In April, she had announced her engagement to Michael Coughlin, who had been in prison in Chicago for political activities. Only weeks later Miss O'Dell was found in an arbutus tree, strangled.

The tree stood in the yard of the cottage she rented right here in Victoria, only a few streets, in fact, from the Greyland-Smiths. Inspector Osmo Beattie had investigated. The case seemed straightforward. Coughlin was not only a felon but a bit of a lad who'd been engaged twice before. Inspector Beattie conducted interrogations and was not, however, convinced of Coughlin's guilt for the man had an airtight alibi, and besides, where was the motive? Yes, Penny O'Dell was famous, but she was also a spendthrift who had no property and lived from performance to performance. Beyond her wardrobe, ape, six cats, and two blind Irish wolfhounds, she had nothing. Furthermore, she and Coughlin were by all accounts in love and shared a joy in dancing. They danced the tango in the ballroom of the *Empress of Hong Kong* in Victoria Harbour the day before she was found dead in the arbutus tree. She was a tiny woman, ninety pounds; still, it would take a man of Herculean strength to perform such a feat whereas Coughlin was a mere ten stone. No, it was not Coughlin but the ape, concluded Inspector Beattie. The beast had been discovered in Penny's closet wearing one of her frocks and a white wig, with red lipstick smeared all over its face. Examination of the beast's paws revealed that they matched the bruising on the victim's throat.

"It was jealousy," said Beattie, "a crime of passion. Before Coughlin appeared on the scene Ulysses had shared Penny's room, they'd gone to restaurants together, and on Sunday rides in her carriage. Suddenly it found itself shut out." He went on to explain that instead of murdering Coughlin, the interloper, it took its broken-hearted vengeance upon Penny, the betrayer. And yet how to punish an ape? There was precedent in France and Germany for executing hogs that had eaten children. Ulysses was sentenced to hang but before the sentence was carried out, he expired of grief in his cage.

"It would appear that the inspector enjoys a deep insight into the simian brain," said Florence.

"Perhaps that is why he is an inspector," said Pearl.

"He's a fine figure of a man," put in Carpy, entering with the tea tray.

Pearl and Florence regarded her, wondering if it was Inspector Osmo Beattie upon whom she had set her sights.

"You have seen him then?" asked Florence with studied indifference.

"Everyone's seen him. A highly respected man. Dutiful."

"And are you very close friends?" asked Florence.

"We're not friends at all. I keep me distance from plods."

"How sad Ulysses must have been," said Pearl. "Alone and heartbroken." She also wondered whether Ulysses and Penny O'Dell had been intimate. The dark notion was inspired by the illustrated copy of Ovid's *Metamorphoses* on their bookshelf in which all manner of unnatural encounters occurred, followed by strange transformations—from women becoming trees to gods becoming swans.

Chapter Three

INTIMACY BETWEEN PENNY O'DELL AND her ape, Ulysses, was
an idea as appalling as it was fascinating. Pearl lost no time
in putting it to her dearest friend, Miranda Robinson, who,
as Pearl's mother had observed, was never lost for opinions.
Miranda had travelled widely, having been to Japan, Formosa,
Hong Kong, Singapore, Siam, and Calcutta, in the last of which
she had visited a bestiary.

"A zoo?"

"Do not interrupt, G-Smith. A bestiary."

Pearl apologized.

"There were apes of every variety, and I can tell you that
they were in a perpetual state of orgy."

Pearl glanced about in terror and fascination. They were
alone in Miranda's room in the Lady Tweedsmuir dormitory.
The atmosphere had turned deliciously scandalous. Leaning
close, she whispered, "Shall we close the window?"

"Whatever are you on about, G-Smith? You're not one of
those medieval creatures who think plague is borne on the
wings of moths, are you?"

"The apes," prompted Pearl.

"Filthy things," resumed Miranda. "Utterly without scruples
or dignity. Forever pawing themselves and each other. I leave
you to imagine the rest. Now, rub my back." Miranda positioned

herself face down on her single bed and Pearl straddled her and began to knead her lower back with her knuckles the way Miranda had taught her, not so hard as to hurt then again not so lightly as to tickle. Miranda groaned and sighed and vowed to write a letter of complaint to the head, Miss Redden, and get Meara, the cook, dismissed.

Pearl found Meara's food and Meara herself perfectly decent but made sounds of agreement for Miranda did not tolerate contradiction. Still, she did not like the idea of Meara, and her daughter Jane, being out of employment. "Perhaps they could be spoken to."

"I've not had a movement in three days, G-Smith," Miranda reminded her for the umpteenth time.

Pearl massaged more deeply, forcing her knuckles into the fleshy bits above Miranda's hip bones, causing her to groan. "I like Meara," said Pearl.

"Some people like eating oysters."

"So, you have seen this Inspector Osmo Beattie?"

"Everyone has seen Inspector O. B. He is a respected and dutiful man. Honourable and stalwart. Why? Are you deeply and eternally in love with him?"

"He was the one who unmasked the truth of Penny O'Dell and Ulysses."

"Lower. Yes. More. What is this unnatural fascination with apes, G-Smith?"

"It is a sad story."

"Sometimes I think you are a sad story."

"Perhaps I ought to become a lady novelist. I do not believe Victoria has one as of yet."

"Would you write about ladies and apes?"

At which both Miranda and Pearl screamed with laughter and bounced up and down on the bed.

Eventually Miranda rolled onto her back, grasped her legs behind the knees and pulled them into her chest and groaned deeply. "It is a boon to the back," she said, sighing. "Everyone in India does it."

Pearl looked out the window at the trees then at the various tins and jars and decanters on the dresser. These included ointments and salves, a bottle of port as well as a half-bottle of brownish liquid with poppy heads floating inside.

Miranda released her legs and rolled upright and sat cross-legged on the bed. "Give me a kiss, G-Smith."

Pearl put her hands on Miranda's shoulders and leaned in and kissed her on the mouth. Miranda held Pearl's hips and murmured while tilting her head side to side. "There," she said. "That is how I will kiss my husband."

"Will he be a count or a duke?"

"I have not decided."

"Do you miss your father very much?" asked Pearl.

"Muchly. He was in Rangoon last he wrote. I would like a cheroot. Do you have any cheroots, G-Smith?"

Pearl thought of her father's cigar box. "Not on me. Do you like Havanas? My father smoked Havanas."

"And do you miss *him* very much?"

"I never knew him." Pearl had won status among the girls by having a father who had died in defence of Empire. This had helped make up for the fact that she and her mother were living in reduced circumstances, had little social presence, few connections, no horse, no buggy, and were forced to endure Carpy for a domestic. That Pearl had become Miranda's closest friend was the reward of a calculated siege that Pearl had begun the very first day of her enrolment: she would align herself with power.

Looking at the clock in the form of a barque on the dresser, she saw that it was approaching 5:45 PM. She would like to invite Miranda home to dinner. She had made noises about this to her mother and received troubling replies. Even when Pearl emphasized Miranda's superior standing as the top girl, the responses were evasive. Pearl did not press, for she was not so utterly naïve or unworldly as to be unaware of their tenuous standing and modest home. Or was it possible that her mother knew things about Miranda Robinson that Pearl did not? That her mother might know anything that Pearl did not was a possibility she found difficult to accept even though she had to allow that her mother's age logically implied the likelihood of a larger store and broader range of accumulated experiences. Pearl tried to view the situation from her mother's point of view, which made her sad. Her mother was, and ever would be, a grieving widow, not that remarrying was utterly out of the question, she supposed, but to whom?

It was now nearly six and time for Pearl to go home and for Miranda to descend into the hell realm of the dining hall and join the other live-in girls and endure Meara's stew or chop. Pearl affected a long yawn and said that she supposed she must toddle off.

"So you must," said Miranda wearily. "So you must. Oh, my kingdom for a cheroot."

"Were you in the habit in Calcutta of smoking cheroots?"

"*Pa-pah* did not approve. I of course disobeyed, for the smoke keeps the mosquitos off and quickens the brain."

Pearl envisioned Miranda's father the admiral and her father the hussar being great friends. A photograph of Admiral Robinson stood on the dresser. He was smiling the satisfied smile of a contented man. Pearl wondered at this, for did it not mean that he was contented with his life so far away from his one and only daughter? Then again it wouldn't do to have a photo of himself looking glum. "When did you last see him?" Pearl had picked the photo up and was studying it.

"Christmas. In Calcutta. Year before last."

Christmas in Calcutta, repeated Pearl to herself. "And that is when you saw the apes."

"And a great many other things. I saw a man who could touch the middle of his forehead with his tongue. This is called yoga."

"Yoga?"

Pearl and Miranda tried touching their foreheads with their tongues but failed.

"Is yoga God?"

"Honestly, G-Smith, you are insatiable. How should I know? I'm C of E."

"It's just that I have heard they have many gods while we have but one."

"I'm sure ours is bigger."

"But isn't one of theirs an elephant?"

Miranda regarded her. "Your mind, G-Smith . . ."

"The Catholics say the pope is God's right-hand man." The image came to Pearl's mind of the pope riding a flying elephant, then she rediscovered the photo of Miranda's father. "Do you speak to the photo?"

"G-Smith, you are a queer duck. I write him each Sunday."

Pearl decided not to mention the business of the eye being the window onto the soul for fear that Miranda would pooh-pooh it. It seemed to Pearl that a postal system between this and the Afterworld would be most welcome. But that, she supposed, was where tarot card and tea leaf readers came in. She and Miranda descended the stairs. At the dining hall entrance Miranda paused. "Well, once more into the breach." She opened the door and Pearl saw the other girls at the tables. "Wish me luck, G-Smith, wish me luck."

"You do not need luck, for you are Miranda Robinson."

Miranda's smile was amused and bemused and yet her eyes wavered. Self-doubt? Miranda Robinson? Pearl hoped not for she wished Miranda to be mighty.

Pearl's walk home took her past the foot of Fort Street and glimpses of the sea. Ships' masts stood like a forest of limbed trees. From an alley staggered two men, one carrying the other sitting upright on his shoulders who held aloft a near-empty bottle and was singing something in what might have been Welsh. She assumed it was a rum bottle because she assumed they were sailors and she assumed sailors drank only rum. It was April, the sky clear even if the air itself was dense with a variety of stenches, including ordure from a horse plodding past and doing its business without breaking stride, incense from a shop, tobacco smoke, wood smoke, coal smoke, urine from a fellow performing his watery business in an alley, fish, muck, tar, leather, brine, sap, and much else. A pair of grey cats on a balcony tracked a flock of starlings while gulls cried their ceaseless complaint against the shouts and clangs and raps from a workshop, the wobbling *wow-wow-wow* of a fallen barrel hoop going round and round. Glass rattled in a slammed door; a dog yelped as it bolted from a shop followed by the roar of an aproned man pursuing it with an axe handle. Two Songhees ladies sold clams displayed in elaborately woven baskets and a man sharpened knives. Up ahead a crowd gathered near the cemetery. Pearl's height stood her in good stead for she was able to stand on her toes and behold a fellow curled up in a glass jar scarcely bigger than a slops pail. He seemed perfectly at his ease and was even puffing a cigar within the confines of his jar, sending out plumes of smoke as though taking his leisure after a satisfying meal. In fact, one wag stepped forward and presented the contortionist with a glass of beer, which the fellow sipped most appreciatively to the delight of the audience. When the man's glass was empty, they filled it with coins. Pearl envisioned him bursting from his jar like a chick from a shell only more dramatically, glass shards exploding outward. She clutched her school satchel tight under her arm, not from fear of robbery but to feel the strength of her muscles. Of course, young ladies were not meant to have muscles, much less flex them, but Pearl liked to feel her sinews and fibres at work.

She moved on past the cemetery and church to the next street and paused at a shop with ships in bottles. What a strange hobby, though she supposed it was no stranger than curling up inside glass jars to earn a living. Likely it made sense for sailors what with all their empty rum bottles and bits of wood and idle hours. She tried to imagine what an empty horizon must look like from the middle of the ocean and concluded it was similar to a pebble on a plate. The word *plate* reminded her of *late*, which she was, so she began to run.

Her mother was in the yard admiring the last daffodils and the first roses. She wore a black shawl and a plain grey hat and gripped a pair of shears with which she was snipping select stems and laying them in a basket. Seeing that Pearl's bunned hair had fallen loose and that she was out of breath, Florence fought the urge to remind her daughter that she was now fourteen and it was unseemly for young ladies of good standing to run through streets.

"I take it that punctuality is not on the curriculum at Lady Tweedsmuir."

"I was consoling Miranda Robinson."

"Has she suffered tragedy?"

"She saw lewd apes in Calcutta."

Florence regarded her daughter and decided not to ask for details. "The fish stew is waiting."

"It's a lovely evening, Mother."

Florence detected a note of admonishment, as if her wise daughter was cautioning her to savour every moment of this transient existence. "Come."

They ate in the alcove that passed for a dining room. Pearl had seventeen fish bones lined up along the painted rim of her plate when Carpy appeared in her black shawl and felted red hat with a white rose and announced that she was off out and would sort everything when she got back.

"Will you discuss the soul?" asked Pearl.

Carpy was enigmatic about her monthly Theosophical Society meetings. And while Carpy knew that the young miss was a shit disturber of the first order who had a genuine interest in matters existential, her nibs, the Lady of the House, might frown so she said nothing. When Carpy was gone, Pearl suggested they both accompany Carpy some evening. "Miranda says that the Queen is a theosophist. She and Madame Blavatsky take tea."

"What troves of knowledge Miranda enjoys."

"May I invite Miranda to dinner sometime? The school food leaves her bunged up and the dining hall is depressing."

"And our dining room, as you can plainly see, is miniscule," said her mother, gesturing around at the cramped space.

But Pearl was no longer listening. "Excuse me, Balthazar," she said. Shifting a leaf on the massive split-leaf philodendron in the alcove window, she peered out at the deepening light lending lustre to the evening and saw a dog crossing the back yard. It was Grandfather Snead's mutt Medusa, who liked to come over and sleep near the Greyland-Smith's compost pile.

Are you going to die soon, Medusa? Pearl wondered. Grandfather Snead predicted Medusa's death every morning and yet Medusa carried on and on. She was not a lively creature, she declined to roll over, much less fetch, and so Pearl had lost interest in her, though each time the ancient dog entered the yard, Carpy would bring one of her bottle-and-tube-and-mask contraptions and kneel and speak to her, or so it appeared from the window.

"April is the bestest month."

"Why is that?"

"Because winter is past and spring is as yet unsullied."

Florence looked through Balthazar's leaves and saw what Pearl meant: the light was all deep reds and rich greens and the season was portentous. The grass was lush with weeds and flowers alike thrusting forth with blind optimism.

Instead of finding strength in this, Florence suffered remorse, the causes of which were varied: Pearl so childlike and yet so sophisticated, so optimistic and yet so jaded, so much to live for and yet such an uncertain future. Then there was Florence's own precarious condition: in a word—alone. She looked down and observed that Balthazar's soil was dry and that he could use a drink. The plant was huge and old; Pearl had named it after the magus who gave the infant Jesus the gift of myrrh. Florence had placed it there in order to prevent anyone looking in while allowing them to look out. It had grown all out of proportion and she had often wished to replace it with slatted blinds or some other plant, but Pearl would not hear of it.

"You are very loyal," Florence stated, thinking of her faithfulness to Balthazar and Miranda. "What are you doing?"

Pearl was holding up her right forearm and swivelling her hand to the left and then to the right. "I am marvelling at what a mechanism I am. I think to myself, turn your hand, and it turns." She spread her fingers and then made a fist and looked at her mother. "Am I not miraculous?"

"You are, dear, you are indeed."

TWO DAYS LATER PEARL ARRIVED home from school to see Carpy kneeling by Medusa in the backyard. The dog, never lively, looked like a dark brown lump, and it was clear by Carpy's urgent manner that something was up, for she was fiddling with her bottle-and-tube-and-mask contraption. Pearl hurried down the rear steps, past the roses and over the spongey grass and when she reached Carpy discovered that the dog was dead and Carpy was packing up. Done, she placed her palm on Medusa's brow and whispered a prayer.

"She's gone?" said Pearl.

"Well, in a manner of speaking," said Carpy.

"What do you mean?"

"You should let Grandfather Snead know," said Carpy.

Pearl asked what she'd been up to with the bottle and tube.

"Preserving her last words," said Carpy.

"And what were they?"

"How should I know, they was in dog."

"Then what was the point?" asked Pearl.

Carpy started back toward the house.

Pearl followed. "What about Medusa's soul? Do dogs go to Heaven?" Pearl imagined angels walking dogs on leashes, or did dogs in Heaven not need leashes for they were so well behaved?

Chapter Four

POSING BEFORE THE MIRROR, PEARL let her robe slide. What a delicious sensation was cloth slipping from skin. She turned her back to the mirror and cast a glance over her left shoulder and widened her eyes and pouted her lips; then she positioned herself in profile and stood tall and drew in a deep breath and pushed out her chest. She felt herself trembling even though it was a warm June day. Now she faced the mirror full on and held one hand Eve-like across her sex. Then, bold, she clasped her hands behind her back, raised her chin, and gazed with blunt and brutal calm, no, with imperiousness; had not Elizabeth the First and Catherine the Great been imperious? You, she said to her reflection, you torment the souls of men, transport the poet, beguile the mystic, and inspire the painters and sculptors, it is you to whom the balladeer sings. Extending her arms high above her head she felt the tongue of the air caressing her armpits. You are Eve. You are Aphrodite. You are Venus. Tremble, all who approach.

A knock at the front door down the hallway sent Pearl diving for her robe. Pulling it on, she snugged it tight then crept trembling to her bedroom door and listened. Another knock. She glanced around. Her window blinds were shut; she had made certain of that, just as she had locked her door. Where was Carpy? Where was her mother? Heart pounding, she listened for steps retreating down the porch and the clap of the gate. Instead, she heard a third knock. Dressing hastily, she unlatched her door and opened it a crack and peered down the corridor and saw a shape in the coloured glass beside the main entrance. Some tinker? Some cobbler or ragman? But they always had the decorum, the good grace, to cry from the street. Perhaps one of the neighbours? Mr. Strickland with his latest batch of chewing gum for them to try? Pearl approached. Flushed, flustered, heart clattering in her chest, she opened up and found a woman in a tattered shawl wrapped high and tight even though the afternoon was bright and balmy. The woman jumped a smile to her face. One of her upper teeth was gone and there were smuts on her brow; her oily blond hair was tied back in a hasty knot and, while she was pretty, she was pallid and her gaze twitched as she sized Pearl up with such a swift and feral intensity that Pearl wanted to shove the door shut and slide the bolt.

"And a good afternoon to you, miss. I'd be looking for Sinead Molloy."

Pearl thought the creature must be drunk and slurring her words. Her confusion was apparent, for the stranger repeated the name more slowly in an accent that echoed Carpy's. "I believe she lives here."

"We're Greyland-Smith," stated Pearl, a hint of indignation colouring her tone.

The stranger clutched the ends of her shawl as a spasm twitched through her entire body. Pearl retreated, fearing she carried some sickness—her mother was always cautioning her to avoid anyone who coughed—but the stranger took this as an invitation and stepped on in. And just like that Pearl had company. The woman bore the metallic scent of clothes washed without soap and wore hoop earrings in the form of snakes biting their own tails which swayed as she looked around the entry- way. Pearl looked around too and saw it through the woman's eyes: small but neat, not poor but by no means rich. This was an undeniable fact that Pearl had been forced to accept and cover up ever since starting school. Giving in to the demands of decorum, she extended her arm indicating the parlour then asked the creature to please sit though she wished she'd leave, for the way she eyed everything was unnerving and invasive and predatory. Once something came to her attention it seemed she owned it. Pearl saw her note the two leather wing chairs, pride of Pearl's mother's life, and the small round brass table between them on which Carpy had laid the morning's post, a sizable stack of envelopes. There was the fire screen, the chimney piece with six small Chinese vases, the bookcase with leaded glass doors, the fresh bouquet of roses on the three-legged stool, the picture of Pearl's father, the hussar. The woman's gaze fastened upon it, and she asked who it was. Pearl explained.

"Your father? Is it?" Her question seemed like that of a patient schoolmaster offering a slow student a second chance to state the correct answer.

Pearl did not like the tone and nodded adamantly that it was indeed her father.

The woman smiled. Was there a hint of pity in it? Even condescension? She sat on the bench in the bay window, scooping her skirt from behind to avoid creasing it, an absurd effort, no doubt a habit or affectation, for the cloth was stained and rucked, the hem frayed and patched, and her shoes worn utterly beyond repair. Touching one of the gold-tasselled cushions with her forefinger—the nail bitten and foul—a fond look came into her eye as though recalling happier days. Pearl wanted to be sympathetic and yet was too fearful. Who was this creature and what did she wish? If her mother was here, she would take charge.

Pearl said, "I'm afraid there's a mistake."

"No, no," said the woman. "There is no mistake, Sinead Molloy lives here and you are her daughter, the resemblance is undeniable." She stated these things with an eerily disturbing confidence and again Pearl wondered where her mother was and where Carpy had got to. The woman smoothed her skirt some more and picked away bits of straw, which caused Pearl to wonder where the creature had passed the night and in what order of company. Was she part of a gang who preyed upon their betters? Were there men lurking down the road or out back awaiting a signal? "We were girls together," said the woman. "We came over on the same ship. Has your mother never told you? I'm Cassidy." She smiled wider now, as if expecting Pearl to light up with recognition, perhaps even throw her arms around her as if at a long-lost and much-loved aunt returned from afar.

Pearl did not recall any Cassidy. Then again, she knew precious little of her mother's past, a realization that suddenly seemed to avalanche down upon her. "Which ship?"

There was that smirk again. "The *Ajax* out of Belfast." There was no denying the music of her accent. For all her wretchedness, her speech could be undeniably eloquent and engaging. Cassidy looked off out the window where arbutus leaves shimmered in the breeze, then she began to laugh, a delighted laugh, her head back, and Pearl tried to see what had caused this but there was nothing, the street was empty and Pearl assumed that perhaps the woman was not right in her head, she having seen many lunatics out and about, talking to themselves, arguing with crows, weeping or laughing at the air.

In a fondly mocking tone Cassidy said, "She worked so hard on her accent, you know. Plumping her vowels here and flattening them there. '*E-nun-see-ate*,' she would say. 'I would rather, he would rather, they would rather, we would rather, thank you ever so very much, kind sir.' Yes, she laboured like a mason to smooth the edges and flatten the bumps." She shook her head, fondly recalling such antics.

Pearl tried taking this on board. Her mother? Belfast? Irish? What madness.

"Ah," said Cassidy. She stood.

Footsteps hit the porch—then paused. Pearl could feel the very air tighten and then after a long moment, the steps resumed and the front door opened. There was murmuring and her mother appeared in the doorway with Carpy lurking behind. Cassidy advanced with her arms wide in welcome as though it was not she but Florence, or rather Sinead, who was the long-lost visitor.

With visitors Florence was ever a study in decorum; face to face with Cassidy the best she could manage was neutrality, her throat churning as she swallowed, as though she was fighting back nausea, her hands pressed to her sides as she fought to master the expression on her face. Never had Pearl seen her so thrown.

"Will you not hug me, Sinead?"

Florence made no move.

"Then will you offer your old friend a cup of tea?"

Florence turned to Carpy and asked if she might be so kind as to bring tea.

"It's been a long time," said Cassidy.

"You've met Pearl."

"I have indeed and a fine lass she is. In *that* you've done well." She smiled a smile of vast understanding, but what criticism there was in her emphasis upon *that*, as if there could be no point denying how far short she'd fallen from the heights of her aspirations. She opened her arms again. "Won't you kiss me?"

"Pearl, will you lend Carpy a hand."

She reluctantly obeyed and at the same time felt relief at being able to escape. As Pearl went out her mother closed the door. Lingering, Pearl heard only murmurs. In the kitchen she found Carpy waiting for the kettle to boil.

"Who the be-christly-jaysus is that?"

"I've no idea. Some old friend."

"Friend, me arse. I know a rat when I see one." Carpy pressed the tip of a Sultan to the stove top and held it there until it began to smoulder then inhaled hard, eyes narrowed against the smoke.

"Sinead Molloy. That's what she called Mother."

"Molloy?"

The kettle began to tremble.

"Did you tell her anything?"

"Like what?"

"Like anything."

Pearl tried to think what she'd said, or more importantly what she shouldn't have said. "No. I don't think so. I mean . . . Why?"

But Carpy wasn't listening. She exhaled toward her spirit jars on the ledge and the smoke enshrouded them, spreading over the windowpanes and curling back down. The kettle began to shriek and Pearl thought of a soul in torment then wondered if souls had voices or were condemned to silence. Carpy poured water into the pot, swirled it once, poured it back into the kettle, added leaves then filled the pot all the way and plopped the lid in place. "She's a right cunt's what she is."

Pearl giggled at such language and Carpy said she'd do well to keep her lips buttoned around this one. When they returned to the parlour Cassidy was gone and Pearl's mother stood in such rigid silence at the window that Pearl wondered how curious it was that one could stand still and yet stand even more still, just as there could be silence and even more silence.

"Give her the boot then, did you?" said Carpy.

Florence did not turn from the window. "Yes, but she'll be back. Depend upon it."

✛

THAT EVENING AT SUPPER FLORENCE avoided Pearl's questions about Cassidy, directing the conversation back upon Pearl herself and whether she had spent her day profitably.

"Mother," she reminded her, "the school term has ended. Summer vacation has begun. I was idle, slothful, indolent, indulgent, and lazy. Who was she?"

"Did you read?"

"Three hours of Latin declensions and then I put on my hair shirt, knelt down on some crushed glass, and read the Bible."

"What is that spice I detect?" Florence nibbled curiously at a spoonful of the stew.

"Bullfrogs. There are bullfrogs in the stew. Carpy sang to them in Irish and they hopped into the pot."

"I do not think that bullfrogs are a spice. Though your father and I once enjoyed a rather savoury plate of frog legs in a bistro in Montreal. Crisp and tender at the same time, like chicken legs."

"That woman said you and she came on a ship from Belfast."

"The deranged say many things."

"Who are we really?"

"That is a large question best left to the priests and philosophers. I would rather focus on things more concrete, such as dessert. Is Carpy surprising us?"

"Who was that?"

"Who was whom?"

"You know very well who—whom."

Florence set down her spoon, pushed her stew away, and then dabbed her mouth with her napkin. "One of the many deluded souls adrift in the world. By no means the last you shall encounter."

"She said we were Irish."

"As I told you, the deranged invent all sorts of things."

"But how do you know her? How does she know you? Tell me. You must tell me. I demand to know!" She was about to pound the table with her fist but held back.

It occurred to Florence that she could reach across the table and give Pearl a slap. It also occurred to her that she could tell her any number of truths, half-truths, or utter fabrications, any one of which might well bear some relation to reality. But there were the consequences to consider, the long-term consequences, and what would serve Pearl best. That, ultimately, was the salient concern: what would serve Pearl best. In her experience, it was not always the so-called truth, indeed the truth could often make things worse. She exhaled long and hard and shut her eyes. "HMSS *Ajax*. Mid-Atlantic. Your father had resigned his commission and we were on our way to Montreal. One dawn we were strolling the deck when a young woman emerged from an air vent in which she had apparently passed the night, having crept up from steerage. She looked even worse than she did this afternoon. She was wretched, half-starved, and covered head to foot in filth. We befriended her. We let her stay in our room. When we reached Montreal, we gave her money and she went her way and we ours and that was the end of it. Or so I foolishly thought."

"But all those things she said."

"As I said, we became friends. Or rather became friendly. After all, there was no cause to be rude. She was in a bad way. We brought food into the room for her and inevitably we talked. The crossing was many days. What were we to do, stare at each other in silence?"

Pearl mulled this. " . . . But Father. How did he . . ."

"Yes. Well." Florence looked away. "He was a great believer in duty, your father. And to be honest, I don't think civilian life suited him. Certain business opportunities in Montreal and then in Toronto failed to materialize. He was a fine man, brave and honourable, but the world of business was too sly and subtle. He could wield a sabre but not a pen. Our funds vanished and when his regiment was mobilized, he rejoined. Ah, custard. Is that cinnamon I detect?"

Carpy set a small scalloped white bowl before Florence and then set one before Pearl. Leaning to inhale the scent, Florence stated that Carpy had outdone herself.

Carpy sniffed dismissively. "Tea or coffee?"

"I think a glass of sherry. Will you have one with us, Carpy?"

She sniffed again and said she might do. She poured and joined them at the small table. If Pearl thought that her mother had assembled them to make further explanations regarding the stranger, she was wrong. Florence raised a toast to Pearl.

"To me?" Was this one of her mother's arid little ironies? She could be as dry and ironic as evasive, all of which made her as formidable as she was frustrating.

"To you," said her mother. "To you at the Dunsmuirs' solstice fête, for which we must find you a dress." And then she did something she did not often do, certainly not often enough: she smiled, and not merely a reluctant thin-lipped smile, but one that showed all of her teeth, most of which were white.

The fête. This reminder was more than enough to divert Pearl. Only a few days ago, on the last afternoon of school, Miranda Robinson had accosted her on the very subject of the Dunsmuir fête. Pearl had of course done the only thing she possibly could and lied and said that naturally she was going, who wasn't going? Well, explained Miranda, a great many people were not going, for only the elite of Victoria would be there, the *crème de la crème*. When Pearl had asked her mother about it, Florence had done the only thing she could and lied as well and assured her that naturally they had been invited, that on no account would they miss the social event of the season, at which Pearl had thrown herself into her mother's arms in joy.

In fact, they had not been invited. There was only one possible way of attending the Dunsmuir gala in their newly completed mansion, Craigdarroch, and that was via Mr. Charles Gloster.

Chapter Five

FLORENCE HAD FIRST SEEN CHARLES Gloster last summer at the beach as she waded the shallows admiring the bioluminescence swirling like aquatic fireflies about her bare legs. The outing had been Pearl's idea. She'd insisted on calling the luminescence Angel Glow, as did Carpy, who'd brought along a jar she filled and held aloft while whispering to it like some mad crone. Florence had not been enthusiastic about this expedition and she kept glancing about to reassure herself that there were other respectable persons present. It had been midnight and overcast, no moon, no stars, but a great many people. That is when she noted the man of about forty wearing a bowler hat with his trousers rolled to his knees, sleeves rolled to his elbows, scooping the glowing water into glass flasks that he labelled and then slotted into the pockets of his embroidered waistcoat. He appeared deeply absorbed in his work, though was not so oblivious that he didn't offer her a "Good evening," and a courtly bow. When he raised his hat she noted his bald pate, heavy eyebrows, and the thick fringe of dark hair that fed into his well-trimmed beard.

The following Sunday after church Gloster's umbrella had collided with Florence's, causing a cascade of water to splatter her cream-coloured button shoes. Horrified, he'd apologized profusely, a little too profusely she thought, given the fact that everything from her feet to her knees was already soaked from the warm summer rain. He insisted on offering Florence and Pearl a ride home in his buggy, its batwing canopy promising a dry and comfortable journey. Florence would have loved a ride home, for the sermon had been long and tedious, something to do with The Great Chain of Being—or a Being with a Great Chain, unless that had been the week before—but was it proper to accept such an invitation from a stranger?

Pearl had solved the dilemma by stating in a well-modulated tone that a ride would not be at all unwelcome.

As they set off, Gloster remarked that he had seen Florence and Pearl at the beach the week before.

Florence politely noted, "You were collecting water in bottles."

"I was. I am devoted to the natural sciences. Though a mere amateur in the field. And yourself?"

Acutely aware of Pearl waiting for her response, Florence weighed her choices. She could go with a judicious fib, she could be bluntly honest, or she could admit a reasonable interest in what was undeniably a curious phenomenon.

Noting her hesitation, Gloster graciously proceeded to another topic. "Did you enjoy today's sermon?"

For Pearl's sake, Florence said, "Bishop Hills is a learned man."

"Very learned indeed," acknowledged Gloster.

"He has hairy ears," said Pearl, unable to restrain herself.

Florence cringed. "Thank you for pointing that out, my dear."

"Well, he does. And hairy nostrils." Pearl had noted that Mr. Gloster's ears were free of hair, in spite of his having a thick beard. Did he shave his ears, pluck them? She imagined his manservant diligently wielding tweezers.

Gloster laughed loudly.

"What is the point of ear hair?" asked Pearl, taking Gloster's reaction as a cue to continue, knowing all too well that she was being unladylike.

"Thank you again, Pearl," said Florence. "Why don't you ask Bishop Hills yourself next week? I'm sure it will stand us in good stead in the congregation."

"He doesn't keep his promises," said Pearl.

Florence was growing alarmed. "Whatever are you on about now?"

"The plaque for Father. He was supposed to get one for the church wall. Years ago."

"From my own experience," began Gloster, "Bishop Hills has an excellent memory, only it is rather short in duration and selective about what it retains."

"A man of God has many weighty matters on his mind," added Florence, grateful to Gloster for his measured irreverence.

"Very weighty," agreed Gloster. "The welfare of so many souls must be a burden."

"How much does a soul weigh, I wonder," mused Pearl.

"Ha. There is a question you might put to him," said Gloster. "And are some souls weightier than others?"

"Fat souls and skinny souls," said Pearl, warming even more to Gloster.

The ride home led to an invitation to dinner. Declining graciously was much more complex than simple acceptance, and so Florence said that they would be honoured. When the door shut and the sound of Gloster's carriage had receded, Florence asked Pearl to explain her performance.

"I was making conversation."

"You were making yourself ridiculous."

"I was bored. We were having fun. *He* was having fun. He likes you and wants to marry you."

"An expert on the minds of gentlemen, are you?"

"One does not need to be an expert," intoned Pearl sagaciously. "Really, Mother, you are a very serious person."

In bed that night, Florence had to acknowledge that Pearl was right, she had become a stick. What a dreadful thing it was to be a parent, and even worse a solitary one. She was a service, a function, a device, a means, something to be sucked dry then cast aside like a husk. She had not been herself since before Pearl was born, and even then she was not who she was—on that point she had been determined.

✦

THE FOLLOWING SUNDAY AFTER SERVICE they joined Gloster and went to his house. It was new but looked old and dark, being surrounded by a fifteen-foot hedge of laurel and shaded by gigantic firs full of crows that set up a fearful cawing upon the arrival of the carriage.

Pearl wore a new frock, cream with pink rosettes, with a not inelegant neckline that showed her collarbones to advantage and gauze sleeves that reached mid-forearm. New clothes were rare enough, so she had promised to comport herself well.

"I shall be an epitome."

"An epitome of what?"

Pearl had traced a curlicue in the air. "Elegance." Seeing her wrist, it occurred to her that a bracelet or watch might complete her look but thought it best not to push it.

They had lamb grilled with lemon and thyme, baby potatoes, and two sorts of pudding, one bread, one rice, followed by coffee and brandy for Gloster and Florence, and sweet cardamom tea for Pearl. It was served by a tall, stern, grey, disapproving Scottish woman with thin lips, no chest, and a limp, the sort of maid that Florence had hoped to secure for herself.

Gloster was a traveller and amateur scientist and an investigator of phenomena natural and supernatural. He had seen men whose wounds glowed in the night. Not only living men but dead ones, corpses that gleamed like banked embers. "A form of bioluminescence," he said. Then he added that some regarded it as the Guardian Spirit of each individual coming down to escort them off to the Afterworld. If the wounded man recovered, the glow faded because the angel had withdrawn to wait.

"Angel Glow," stated Pearl with sober conviction and a solemn nod, as though she knew it all too well. She was determined to demonstrate her maturity before Mr. Gloster who, after all, might very well become her new father. She had spoken to Miranda Robinson about Gloster after Miranda had seen Pearl and her mother trotting off in his carriage the previous Sunday.

"G-Smith," Miranda had begun in her lofty style, "one was unaware that you and your estimable *ma-ma* were so well acquainted with the singular Mr. C. Gloster."

Not wishing to put her foot in the works and send the whole affair veering off course before it was scarcely underway, she'd told Miranda that Gloster and her mother were cousins, a spontaneous fabrication that allowed for familiarity and social status, and yet did not preclude marriage. She judged herself clever indeed.

"Cousins?" said Miranda. "Does the madness then run in your branch of the family as well?"

Pearl, alarmed, thought it best to play for time until she learned more. "There is madness and there is madness."

"What type of madness is leaping from German cathedrals?" enquired Miranda.

Had Mr. Gloster leapt from a cathedral in Germany? Pearl could scarcely credit it. No, the only possibility was that he had lost his footing and fallen. "Germany is a very rainy land," she said. "The cathedrals are slippery."

Miranda reluctantly accepted this.

But Pearl was determined to get to the truth.

Now, over dinner, Mr. Gloster warmed to his topic. He had tried to photograph Angel Glow but the technology was as yet too primitive to yield anything but the blurriest results. He spoke with a velvet voice and with a smile that revealed exceptionally white teeth, so exceptionally white that Florence assumed they must be made of porcelain. His eyes were yellowed, likely from the many fevers he had suffered on his travels. He had been to Egypt and spoken to the sphinx, had seen the rainbow arcing across the back of the Gangetic dolphin when it breached against the light of the newly risen sun at Benares. He had brought home an Indian cobra upon whose eye he meditated a quarter of an hour each morning. If these were meant to beguile and enthrall Florence Greyland-Smith they failed utterly, for she was beginning to think that he was cracked.

Pearl felt differently. "Can we look at your cobra? Can we look?"

He led them from the dining room to the library. The gas cast a mustardy glow over the pine panelling. Gloster explained that he liked the way the gas flame danced like a joyful little god; Pearl saw exactly what he meant; Florence thought it absurd. On the walls hung photographs of weeping madonnas from Sicilian churches, dervishes from Turkey, miracle workers from India, holy men from Tibet, feluccas on the Nile backlit by fantastic sunsets, the Parthenon at sunrise, a Mayan pyramid in the steaming jungle of southern Mexico. There was also a row of framed photographs of portrait paintings. "My ancestors," he said, explaining that he could not take the originals from the family home, adding that it was good to know one's lineage, that without it one was apt to go astray. Florence felt that Mr. Charles Gloster was already more than a little astray in the fields of whimsy.

Pearl was intrigued by a portrait of a woman with a black eye patch.

"That is the poet Sarah Jennings Gloster," he said. "She was known to write only with quills harvested from the left wing of live ravens."

"What happened to her eye?" asked Pearl.

"She blinded herself."

"Had she seen too much?" Pearl was in awe. How splendid to be a poet and have seen too much.

"I'm afraid I never met her."

"And do you have her books?" asked Pearl eagerly.

"She burned everything she wrote." Now Gloster turned to Florence. "Greyland-Smith," he said. "There are Greylands in Dorset, are there not?"

Florence endured a surge of panic. She had often consulted the almanacs and registries and knew that there were indeed Greylands in Dorset, yet was it wise to claim a connection? She had thought of tracing a circuitous lineage full of bumps and cul-de-sacs and second marriages but feared tripping herself up with her own cleverness. "Ulster."

"Ulster?" He nodded noncommittally, then smiled brightly. "Orangemen."

"Proud Empire Loyalists," said Florence.

"Of course."

Pearl's interest in her own past was trumped by all the photographs of faraway places. Feeling freed from the obligations of propriety, she announced that she would very much like to visit Hades.

"I should think it gloomy," said her mother.

"It sounds far more interesting than Heaven," stated Pearl. "Heaven sounds ever so humdrum." She looked to Mr. Gloster for support and wondered if he knew about the Bardo.

"Someday you will travel to Greece," he assured her, "site of many oracles and, it is believed, caverns that descend to Hades. But here is Cleopatra," he said, directing them to a corner. He tapped the glass of the terrarium with the ruby on his forefinger. Pearl leaned in close while Florence kept her distance. The snake, resembling a long coil of burnished and braided rope, did not stir.

"Do you feed it live rats?" asked Pearl, desperate for a demonstration.

Gloster could not mistake the aversion on Florence's face at this question. He coughed and cleared his throat and mumbled that a snake was a snake. "Can I show you my cats?" He led them to a row of onyx cats, polished and black and luminous.

"Were you very long in Egypt?" asked Pearl.

"Only a year."

"And what about Germany?" she asked, rating herself clever for such a smooth segue.

He frowned. "Germany? Why, I have never been to Germany."

Pearl thought it best to change topics. "I would like to see more Angel Glow. We must go to the beach again at midnight. All of us. Together."

"It is late," said Florence. "We should be off home."

"What about mermaids?" asked Pearl, ignoring her mother. "Carpy believes they are souls set loose in the sea." She looked to the wonderful Mr. Gloster, hoping he had seen one or, better yet, kept one as a pet in a pool.

Gloster withheld comment. He saw them to the door where Florence wouldn't hear of using his carriage for it was a balmy afternoon and she insisted upon the benefits of exercise.

Florence and Pearl were scarcely down the road when Pearl asked, "Will you have a very big wedding?"

Florence responded that she really should have beaten Pearl more when she was young.

"Then I should hate you," said Pearl. "I shall be your brides-maid. We can hold the ceremony on the beach at the full moon. It will be romantic. Carpy can call up the mermaids who will dance." Suddenly Pearl halted. "But what about Carpy? How will she get along with Mr. Gloster's cook? Will they not clash?"

Florence did not bother to respond. Gloster was courtly and kind and maintained an excellent table, he was stately and decorous and apparently a man of good breeding and decent hygiene, but all this talk of Angel Glow and Gangetic dolphins and one-eyed poetesses was ridiculous. And it was clear that the man had feelings for her. Men were simultaneously simple and enigmatic, mulish and fickle, sober and silly, characteristics they also applied ox-like to the realm of romance. Then again, here in Victoria, on this far edge of Empire, they must all, men and women alike, make do. Perhaps it was as simple as that: she was available. Or so *he* thought. The *Colonist* reported that there were five males to every female, which made Florence feel like little more than an object on an auction block. In church, she'd made a point of studying all the women present. Of the approximately one hundred and twenty people, some eighty were female and of those about fifty were ancient and twenty were children, leaving ten. Yet of that ten, six seemed to be married, or at least in the company of males. Of the remaining four, one was a spastic in a wheelchair accompanied by a nurse, one wept continually, and the remaining two appeared determined to be alone.

Charles Gloster was persistent, though mercifully not intrusive or overbearing, and Florence was intrigued and flattered by his attention, and so throughout the rest of the summer and into the autumn she'd watched and she'd waited. He was, after all, the only spark in her life.

Pearl watched and waited as well. It was clear that her hapless mother needed aid in the realm of romance. She and Miranda met at the Tipperary Tea Room and conferred on the topics of men, marriage, and German cathedrals. Miranda, to her credit, admitted that the creature who had leapt from the cathedral of Mainz was perhaps not Gloster but Kloster. Pearl was both relieved and disappointed. Danger aside, throwing oneself off a cathedral seemed a wonderful thing to do. Still, Mr. Gloster was intrigued by Angel Glow and owned a cobra, and that counted for much. Miranda cautioned against eccentrics for it suggested madness, and you could only be mad if you were an aristocrat, like King George, otherwise you were merely a nutter, and nutters were merely aggravating.

"I think that Mr. Gloster is learned," said Pearl.

"The learned are often nutters," said Miranda. "Some say the one leads to the other. Hence, beware of books."

Their Darjeeling tea and black currant scones arrived.

In a manner of infinite boredom, Miranda gazed around at all the females in the Tipperary and rated them a herd of mindless old cows munching their cuds. "There are times, G-Smith, when I want to swim naked in the South Seas. We must seize the day, G-Smith, we must seize the day."

Pearl wondered: what will I be doing in five years? Will I have travelled, written, loved? One thing she knew was that in order to seize anything she must encourage her mother to marry Mr. Charles Gloster.

✦

FLORENCE AND PEARL DINED TWICE more with Gloster during the autumn, and then accepted an invitation to Christmas dinner. Florence gave Gloster a ship-in-a-bottle, one of a pair that she had seen in a pawnshop where she was selling some of her jewellery. It intrigued her. In the days before giving it to Gloster, she would set it on the brass table in the parlour, shift her chair closer and peer in through the curved glass at the intricacies of the ship within, admiring the rigging, the masts, the sails, studying the foredeck, afterdeck, and cabins. There were tiny figures, tars and officers, each one individual, their clothes painted with the keenest attention to detail. There was also a woman posed in a doorway who appeared to be emerging from the lower decks. One hand gripped the rail and the other held her wide hat to her head as though against a breeze. The bottle glass caught the light tilting into the room and dispersed it over the ship. Florence envied this woman, contained and yet somehow free. She wanted to keep her, so returned to the pawn shop and to her great relief discovered that the matching ship-in-a-bottle was still there, so she purchased it as well.

Gloster's Christmas gift to her was a letter.

That you are and ever will be a grieving widow I acknowledge and honour. That I might ease these pains I can only hope. Yet it is an offer I must make for it would improve my own life beyond what I can ever reasonably expect. I ask no questions and make no demands.

Through the depths of winter Florence had weighed the pros and cons, tallied the credit and debit, took the long view and the short, considered what was best for Pearl and for herself and Charles as well, for a miserable union would serve no one. He had means and breeding and status. Yet cobras and sphinxes? And those white teeth and yellowed eyes were eerie. What had he to gain by attaching himself to a marginal creature such as herself? Sex? He said he made no demands. Seated in her parlour by the fire, the February rain lashing the windows, Florence had raised her head, slid her jaw to one side, narrowed her eyes, and gazed into an imagined future. Would she find herself hosting seances and feeding mice to snakes? Pearl would approve, and it was perhaps a small price to pay to so hugely improve the girl's prospects.

Florence wrote Gloster a card a week before the summer solstice and the Dunsmuir fête. In fact she wrote him many cards, all of which she crumpled and dropped in the bin. She rubbed her temples and chewed her pen. He had been direct with her so she would do him the same courtesy. She wrote stating that the foremost concern of her life was Pearl's future, and if she was to have any chance in the world then appearing, in full flower, at the Dunsmuir fête was paramount. Which is how, a week later, Florence and Pearl came to be riding with Charles Gloster in his carriage to Craigdarroch.

Chapter Six

PEARL WAS DELIGHTED, FOR NOT only were her mother and
Mr. Gloster keeping company, but she herself had new clothes
and a gala at which to display them. She and her mother had
spent the entire week finding the right fabric for the right
dress of the appropriate style. They'd gone to the Palace, the
Gown and Glory, the Victorian Woman. They'd paged through
catalogues and it soon became clear that her mother's concept
of what was appropriate differed dramatically from Pearl's, for
what Florence rated elegant Pearl called frumpy, and what
Florence called beautiful Pearl called a sack. All the while the
clerks looked on with wry indulgence, familiar with such scenes
even as they tried to placate them both, smiling first at the
daughter and then at the mother.

Pearl said, "This business across the front sags like a fruit
picker's apron stuffed with apples. And does it have to be
charcoal?"

"There is burgundy," offered the seamstress.

Pearl pointed to a different one, all cream and gold, causing
her mother to wince and state that it would draw attention.
"You want a calm and quiet elegance," she said, "not to be
mistaken for a giant canary."

"What about the red?"

"I don't see that resembling a woodpecker is any better."

"Perhaps I should go in purdah?"

They compromised on a colour the seamstress called Siena Sandstone in September, a golden tan with a black bib and cuffs, a slim side stripe also of black, grey velvet buttons, with a not altogether unbecoming drape that put Pearl in mind of ripples upon a pond at sunset.

"Satisfied?"

"I need a hat."

They proceeded to Sharpe's. Entering was as though stepping into an aviary of tropical birds. There was a profusion of plumes and feathers and flowers ranging from the funereal to the fantastic, many involving veils and gauze while some resembled platters of fruit and others included actual stuffed wrens and sparrows. They agreed that Pearl didn't want anything that exaggerated her height, and for a moment she was taken by a hat resembling a black velvet tiara with a gold fringe. The clerk suggested a circlet of braid currently à la mode in France that included what looked like a set of bat ears.

"No."

"What about ribbons?" asked her mother.

She groaned. "I'm not Little Bo Peep." She could just imagine Miranda rolling her eyes and shaking her head should Pearl show up looking like a child in a nursery rhyme.

She was drawn to the riding hats, which were small and elegant and possessed the right degree of deportment and yet the implication of adventure. Did it matter that Pearl had no experience of riding? Perhaps it would be an opportunity for some blade to teach her, at which her imagination galloped off upon various escapades featuring some young gallant and Pearl cantering together through the forest, racing along the beach and across grasslands before slowing to a stately walk up a cobbled lane to take tea in the sunroom of a manor house. She chose a tan hat with a black brim that came to a V-shape down the middle of her forehead and had a small plume at the back.

"Are you sure?" asked her mother.

"It is admirably clean of line," said Pearl.

Florence expected that Pearl had read this *clean of line* business in some novel.

"Sleek," explained Pearl, seeing her mother's frown.

Florence suppressed her indignation that Pearl rated her too old and provincial to know when something was *clean of line*. The false sophistication of youth, she thought wearily. "Very well." What Pearl did not know was that her mother had pawned a set of ruby earrings to pay for it all.

Pearl spent the evening before the party in her room deciding what to do about her hair. It wasn't her best feature, sometimes she couldn't even tell what colour it was, a sort of brown, not tan, not auburn, not chestnut, neither lustrous nor rich; rather it was a greyish shade of brown. Dust brown? Ash brown? Mouse brown? Miranda's hair was golden. Her mother's was auburn. Even Carpy had better hair. Pearl piled hers up in order to expose her neck, which though admirably long lacked anything approaching a curve that could be even remotely described as elegant. Miranda, of course, was a veritable swan. Going for the least bad option, she decided she would pile her hair up—then chastised herself for of course that would make her too tall. What if the young officer whom she captivated with her charm and conversation was himself not overly endowed with height? She decided to leave the issue of her hair for later and devoted herself to the question of deportment, which involved posture and how best to hold her head, pitch her voice, occupy her hands. Finally, there was conversation, or *conversazione*, as Miranda put it, for it was essential that she both intrigue and delight if the evening was to be rated a success. She began compiling a list of suitable topics. World events? Theatre? Novels? Fashion? She decided that she would attach herself to Miranda and take her cues appropriately.

✦

TORCHES BURNED ALL ABOUT THE grounds where tea roses, lavender bushes, and Spanish broom sweetened the summer air. The stone blocks and towers of Craigdarroch were stolid and solemn. Chained black mastiffs watched everything, their eyes reflecting the torches, their sleek fur rising and falling in slow ripples as they breathed. The turf upon which the dogs rested was deep and plush. It had rained all week though that morning the sky had cleared and the sun shone hot through the afternoon resulting in such a flush of mosquitos that Lady Dunsmuir, consummate hostess, caused a selection of veils and hats to be waiting for the comfort of her guests.

Florence and Pearl chose sheer scarves that they arranged across their hats and down over their faces and under their chins. Suddenly the problem of Pearl's hair was rendered null and all the ladies were anonymous, which lent the evening an air of almost Venetian daring. Florence, Pearl, and Mr. Gloster stood to one side taking it all in. Florence was apprehensive, Pearl ecstatic, Gloster enigmatic, his expression hidden behind the smoke of his cigar, which kept the mosquitos at bay.

A murmur moved through the crowd like a wind and the guests parted as a sedan chair trimmed in sandalwood and draped in mosquito netting appeared. They all watched as it was positioned by four liveried bearers inside a curtained pagoda.

"It is the Widow Dunsmuir," whispered Gloster.

"Miranda says that she is as terrible as the Empress of China," said Pearl.

"Pearl," said her mother, suppressing a smile.

"She's a pompous old bat," said Gloster out the side of his mouth, "and rates me a queer duck. But her late husband and I shared an interest in antiquities, therefore she tolerates me."

Florence was relieved to detect this awareness as to how he appeared to others, and made so bold as to pat his arm placatingly while breathing the aromatic smoke of his Havana, which caused her a nostalgic light-headedness verging on euphoria. All she needed now was a glass of punch and a deep wicker chair in which to recline.

"Perhaps a glass of punch," suggested Gloster.

Florence and Pearl watched him plough his ballasted course through the crowd to the torchlit tables. Pearl tried to think of some compliment. Mr. Gloster was not fat, then again, he was not thin, nor was he bulky or even particularly rotund, *barrel chested* gave the wrong impression, for he was not a stevedore, perhaps he was stout, then again that suggested a dark and heavy beer; she finally settled upon the word *substantial*.

"He is a substantial man," said Pearl, as though knowledgeable in such matters.

Her mother regarded her. Was Pearl commenting upon his physique or his bank account? But the evening was too pleasant for conflict, better to take the course that flowed more easily. "You like him."

"I do," said Pearl with adamance, for she did. "Muchly."

The scent of the Spanish broom invited Florence to shut her eyes and inhale deeply. She had not been to a social event other than church for years. A brief urge to weep spasmed through her, and she thought what a simple and straightforward affair life seemed for some people and yet how complicated for her. She was exhausted and yet relaxed; when was the last time she'd been relaxed? Yet to be lax was to be sloppy, and that did not do for a woman in her position, or more to the point, lack of position. She heard Pearl say, "Thank you." Opening her eyes, Florence found Gloster standing before her with a glass of punch and a napkin. Pearl was already halfway through hers.

"How gallant." Florence took the glass in both hands, it was wet and chill and smelled of citrus and mint. She sipped and her eyebrows shot up for it was sturdily laced with rum. "It would appear that Mrs. D. is eager that we get in the party spirit," she observed and sipped again.

Pearl and Gloster made eye contact and exchanged small nods. Florence noted this and was about to chastise them for being covert collaborators but sipped more punch instead. Even as Florence drained her glass, she cautioned Pearl against getting carried away.

"What do you mean?"

Her mother waved her empty glass like a red flag.

Pearl rolled her eyes. Then, feeling that she had completed a good job of work, she decided that it was time to find Miranda. Scanning about, she spotted a crowd of veiled girls following one rather exalted creature whose posture could not be mistaken. "Mummy," she said in a tone all balm and honey, "do excuse me, for I should very much like to say hello to my schoolmates. It would be rude not to," she added.

"Of course."

Pearl went off to join them. Growing uncharacteristically shy at the last moment, however, she detoured to the refreshments table where, affecting a worldly manner, safe within the anonymity of her veil and as tall as any woman thereabouts, she was served another glass of punch, which, raising her veil just high enough, she promptly drank. It was pink and tumultuous with fruit and even though full of ice, the liquor burned in her stomach, a welcome sensation that not only fortified her body but cleared her mind. Shoulders relaxed and head high, she proceeded to the other end of the table and received another glass from a different steward. Emboldened, she cast around for Miranda and her acolytes. There. The veils hid their faces but Miranda's voice, so high and confident, so poised and clear, was unmistakable. Fuelled by punch, Pearl launched herself forward like a mighty ship. "Ah, Robinson," she said, as if surprised to find Miranda, of all people, in attendance.

"Ah, G-Smith," said Miranda, keen to the tone of challenge. "Have you seen Lady D.? We are screwing up our courage."

They all regarded the queue assembled to enter the pagoda

and pay their respects to the widow.

"Courage," said Pearl, as at a quaint concept. She had three glasses of courage inside her; her cannons were primed. Conscious of the others watching, she stepped smartly forward and joined the line where she stood tall and noble and, she hoped, splendid, for once glad of her height.

Shouts of laughter came from within the pagoda and all agreed that this was a good sign: the Dragon Lady was in fine humour. Judge Begbie emerged singing an Italian aria. Major-General Givner and his one-legged wife went in next and they merited five minutes. Others, lesser, were in and out in one or two. Pearl waited, the rum spiralling in her head, heart thumping in her chest. Lady Dunsmuir was said to be as cruel as she was rich, to hate her sons and dominate her daughters, and she was rumoured to eat sliced lemons on burnt toast for breakfast, which caused her teeth to ache and her gums to bleed.

When Pearl's turn came, she took a deep breath and stepped up into the octagonal building with its dragons glaring from each of the eight corners. Inside, Lady Dunsmuir sat in a carved chair. A spirit lamp whispered on a table to her left and joss sticks fumed in a black bowl of white sand on a table to her right. Behind her stood a fortyish woman who, judging by her expression, was in pain.

"You may remove your veil," said Lady Dunsmuir. "There are no mosquitos in here." Her tone implied that so great was her power, so far reaching her dominion, that neither mosquito nor any other creature large or small, human or animal, stinging or benign, would dare sully her personal atmosphere. Lady D. was small and severe, her eyes deep and dry, her forehead smooth, nose fine, chin defiant; overall she exuded the iciness of an obsidian cat.

Pearl folded back her veil.

Lady Dunsmuir studied her up and down. "You are tall."

"Yes, ma'am."

"You must beware of height," she said, "for it can lead to airs."

Did she mean delusions of superiority or tainted atmospheres?

"You must be one of Bradley's acquaintances."

Pearl knew no Bradley. "I've been out of the country," she said, as if to excuse her height, ignorance, and obscurity.

"Where?"

Mr. Gloster had mentioned Philadelphia on the buggy ride over. "Philadelphia."

"I prefer Baltimore."

"It's a lovely party," said Pearl.

"I wouldn't know," said Lady Dunsmuir. "I loathe parties. But one does what one must. It has been a very long day."

"You and Judge Begbie were in high humour."

"The judge and I understand each other," she said in a high tone, and then looked away. "How late it is. Will this day never end?"

Pearl took this as a signal to leave, but didn't want to, not just yet. "Have you been to Helsinki?" she asked. Mr. Gloster had spoken of viewing the aurora borealis from Helsinki.

This alarmed Lady Dunsmuir. "Do I look as though I've been to Helsinki? Do I look Finnish? Hazel, do I look like a Finn?"

"No, Mother. You do not look like a Finn."

"The light," Pearl explained. "At this time of year, it stays light—"

"Yes, yes." She shut her eyes as if pained by the very thought of so much light. "All that glare, it must be awful." She offered her hand, fingers like sticks, and Pearl held them for a moment during which she asked about the incense in the bowl, quoting Mr. Gloster who said that the Chinese emperors had an incense for every day of the year as determined by their astrologers.

"Is that so."

"It is what I once read."

"You are in the habit of reading?" Her tone was admonishing. At the same time, in spite of herself, she seemed intrigued and said that she had once met another young lady who was a great reader. "It was aboard the *Ravenna*—was it the *Ravenna*, Hazel?"

"I don't recall, Mother."

"The *Ravenna* or the *Syracusa*, something Italian. Why British ships should be given Italian names I do not know. At any rate this woman, this young lady, was forever walking the deck and reading at the same time. And then one night, not seeing where she was going, she fell overboard into the Red Sea. Why they call it the Red Sea is another mystery. I saw nothing red. She was very young and was going to India to be married. Some suggested that she'd thrown herself overboard in despair."

"Perhaps marriage is not for everyone," said Pearl.

"Just so. Hazel will not marry. Will you, Hazel?"

Hazel looked away. "It is not likely, Mother."

"Bradley's friend, did you say?"

"It's been some time."

"Time," she said, as if Pearl had introduced a troubling topic. "There is so much of it about and yet it seems rather haphazardly distributed. Cads live long and saints die young. Why were you in Helsinki?"

"Philadelphia, Mother," said Hazel with no attempt to mask the exasperation in her voice.

Lady Dunsmuir was impervious. She said, "I had a friend from Baltimore who had her foot amputated due to an insect bite. She was young at the time and had been a spirited dancer. Do you dance?"

"Not often enough."

"She was fat, though nonetheless graceful. I have observed that there are a great many large people who are graceful. She liked to dance barefoot on the grass in Baltimore. Very dangerous. Grass teems with insects." Lady Dunsmuir grimaced as though she could smell the sharp stink of these vile creatures.

"It was her undoing. So, take heed, young lady, take heed. And do be sure to refasten your veil when you leave."

Pearl thanked her ever so much and, rearranging her veil, withdrew. Exiting the gazebo in triumph, she ignored Miranda and the others and strode straight to the punch bowl where she received another glass. So flushed was she with her bravura, however, that she forgot her veil and tried drinking right through it; coughing, she turned from the table and bumped into a man, slopping punch on his suit as well as down her own bodice. Horrified, she apologized even as she continued to cough, while he merely smiled and introduced himself.

"Osmo Beattie," he said, offering his hand.

Pearl wiped her punch-sticky fingers on her hip before touching him, all too aware of the punch dribbling between her breasts. "*Inspector* Osmo Beattie?"

"I'm afraid so."

"I've read of you."

He rolled his eyes. "Hearne and his articles," he said as if at an ongoing embarrassment.

"He's a great fan."

Beattie murmured that one could be undone by such a fan and Pearl said that it sounded ominous and he said that Hearne had no scruples.

"Well," said Pearl, "he has to entertain his readers." How worldly she sounded, as if she herself was in the habit of tippling with hacks. In the torchlight she could see that Inspector Osmo Beattie was a handsome specimen, dark haired, dark eyed, with a solid chin and full mouth.

As though it were the most natural thing in the world they began to stroll. They passed a bonfire and felt its heat. To Pearl's embarrassment, the sensation of the slopped punch in her cleavage caused a heightened awareness of her bosom. She asked, perhaps a little too loudly, how his interview with Lady Dunsmuir had gone. He glanced around and, seeing that they had proceeded out of earshot to the fringes of the party, said, "My minute felt like an hour. And yours?"

"We discussed the dangers of dancing barefoot in Baltimore."

Unsure what to make of this, he frowned and smiled and studied her.

Pearl stood taller, though not too tall, for Inspector Beattie, while not short, would never be rated a large man. She had to force herself not to squirm or scratch at the spilled punch on her chest, while at the same time scandalizing herself by imagining him leaning to kiss the sweet liquor from her skin.

He said, "I can't imagine Lady Dunsmuir ever having danced anywhere, much less barefoot in Baltimore."

Pearl heard the bemusement in his voice and said that she must have been the belle of the ball in her day.

"In her day," said Beattie implying that was an eon ago.

"Are you mocking our hostess?"

"Never."

Pearl found herself grinning idiotically under her veil. All thoughts of rejoining her mother or of finding Miranda had vanished, though she did hope that Miranda and the others saw her strolling in the company of the inspector. Perhaps she should try and steer their way past them so that they might be seen. How secure she felt being chaperoned by a policeman.

"Well," he said, "time to rejoin the others."

Yet he made no move to turn back toward the lights and the people, but continued down the sloping lawn where he plucked a torch and went through an arch in a tall dark hedge. Pearl remained where she was and felt bewildered, somewhat relieved, but mostly abandoned. The punch seemed to slosh in her skull as she looked around, noting how distant the other people seemed, and how trivial. She turned back to the arch through the hedge. And then followed.

She found Beattie in a gravelled circle in which stood an enormous plaster sphinx.

"Sadly, it will go the way of Napoleon's plaster elephant," he said. "The rain and the elements will degrade it all too soon in this climate."

Pearl stroked its flank, which was as coarse as unfired clay. She wondered if Mr. Gloster knew of it. Perhaps he and Lord Dunsmuir had discussed it. "Unless they intend it to return to nature like a totem pole," she said.

"Then why build it at all?" asked the inspector musingly and they stood there, frowning at what seemed a great conundrum. "I understand that Lord Dunsmuir was fond of Egyptian arte-facts," he said, as if seeking an explanation. "He has a collection of mummies. Two humans and a cat."

"A cat?"

"Apparently the ancient Egyptians venerated cats."

Pearl knew this from Mr. Gloster, though she made her eyes round as though much impressed by this fabulous information, for Miranda had counselled her that it was important to men that they appear knowledgeable.

Inspector Beattie freed a latch, causing a panel to drop open. Was this an accident or was he familiar with this sphinx? Had he, Pearl wondered, been here before? Alarmed, she glanced about. Through a gap in the hedge and up the slope she could see the silhouetted guests backlit by the bonfire. Between the dark and the flames, the hedge and the distance, as well as the scrim of her veil, it was a blurred and fragmented picture made even more disorienting by the punch.

The inspector angled the torch and peered inside the creature as though an explorer examining a strange cave. "Comfortably furnished," he observed in a tone of not quite convincing surprise. Reaching in he came out with an oil lamp, lit it, then looked at Pearl with an enquiring expression.

She looked again through the gap in the hedge and up the slope. Guests appeared to be dancing and the flames undulating so that it all seemed suddenly pagan. She felt Osmo Beattie's gaze upon her, the lamp casting his eyes in shadow. Her heart pounded against her ribs and she thought of a woman beating upon a door—but was she desperate to get in or out?

"I wonder what you look like," he said quietly.

She touched her veil though she did not remove it.

When he stepped up and into the sphinx she considered fleeing, saw herself running through the night, veil and hair flowing against a sky of wind-raked cloud and a racing moon ... Yes, she could rejoin her mother and Mr. Gloster, jibber-jabber with Miranda and company, run home and lie alone in her bed in the dark and fantasize over what might have been, or *carpe diem*, she could seize the day, or rather the night. She followed him inside.

There was a small table and a sideboard on which stood a bottle of Wharton's whiskey and two glasses. At one end was a couch covered in a royal blue spread with a fringe of gold braid. Beattie placed the lamp on the table and lowered the flame then found a rod that adjusted a vent in the ceiling. "Ah, better," he said.

"Now we wait for the Trojans to open the gate?"

"Or we can open it ourselves." He smiled as he poured two measures of the whiskey.

Pearl said, "I think you've been here before."

"Every moment is the first. It is my motto. Only thus can one live a full life."

"How exciting your life must be." She felt as though she were an actress in a role, then she reminded herself that it was not a play, that she was swimming in dangerously deep water. "Chasing evildoers," she added, lest he think she was saucy.

"Quaint little Victoria is a nest of villainy," he said, smiling.

They clinked and sipped. Or almost sipped, for Pearl very nearly tried drinking through her veil again. Instead of removing it, she raised it in what she thought a seemly manner, drank, then let the fabric fall back into place. The liquor felt riotous in her mouth and she became aware of her lips and tongue burning. What watery stuff punch was by contrast to whiskey. The cider Desmond had pinched had never been like this. She recalled their chaste kisses, his endearingly soft moustache, his scent of armpit and oatmeal, his fumbling caresses and awkward apologies. But that had been years ago. What children they were.

Inspector Osmo Beattie had wavy black hair, a straight nose, square chin, and an impressively youthful and engaging smile. Was he all that much older than her? She judged him to be about twenty-five or -six. She finished her drink and he promptly topped her up and she repeated the word *topped* to herself and thought of the old black ram tupping the white ewe and flushed all over, for here she was, seventeen and drinking whiskey in a sphinx with a man; it was as delicious as it was terrifying and she tried to feel as drunk as possible, which was not difficult what with the punch and the whiskey on an empty stomach for she'd not eaten for fear of looking fat, and yet her senses were heightened as well, and for all that her body seemed wobbly, for all that the world tilted at an unfamiliar angle, her mind was keenly present as she studied her companion.

He had a calm confidence that came, Pearl assumed, from being a police inspector, a man of authority, which, along with his broad shoulders and handsome face no doubt contributed to his self-possession. It was as if he suffered no doubts whatsoever. This was impressive but aggravating as well, like a child born to privilege who assumes superiority. She thought of Miranda.

"You are statuesque," said Osmo.

"Thank you."

If Osmo Beattie had a flaw, it was that he stood no more than five foot six whereas Pearl was five foot nine. Did he wear heeled boots? Meaning he might well be shorter still? She thought of the cartoons she had seen in *Punch* of eminent ladies towering over their paunchy and balding husbands. Was not the great Bobs a shrimp?

"Shall I turn down the light?"

She was about to respond that the light wavered so wonderfully over the arcing sides and ceiling that it was as if they were inside a magic lamp, then understood by his softly suggestive tone that she had arrived at a crucial juncture where the path branched and she was not sure which one to take: one the route of prudence and caution and the other, well . . . How quickly it was happening. Rather too quickly. Osmo—what a curious name—was gazing at her, heavy eyed and waiting. "Did you ever consider becoming a Mountie?" she blurted.

He continued to gaze at her. Did his dark eyes darken? Did irritation flicker like lightning across them? He cleared his throat heavily.

She saw that she had stumbled. Perhaps he did not ride or was afraid of horses. But that was impossible, a police inspector who tracked murderers afraid of horses?

"In fact," he said, "I did attempt to join the RCMP. But I am afraid they have a . . ." He coughed again. "A height requirement, and I came up short."

Pearl felt herself shrinking in horror at her blunder. How typical that she should find the absolute worst thing to say. Was it some perverse skill she possessed?

But now Osmo smiled, and it was a handsome smile indeed, and said that it was for the best as he was a city boy at heart and he was more interested in people than moose.

"Even a moose such as myself?"

"You are a gazelle." He touched his finger to the lamp dial and looked questioningly at her.

Now her dilemma was complicated by the fear that he might think she disdained him due to his height. What, she wondered, would Miranda do? *Seize the day, G-Smith, seize the day.* She tried to speak but choked, and so merely nodded her head that yes, he should turn down the light.

LATER, HE OBSERVED THAT SHE hadn't told him her name and she responded by asking if there was more whiskey. He was sure there was and relit the lamp, which required some fumbling. This offered Pearl a moment to feel confused and disappointed alongside a spasm of remorse—was that it, was it over, was this what all the fuss and muss and mystery was about, the rumours and whispers, the gossip and scandal, the poetry and painting, the songs and operas, the duels fought; was this indeed what the Greeks and Trojans had gone to war over? Or had she done something wrong? Osmo, however, appeared quite content. Wet and uncomfortable and embarrassed, Pearl wanted to cry. She took the opportunity of Osmo's focus on lighting the lamp to slip out the door of the sphinx, her face and her identity still a mystery, and thus, she thought, her dignity intact. He made no effort to follow, but as she fled he called after her in a quiet but penetrating tone the vow, the promise, the certainty that they would meet again, that he would find her.

She darted through the gap in the hedge and up the slope then slowed to what she hoped was a stately stroll lest she draw attention. Where was her mother? Where was Miranda? She wanted to go home. She wanted to wash. She kept glancing back to see if Osmo was pursuing her and was unsure whether she was relieved or disappointed that he was not. There was her mother. She and Gloster had been joined by Doctor Giles Meadows.

In a yellow suit, the doctor was as bright and lively as a bird. Mr. Gloster seemed stolid and solemn by contrast while Pearl's mother portrayed a polite interest in what the doctor, who stood between herself and Gloster, was saying. Meadows's hands danced as he described the benefits of galvanism in treating depression and paralysis, maintaining that the French were far and away ahead of the English and that he himself was having excellent results administering three milliamperes to patients stricken with melancholia and numbness and that he hoped to publish an article soon in no less a journal than the *Lancet*.

"Far better than cocaine," said Meadows.

"How so?" asked Gloster.

"Dosage. Precision. No lingering after-effects."

Gloster did not appear convinced, in fact, he appeared irritated by the presence of Meadows, especially what with the fellow having inserted himself between he and Florence. "But one must undertake a journey to the physician and undergo treatments with a contraption," said Gloster, "while one can take one's cocaine at home."

"Hardly a *journey*, Gloster. And hardly a contraption. It is an implement, a tool, a device of precision manufacture. One may as well call a stethoscope a contraption." Feeling he had won the point, Meadows turned from Gloster to Pearl. "Ah," he said. "Here is one in no need of electricity. Youth is its own fire."

"And what have you been up to?" Florence asked Pearl. "Not badgering Lady Dunsmuir, we hope."

"We discussed dancing barefoot in Baltimore," said Pearl. And though she felt like weeping, she forced herself to laugh.

Chapter Seven

FLORENCE WAS RIGHT THAT CASSIDY would return. On a sweltering August evening she appeared at their door looking as if she had been attacked, eyes pouched and purple, a scrape down one side of her cheek, a split at the corner of her lip. Her clothes were of better quality than previously but that only made the contrast with her face that much more drastic. Her attitude, however, was bright and energetic and she wore the same pair of snake-with-its-tail-in-its-mouth earrings. Noting Pearl's interest in them she drew one from her lobe and presented it to her.

Pearl protested that her ears were not pierced.

"Keep it anyway. As a token between friends. After all, I'm almost your auntie. Do call me Auntie, won't you? It would make me ever so happy." She lay her none-too-clean palm alongside Pearl's cheek and, smiling fondly, stepped past her into the parlour and stood with her back to the round brass table and her hands clasped behind her. She said that her own daughter would be her age. "Do you go to school?"

"She attends Lady Tweedsmuir," stated Florence, entering.

Cassidy was impressed. "Yes," she said, as if continuing a conversation from her last visit, "you've done well enough by your daughter, Sinead. Though to be frank, and all things considered, I'd have thought you'd've risen higher. You had such plans." She made a performance of appraising the parlour and finding it sadly lacking; Florence's face hardened even further.

The sun had set and the room gone dim. They had electric light—Florence had insisted, the next step was an indoor toilet—and yet she made no effort to use it now, fearing that that would only afford Cassidy the opportunity to pass judgements in even more hurtful detail.

"Pearl," said Florence, "will you leave us?"

Cassidy smiled and winked as if to remind Pearl that they shared a special understanding. Slipping the earring into her pocket, Pearl went out. Cassidy and Florence talked low and tensely so that even with her ear to the door Pearl could not catch what they were saying. When their steps approached, Pearl retreated to the kitchen where Carpy offered her a lamp glass, saying it would serve her better as an ear horn the next time she wanted to Nosy Parker it.

Presently her mother and Cassidy emerged, Cassidy as amiable as ever and Florence as restrained. Cassidy opened the door for herself and departed with a bright "Cheerio!" Florence pressed the door slowly shut and the catch clicked to with an ominous finality. Pearl approached but her mother refused to answer questions, did not even acknowledge them so preoccupied was she with staring at the door.

"Mother," she repeated, "what did she want? Mother!"

Florence went into her bedroom, leaving Carpy and Pearl in the corridor looking at each other.

Three days later two things happened. First, a pair of men came with a cart and took the Kashmir rugs, the Swiss cuckoo clock, the vases, and all the silverware. Second, Pearl accepted the undeniable fact that she was pregnant.

It was the uncharacteristic fatigue and nausea combined with being a fortnight past her monthly, along with the fact that everything tasted of tadpoles. She had never eaten a tadpole and could only imagine, all too vividly it turned out, their flavour and wiggly sensation in her mouth, sliding down her throat and squirming in her belly, but there it was: she was up the duff. She'd overheard the girls at school whispering of such symptoms. Stunned, terrified, alone, too humiliated to turn to her mother, she had no idea what to do or where to go. Presenting herself to Inspector Osmo Beattie was impossible. What could she expect him to do? Marriage? Money? What sort of trollop would he take her for? He would rate her no better than the likes of Cassidy and perhaps she wasn't.

Above all Pearl felt ludicrous. Not even finished school and already a fallen woman; her life scarcely begun now over. Was that what had happened to Cassidy? Some summer evening fête, some innocent costume ball, and one glass of punch too many? She felt a new sympathy, as well as chastened and crippled and sick to the stomach both literally and figuratively. It was scarcely any solace that Victoria was full of such women— furtive, sullen, broken, their clothes torn and faces smeared, with squalling children pawing their skirts, their lapses blatant and futures nil.

To make things even more complicated, in only a few weeks she was slated to start her final year at school where she would be under Miranda's falcon-eyed scrutiny. She would be outed. She could hear the whispers already, see the horrified delight in everyone's eyes. Pearl Greyland-Smith, that great galoot of a girl—preggers, up the spout, wearing the bustle the wrong way. To be mocked by Glynda Bell in her Scottish accent. To have Jo-Ellen Belvedere singing "O Pearl our Pearl is a fallen girl . . ." Clarice Lawrence recalling the half-breeds and half-castes and *chichis* behaunting the lanes of Darjeeling. Even Moira York, yes, Moira York with her hand that looked like a foot, but her family second only to the Dunsmuirs; yes, even Moira would smugly shake her head and who knew, someday, many years from now, when she was happily married with children and a large house—wearing any number of silk gloves to cover her chicken-foot hand—yes, even she would think back upon Pearl with distaste and perhaps a touch, though only a touch, of pity. As for Beryl Morley who could trace her lineage back to Queen Anne, she and Miranda would likely have erased Pearl altogether from their minds, as if Pearl was but a stain, a smudge, a smut, an interloper who had, through the lies, deceit, and all manner of subterfuge typical of the lower orders, slithered her way in among them like a serpent in the grass, only to show her true colours in the end, yet one more instance, one more proof, that breeding will out.

Pearl buried her face in her hands and leaned her elbows on her desk and wept before her mirror. Was she no better than Hetty Sorrel or Lydia Gwilt? Was she too fated to die young? She thought of Cassidy. Had Cassidy infected Pearl with her own fallen state? Was her moral degradation a disease, a pox, a contagion that she exhaled and which Pearl had breathed in? She thought of Doctor Meadows who was so progressive; did he have some potion, some pill, some device? Now, of all times, Pearl understood that she must act with intelligence.

With Herculean effort she sat upright. With another effort she stood, straightened her frock, and, positioning herself before the mirror, evaluated her figure from all angles. Yes, her belly and breasts were bigger. Or were they? She couldn't say for sure. Standing tall, she held her belly in, turned to the left, turned to the right, and took some solace in the fact that, for the present, her frock hid her condition, and in a fortnight when she began school the long skirt and blousy pinafore of her uniform would more than conceal her figure for weeks to come. Yes, she thought, I am safe for the moment, I have time—or do I? No. I have no time. If I do not act immediately I am done for.

But do what?

Whatever it was, she would need more than merely the school uniform as disguise, she would need clothes for occasions, for her final year at the academy involved ever more extracurricular activities demanding formal attire under society's merciless eye. Smoothing her frock, she marched into the parlour and in a high tone announced to her mother that she needed a new wardrobe, that school was starting and it behooved her as a Greyland-Smith to be presentable.

"Yes, well," said her mother, laying aside her gazette and gravely considering her daughter. "As to that, I've been meaning to tell you that you needn't worry."

For a moment Pearl feared that her mother knew, that she had somehow sussed her condition already; horrified and at the same time relieved, Pearl very nearly dropped to her knees.

"I don't think you shall be returning to school. I do hope you're not too disappointed."

It took a few moments to grasp what was being said, and once Pearl had she did all the things people do in moments of trauma. She swallowed, she blanched, she felt her bowels loosen and her heart seize and the very floor beneath her feet tilt and roll. Reaching out she gripped the wing chair for support. "But whyever not?"

"As you have noticed, I find myself in somewhat reduced circumstances. I am sorry." Florence had rehearsed this speech a hundred times and managed it without sobbing, though now was forced to avert her face a few degrees and blink quickly.

"But—"

"As I say, Pearl, I am sorry, I truly am. Perhaps in January."

Not return to school? Miranda would demand to know why. All of them would demand to know why. Which meant rumours, a plague of rumours right from the very first day. Pearl could see Miranda and the others putting their heads together in discussion. There would be theories. Where there were theories, there was invention and speculation and inevitably scandal. Someone would recall having seen Pearl walking with Inspector Osmo Beattie at the Dunsmuir's party. In point of fact, Miranda had indeed seen them and made mention the last time she and Pearl had taken tea at the Tipperary just last month. How proud and sophisticated Pearl had felt. Miranda had of course demanded details and Pearl had supplied them in abundance, some true and many false, from the timbre of his voice to the scent of his cologne to the grade of his diction and the themes of their conversation.

"Did he woo you or was he the perfect gentleman?"

"A bit of both," said Pearl.

Eyes down, eyebrows up, Miranda had toyed with her sugar biscuit and enquired if he had made so bold as to touch her hand.

"Twice."

Miranda's sugar biscuit broke between her fingers. "You are a dark horse, G-Smith. I don't know whether to admire you or hate you."

+

PEARL CERTAINLY HATED HERSELF. AT times she felt a delicate crackling within her, and recalling the midsummer phosphorescence imagined it seething richly in her womb. At other times she knew the course she must take yet could scarcely utter the dread word *abortion*. It was terrifying and dangerous and obscene, but it was there, lurking like an odour from a drain. She had heard rumour of girls who had vanished only to be seen months or years later begging in the street with a child in their arms. Or they were never seen or heard of again having bled to death on the butcher's table. Then again, Pearl had read the advertisements in the back of the *Colonist* for pills that were understood to induce miscarriage. How she had come to understand this she was not quite sure. Carpy? Miranda? Some sort of psychic osmosis? She found the most recent edition of the newspaper in the basket by the hearth in the parlour where it was used as fire starter, took it discreetly to her room, and pored over the various ads in the back pages. Cummer-Dowswell Washing Machines, Coca-Cola, Aunt Jemima's Pancake Flour, Platinum Anti-Corset: the perfect figure without danger to health, and there, Madame LaBuda: Physician, Surgeon, Apothecary.

Madame LaBuda, trained in Vienna and Budapest and Prague, Specialist in the treatment of diseases, maladies, and conditions peculiar to Females. Her tonics, oils, and tablets address the complaints of Ladies on the point of Confinement and those who wish to be treated for irregularities in their Lunar Phases. Madame LaBuda can be consulted at her residence at 43 - 312(a) Wharf Street.

Pearl had no idea how much Madame LaBuda charged for her services though did not doubt that it must be expensive. She went to the drawer in her bureau and counted thirteen Canadian nickels, seven English pence, a florin, three American pennies, and a Peruvian peso. She went to the drawer in her vanity and stared at her rings, brooches, bracelets, and pins, gifts from her mother. She picked out the pearl set in a silver band, slid it onto her finger, extended her arm, and admired the gloss of her namesake jewel. How much would it fetch at the pawnbroker? She took it off and slid it into her skirt pocket along with a gold brooch and a fistful of bracelets. She saw the snake earring that Cassidy had given her but, superstitious, left it in the drawer. Then she took it out and thought she should bury it or throw it into the sea, for it might be cursed. Better yet, she should pass it on to some other person, slip it into their pocket or bag. But was that not evil? Would it not follow her, would it not find her? Perhaps if she had the earring recast into some other shape, say a dove? Then again, she might go to the Catholic church and find a priest to perform an exorcism. She even thought of Carpy and her Theosophical cohorts. No. She'd die before letting Carpy find out. She must pawn it, but would that not then curse the money she received? For the moment she returned it to the drawer. Surely the jewellery and coins would be enough. And if not? What did poor girls do? Is that how they were indentured into sexual servitude? Was Madame LaBuda also the madame of a brothel? Pearl sat stricken before her mirror, hands ice and feet frozen even though it was a summer's day. She thought of Osmo. Was he blithely going about his business? And what was Miranda doing this very minute? Was she with friends? Laughing? Disdaining? Proclaiming? Soon she would be sitting with the other girls in French class. Afterward they would gather and gossip and perhaps wonder at Pearl's absence. How innocent and adolescent they were, what children. Pearl disdained and envied them. She wanted to weep but did not give in. She reread Madame LaBuda's ad then paged through the rest of the paper for she was no longer a child but an adult—a foolish one, an ill-fated one, but an adult nonetheless and she was dealing with hard facts in the adult world. War, famine, robbery, execution, politics. Here was a photo of Sir John A. Macdonald with his bulbous nose. What a lot he had achieved. A nation born, a railway built, fame everlasting. A nasty fellow, said some. Cold and calculating, said others. A philanderer as well as a drunk. His first wife an opium eater and the daughter by the second suffering water-on-the-brain. Tragic. No wonder he drank. She got her shawl and her shoes. As she passed the parlour her mother looked up from a letter and asked where she was going.

"Out."

"Yes, thank you, Pearl, quite a revelation, I gathered that. Out where?"

"I don't know. Just out."

"Alone?"

"It's not as if I have friends, Mother. I need air."

"Is there not air aplenty in the house?"

"It's stale."

"Open the window."

"I need exercise. At school we would be learning dance."

"You know how to dance."

"But will I ever have the occasion to do so?" Pearl demanded.

Florence bore this assault. "Young ladies should not gallivant about on their own."

"I am hardly gallivanting, Mother. Besides, I won't be long. And I promise that I will be the picture of dignity and deportment and a credit to the name of Greyland-Smith." Hand pressed discreetly to her hip so as to keep the contents of her pocket from jingling, she departed.

It was hot. The final days of summer, high wisps of white cloud, apples heavy on the branches, blackberry vines laden, the maple leaves weeks away from even beginning to turn, men and boys in their short sleeves, women and girls in light cottons, the dogs panting in the shade beneath wagons, bees tumbling lugubriously about gardens and in the wildflowers that thickened verges and ditches. In any other circumstance, Pearl could have counted herself happy. Or as happy as she was capable of being given her fantasizing, which so often led to drama, and that to tragedy—glorious and sorrowful, inspiring young men to poetry and song on the topic of the beguiling, entrancing, mesmerically fascinating Pearl Greyland-Smith. Yes, she would hover angel-winged in the Afterworld and visit these poets in their dreams. On this afternoon, however, she moved with purpose and did her best to appear serene and businesslike, as if her conscience was as clear as the weather itself. She wore a forest-green skirt, long-sleeved white blouse, matching shawl, flat grey hat with three blue feathers. Innocuous and innocent, a young woman on a domestic chore. Occasionally the crowds diverted her and this was a mercy. A donkey trotted down the middle of Fort pursued by a cursing drayman. A pair of hounds copulated. Boys flung apples at pigeons that whirled up into the air. A Songhees girl strolled along with a tray containing small baskets of blackberries. Two tars lugged a shipmate between them while chanting a filthy ditty concerning "a lady athletic and handsome." Men. Awful and enviable. Foul and free.

On Johnson Street, Pearl saw the three suspended gold balls indicating Shaw Pawnbroker and she paused and looked in the window protected by iron grating. There was a crowd of men and a few exhausted women lined up at barred wickets. High on the walls suspended by hooks were rifles and pistols and knives and sabres. There were glass-fronted cases heaped with everything from glass eyes to telescopes to wigs. She debated whether to exchange her jewellery now or wait until after her consultation with the doctor when she would know the price of her services. Unable to face the crowd in the shop, she decided upon the latter and walked on.

She turned onto Wharf and saw number 312. It was not brick but a wooden building. Newly painted red and grey, it presented a clean and decent aspect, which was reassuring. Still, Pearl avoided eye contact with other pedestrians, fearing that they had only to look into her face to divine her purpose. Above all else she feared seeing, or more to the point being seen by, one of her former schoolmates who would make exclamations and ask awkward questions. She tried to move with the ease of the innocent even as she was crippled with the weight of the guilty. Approaching the building, she had to fight the urge to walk on past. It had four floors and must therefore house a variety of business concerns and perhaps even residences and so for her to enter was hardly cause for suspicion. In the empty lot beside it two tethered horses cropped grass. What could be more natural? Just up ahead was the entry, paved with small black and white hexagonal tiles. She slowed her step.

She turned in. Now she was committed. Or could she merely pretend to read the framed list of occupants and then move on, perhaps muttering aloud for any who might overhear that she had mistaken the address. She saw the name of a barrister, *Fleming & Sons*, and here on the ground floor a shipping office. And there, on the fourth floor, *Madame LaBuda: Physician*. Pearl faced the oak door. It had nine panes of glass and a copper knob. Or was it brass? She didn't know. It didn't matter. Only one thing mattered at the moment. As she reached for the door it opened outward and a man whom, at first sight, for just an instant, she thought was Inspector Osmo Beattie, stepped aside and tipped his hat as he held the door and ushered her on in and then went on his way leaving Pearl, heart pounding, alone in the twilight of the foyer that smelled of vinegar and bleach.

She climbed the stairs thinking of a woman mounting the scaffold. The first flight of steps was marble, the second wood, the third narrowed, and by the fourth the air was warm and stale and dusty. There was number 43. She stood listening before the door. She could still turn and creep back down the stairs and escape. But to what? There was the inescapable question. To what? Once again, her every option paraded itself before her and they were all bad.

She knocked and waited. The dark door had a window of scalloped grey glass. Hearing nothing, she frowned and listened more closely and tried to see through the glass, but it was too dark. At length, however, she heard an inner door open followed by footsteps and then the outer door swung inward.

Madame LaBuda was not tall but stood with an erect bearing. Her neck was long and her chin high, her dark hair tied so tightly in a bun at the back of her skull that it narrowed her eyes, adding to their quality of penetration. Before inviting Pearl in she glanced along the corridor to the left then the right. She did this slowly, carefully, loftily. There was nothing furtive about Madame LaBuda. Finding the corridor empty, she offered a close-lipped smile and inclined her head and shut her eyes in what struck Pearl as almost Ottoman serenity. Leading Pearl into a consulting room she extended her arm to indicate a black leather chair. Her gestures bore a foreign quality that Pearl assumed must reflect the doctor's formative years in *mittel* Europe. Pearl had never had much occasion to think about Budapest. She knew that it had once been attacked by the dread Turk and imagined a towering dark cloud in the form of a scimitar-wielding warrior.

She settled herself on the edge of the chair that seemed to exhale beneath her. How many other desperate women had sat here? For a moment the room was crowded with the ghosts of sad-eyed infants and mourning mothers. Above the dark wainscot the office walls were papered in a dull gold that caught the light of a south-facing window overlooking the harbour. One window was slightly ajar and there was an odour of pepper and sea air and the innocent clamour of men at work. Madame LaBuda wore a long-sleeved dress of burgundy velvet pleated across the bosom but otherwise unadorned except for a plain pearl-and-gold brooch. Settling herself behind the broad expanse of her desk, she considered Pearl who tried not to blanch under her scrutiny.

"You are alone." This was as much a statement as a question, and it raised a sob in Pearl's throat and brought tears to her eyes even as she was suspicious that Madame LaBuda was attempting to determine how best to take advantage of her. A vision arose that she must tread carefully or end up in some pasha's harem for which the madame was a procuress.

"I am here on my own of my own accord," said Pearl.

Madame LaBuda accepted that. She let her eyelids settle and nodded ever so slightly. She folded her hands upon her desk. How shiny her knuckles were. "What exactly is it that brings you to me?"

Pearl's eyes overflowed with tears.

"I see." In a highly formal English with a slight torquing of vowels, she asked how many weeks, her age, details of her health and habits and sexual history. She was direct without being blunt, forthright without being crude.

First, Madame LaBuda congratulated Pearl on coming to her. Second, she observed that Pearl was clearly a young woman of quality and dignity and intelligence. As Pearl blinked back tears, Madame LaBuda began to explain what was to transpire should Pearl choose to proceed, never for a moment denying that there would be discomfort, that the process, though guaranteed ninety-nine percent successful, did vary from person to person and might take anything from a few hours to a few days. Ideally, she would have some support, someone to cool her brow and soothe her nerves; if such a figure was not available then Madame LaBuda, for an additional fee, could place her in an excellent house with an excellent nurse of impeccable discretion. "Do you have any questions?

How ancient the doctor seemed, how sage and solemn and distant, as if she were observing Pearl from dry land while Pearl drifted ever farther from shore, growing smaller and smaller. She couldn't speak.

"You need time to think," concluded Madame LaBuda. "This is natural." She sat back and smiled with grave comprehension. "It is large decision, one not to be undertaken lightly. Just know that I am here for you." She stood and went to the door and put her hand on the knob. "Only do not delay too long. Treatment is most effective the sooner it is initiated. If you so choose, we can begin today, now . . ." She waited. Pearl, again, was stymied, and so Madame LaBuda opened the door, indicating that it was time for Pearl to leave and reflect. Pearl hesitated and Madame LaBuda, infinitely sympathetic, observed that it was an awful lot to take in, that human biology was splendid and terrible and remorseless and Pearl was faced with perhaps the largest decision of her life. Before Pearl departed, Madame

LaBuda embraced her and it was all Pearl could do not to sob on her shoulder.

She took a long time walking home. She did not see anything. People, horses, shops, trees; she passed them all by. Nor did she hear the shouts of men or the barking of dogs or the crying of gulls or the honking of geese. Yet when she did arrive at her gate and walk the shell-lined path to the front steps and cross the porch to their door, she realized that she had forgotten to ask how much Madame LaBuda charged. That, however, did not matter, for she knew that she was having a baby.

+

HER PATH WAS CLEAR. SHE must win Inspector Osmo Beattie's heart and do it as soon as possible so that he would marry her. Having no idea how to achieve this, she gave in to despair. How had a simple summer's eve party gone so wrong? Was it her fault; was it his? Had he seduced an innocent girl? Had she really been all that innocent? Certainly she had been drunk, and that was her fault. Or was it the blind tumble of events, fate terrible in its icy indifference? She had seized the day and like a serpent it had turned and bitten her.

None of that mattered. What did matter was that each day she allowed to pass was a day lost. And yet all too soon a week went by and, with the onset of autumn, the days were already getting ominously shorter and darker and colder. She found herself ever more drawn to the sunlight, as if luminosity were everything; if she couldn't be in the sun, she'd stand under the lightbulb in her room gazing at it until she had absorbed it and, shutting her eyes, the radiance persisted as if having taken up residence in her brain. She thought of Carpy's collection of bottles and the way the sunlight seemed to hover inside the glass like a spirit safe in its own luminous world. How she wished to escape her body and vanish inside one of those bottles. As that was impossible, she set to work and learned that Osmo Beattie lived in Greer's Boarding House, which was not so many blocks away. She resolved upon a chance meeting in the street when the sun was low and the light rich. She'd wear a shawl whose texture and colour would thrive in the lustre of the late September light, making her appear wistful yet vibrant, profound yet playful, intense while at ease, the golds of autumn bespeaking not death but rebirth, spring, and above all else, love. That she did not love Beattie scarcely factored in.

She began walking past Greer's Boarding House each afternoon. And did not see him. He was either delayed or working late or for all she knew out of town. The thought struck her that he might very well have a lady friend. A handsome man such as the inspector must have many admiring females all too eager to land him. This was devastating. Even more devastating was the possibility that there were other girls in Pearl's very same condition! She very nearly gave up and went to the pawnshop with her jewellery and returned to Madame LaBuda. But this, she cautioned herself, was panic, this was fear, she must stay the course. She considered asking Carpy—who had her ear to the grapevine—whether or not the inspector had a fiancée but feared that would trigger suspicion, for Carpy possessed a rat-quick intelligence ever alert to sussing out scandal. She continued walking past Greer's Boarding House late each afternoon.

"I'm off out for my constitutional."

"Be careful of bicycles," said her mother. "There was another pedestrian struck."

Florence had become resigned to Pearl's new walking regimen. Thinking that it was but small compensation for the loss of school, she'd let her initial objections slide. Perhaps Pearl was hoping to encounter some of her former schoolmates? Was that so very bad? The notion seemed unlikely, however. It was more probable that Pearl would avoid them so as to escape making explanations regarding their reduced circumstances—unless she was winning sympathy and notoriety by heaping blame on her evil mother ...

Florence was feeling guilty enough. Had she destroyed all she had worked so hard to build? Pearl had become withdrawn because she too saw their precarious state, and while this was out of character, it was also a relief, for Pearl had ceased pestering her about Cassidy and the loss of their rugs and silverware. What, she wondered, was on Pearl's mind? Had she met a young man? But where, when? No, she was not a woman in love, the very opposite, it was something else, more likely she was punishing her mother for not being able to go back to school, which was tantamount to ruining her life.

And then there was the issue of Charles Gloster. She could not put him off forever. Marrying him would solve many problems; if it also brought some that was only to be expected, and what were those in comparison to the benefits to Pearl, whose welfare was paramount? Unless it all backfired and she was utterly exposed. Would he really investigate her background? She had to accept that it was standard practice to know who was who and what was what in a prospective spouse. And what about Cassidy? If Florence married Gloster, Cassidy would only redouble her extortion, meaning that Florence must do the honourable thing and write and explain everything to him in advance. Florence tore up each letter, resolved to avoid Sunday service for fear of seeing him, and then went anyway for fear that her absence would cause him concern. They chatted afterward and shared wry remarks about the sermon and she thought how perfectly pleasant he was and what a fine couple they made. Standing out front of the cathedral, the autumn light played well upon Gloster's swirling beard and tweed suit. If he was not exactly handsome, he was clean though he did smell of cigar and camphor. Perhaps she could learn to believe in Angel Glow, or at least to indulge such harmless whims.

Then again, was she masking her fears that such things were too serious to trifle with and therefore proving that she in fact believed in them? How exhausting it all was. Perhaps she should simply let Carpy go, for the financial savings might just be enough to put Pearl back in school. Yet how could she hold her head up? Bad enough to have lost their rugs and silverware, but to have no maid? Besides, if she let Carpy go, she'd talk. They were slipping; after so much Sisyphean labour up the slope, they were slipping back down.

One morning, lugging out Florence's chamber pot, Carpy observed that there were people who did things for a price.

Florence was confused. Was Carpy requesting a rise in wages given some of the more ignoble chores in her roster, or was she suggesting they hire some sort of Untouchable to deal with the chamber pot? "You know I cannot afford indoor facilities."

Carpy set the glazed pot down and pulled her Sultans from her apron pocket and lit up. Leaning against the door frame, she said, "Other things."

Florence had been in the midst of her exercises. Isometrics, they were called. Guaranteed to firm the bosom, slim the hips, strengthen the back, provide flexibility to the joints, bring lustre to the complexion and clarity to the mind. She had tried interesting Pearl in them but with no success. "What other things?" She imagined Carpy meant coal lugging and wood chopping.

"People things," said Carpy, taking care to blow her smoke away.

The revelation emerged slowly, like a figure out of the mist, that Carpy meant dealing once and for all with Cassidy. "What are you saying?"

Carpy gazed bluntly at her as if it hardly needed spelling out.

Chapter Eight

THE AFTERNOON PEARL FINALLY SPOTTED Osmo was not
ideal. It was drizzly and grey and the pedestrians carrying
umbrellas impeded the view, not at all conducive to pausing
and chatting, much less kindling romance. Yet there he was,
her Osmo, the randy Mr. Beattie, not gliding forthright and
square-shouldered but hunched and preoccupied. This was only
to be expected for he dealt with life's many darker aspects. Still,
the weather and his demeanor threw her. She had rehearsed
this moment a thousand times. No actress preparing for a role
had worked harder, only now that it was happening everything
was wrong, certainly she hadn't counted on an undeniably
majestic woman under full sail, hat, umbrella, black coat and
wrap, and voluminous skirts, cutting between Osmo and her at
the last moment so that he passed right on by! She halted. She
stared. She darted across the road, nearly being run down by a
cart, and hurried back along and then recrossed—calming her
breathing, steadying her step so as to once again appear serene
and alluring. Now they were within thirty feet of each other,
twenty feet... Only this time instead of a woman interfering
it was the sun; it broke through the clouds illuminating trees,
walls, windows, and faces in a last flush of radiance. The rain
continued to fall but took on an almost festive air while a child
shouted, "Rainbow!" Yet Pearl had eyes only for Osmo who was

in fact looking at her. Yes, at her, he was looking at her, he was! Here was the moment for which she had practiced. As though walking on stage she performed a small frown then began to smile in recognition and watched as he too began to smile, or should have, for in truth he did not smile, nor did he pause; he walked on past as if she was not there. Again, she halted and turned and watched him recede into the evening drizzle even as that sudden flash of sunlight died and night descended. What had she expected? She'd been wearing a veil. He'd never seen her face. He did not know her.

So, she thought, this was tragedy, this was what Homer and Aeschylus and Shakespeare and so many others had meant, except that it was not beautiful or glorious and certainly not romantic; she was wet, cold, alone, and pregnant.

She plodded home and sat on the side of her bed, hands dead in her lap, and stared into the darkness that both filled her and engulfed her until she was darkness and darkness was her. She breathed, she blinked, an itch on her foot came and went, but she did not move, just as the urge to pee came and went, and the urge to weep. Occasionally she swallowed but did not go to the pantry for something to eat or drink. Why bother? What did it matter? How long she sat there she had no idea. She heard distant sounds from the kitchen. There was a knock at her bedroom door and her mother called, and Pearl, or some part of Pearl, responded that she was tired and no she was not hungry, she would go to bed, except that she did not crawl under the covers and sleep, she remained where she was, her body stiffened as if rigor mortis were setting in. As for her thoughts, there was but one: her life was finished, over, done. She was well and truly buggered, as Carpy would say. Once again, she reconsidered Madame LaBuda.

Then in the cell of her room she saw the answer, the only possible answer, the one that had been there all along, the one she had been avoiding. Slowly she stood, sore back, sore feet, stiff neck, crushed spirit. She straightened her skirt and shawl out of habit and little else, for she did not care what she looked like, certainly it didn't matter, not anymore, and before leaving her room she opened the drawer containing her jewellery and found Cassidy's earring and, having no pockets, she slipped it onto her baby finger and then left the house, no attempt at stealth, merely going out the door and shutting it soundly behind her. If her mother called, Pearl did not hear; if Carpy stared from her alcove, Pearl did not care. She went along the walk and through the gate, which clapped shut behind her.

She walked into the autumn wind then turned and went the other way, letting it beat her back and press her skirt to her calves. Most houses were dark but a few were lit, their windows reflecting squares of metallic moonlight. She did not think about the lives going on in those houses, did not dwell upon visions of domestic bliss or strife or indifference, for those were other worlds as distant as stars. Clouds fled and the half moon appeared then vanished then reappeared. She walked without direction other than to avoid puddles and the shouts of men. Buildings blocked the wind, which then rushed at her from alleys with renewed force as if to drive her off, to mock her, to punish her, scornfully hurling gusts of leaves against her legs. Miranda had stated that some winds caused madness but that the doldrums did as well. Osmo could have saved her. He should have known. If he was a real inspector he'd have known that she was the Woman in the Sphinx, if he'd been true to his word he would have found her by now. He was a sorry excuse for a police inspector, a charlatan and a cad, handsome but dim, and she had fallen for him, making her all the more of a dupe and a fool. Perhaps she was mad? Were there more mad men or mad women? Perhaps she should have left a note for her mother. Would it be Osmo who came to the door to tell her that they had found Pearl's corpse? Would that old ghoul Bishop Hills bleat some inanities at her funeral?

She walked on. Gas lamps burned with dirty yellow haloes and the wind blew the odours of woodsmoke and rot. She heard the muted racket of machinery and found herself at the offices of the *Colonist*, the boardwalk vibrating beneath her feet with the churning of the presses, while in the window were pinned sheets from yesterday's edition. The electric light illuminated the news sheets which glowed eerily. *Bodies still being recovered from a shipwreck off Gibraltar. Police fire on protesters in Paris. Earthquake in Japan. Massacre in China.* And there, in a lower corner, a report from Jerusalem on a certain Mirza Ghulam Ahmad claiming to be the Second Coming of Jesus Christ. Truly it was the End of Days. She must have spoken this thought aloud, for a voice responded.

"Ah, but it always seems so. What a dull, flat thing life would be without ridges and chasms for us to traverse. But you are distressed. Why else would a young woman be out and about at this hour? Unless . . . No. No."

The man raked her with his gaze and Pearl felt the very grit of his attention abrading her skin. He was lean and sallow, with large red ears sticking out from under the brim of his tall hat, had close-set, heavy-lidded eyes and long, dark nostrils. She recognized him, for he had been in the paper: yes, Harry Hearne, ever on the prowl for news. It was said that he never ate solid food but subsisted on black coffee and Coca-Cola. She had seen him at a distance, moving in his characteristic gait, cocked forward at the hips, one fist behind his back. Now, up close, she saw something extraordinary—a ferret peeking from his coat pocket. It peeked then darted, flowing about him from place to place, inside his coat, onto his shoulder, up onto his hat brim, down his neck, and along his arm, only to curl around his cuff and disappear back up his sleeve and emerge from inside his waistcoat, as fluid as a fish.

"This is Roderick," he said.

"A ferret."

"Tut. A weasel, a least weasel, *mustela nivalis*."

It was six inches long, tan on the back, white on the belly, with short, furred ears and inquisitive black eyes.

"Hold out your arm."

Pearl obeyed and Roderick ran down Hearne's arm and hopped from his hand to hers and proceeded up to her shoulder and inspected her ear. She could not help laughing, like a sad child diverted by a toy.

"On a recent night I was put to wondering," Hearne began, voice raised as if reciting one of his columns for an audience, "how the youth of our fair city, of the very world at large, view the present and the future, and their place in it, if indeed there is a future to have a place in. Speak of this, young lady. Enlighten me, enlighten my readers."

Her views? He, Harry Hearne, was asking her opinion? Now of all times some man was asking what she thought? The absurdity was too much. She was terrified and at the same time—to her astonishment—strategic. What did he wish to hear, what would please him and at the same time earn his respect, or at least soften his severe expression into one of approval? For she wanted approval, she needed it now more than ever because if she failed to answer intelligently she'd know the humiliation of being critiqued in print, except of course she would not live to see it. Still, the moment was upon her.

"If one reads the papers," she began, "the world appears a bad place." Pearl nodded to the page in the window. "Which tells me two things. I must engage in some good work or cease reading the papers."

The lines angling down either side of Harry Hearne's nose and from the corners of his mouth deepened and Pearl perceived that he was unconvinced and that he would not let her off so easily. In fact, he seemed to suspect that she was quoting, which would not do, would not do at all, so Pearl added that she had heard that Victoria was a nest of villainy.

"Heard?" he said, as if hearing was flimsy evidence indeed. "Heard where?"

"From a reliable source," she assured him.

"Does this reliable source have a name?"

"That would be indiscreet, sir."

He grumbled. He did not like being defied, even if politely. "Teaching, nursing, motherhood," he declared, "these are the paths to consider. You are a Daughter of Empire, the greatest empire on earth, the greatest since Rome, never forget that. It is an incomparable gift and more than enough."

Maybe Pearl should have cast her gaze downward, curtsied and thanked him for this profundity, he being, after all, the eminent Harry Hearne, and she but a stupid girl in a bad way. Instead, she asked, in a tone seemingly innocent, "For whom, sir? The Irish? The Slav? The Chinese? The Indian?"

His head pulled away as if she had assaulted him. "Who have you been talking to? Do not speak to me of the Irish, girlie. They are not all one. There are the loyal and the disloyal, the Protestant and the Papist." At this, as if in total agreement with his master's sentiments and as if to escape this apostate creature, Roderick abandoned Pearl's elbow for the safety of Hearne's.

"Circumstances change."

"Change? Change how? Be specific."

In a softer tone, almost a whisper, she said, "I don't know, I once thought I might find another path."

"And do you think you will find this path traipsing about the night?"

"Oh, sir. I know exactly where I am going tonight."

"Where is that?"

"To the end."

"To the end of what?"

"The end of the night."

Hearne demanded her name.

"I'd rather not say."

"Rather not or cannot?"

"Exactly, sir. A bit of both. And now you must excuse me for I've an appointment." With a half bow she stepped back and turned and continued to walk.

He called after her, severe and yet not utterly without concern, "Take care, young lady, take care."

"I will try, sir. And thank you," she added, sincerely, for as she went it occurred to her that Mr. Harry Hearne had hit the mark: *rather not or cannot*, meaning that her past was shadow and her future fog. Literally and figuratively, she was a wraith plodding from one oblivion to another.

She may have been lost but she was not invisible. Men called from doorways. Two fell into step with her. She hurried on and they, old and drunk and wheezing, gave up. Then a short fellow with a thick beard and a bowler set hard on his round head appeared at her shoulder asking if she liked silk, for he had silk, gold silk and indigo silk, black silk and red silk, silk by the yard, and if she'd come with him he'd let her have all the silk that she desired and more, much more, adding that he did like a big girl, appraising Pearl as if she were a cut of meat. "I like a bit of heft," he said. "What will it be, gold silk or indigo? Or both? Yes, you deserve both. Plus a glass of claret. On a night like this I should say claret. I'm not far from here, just up ahead. And a hot bath, nothing like a hot bath on a cold night. I have a lovely deep tub. Copper. And towels, linen towels, vast linen towels and silken sheets and an eiderdown. Or hot rum, do you favour hot rum with a dash of cinnamon? I can give you that, I should be honoured to give you that and more..."

He fell away at the sound of dogs, which loomed up out of the night then were whistled off.

In her efforts to escape these Lotharios, she'd taken sudden turns and now saw a tavern up ahead on the opposite side of the road. It throbbed with shouts and stomps and snatches of song. A figure appeared from an alley and came angling toward her. She'd have run but saw that it was a woman. Then wished she had run for it was Cassidy. Pearl hesitated then kept on walking and Cassidy strode along with her. She wore a cloak with the hood down and the hem roving about her knees. How easily she moved, all leisure and pomp, a right little royal, as Carpy would have said. Pearl walked faster but Cassidy caught her arm and halted her so that they stood face to face in the cool starlight.

"Out and about, are we? I expect your dear mother wouldn't approve. No, not at all. Doesn't do for a young lady to be wandering alone after dark." Cassidy angled her head as though to better gauge the depths of Pearl's rebellious character. "Or did you finally have a sit-down with dear Mama? Laid the cards on the table, did she? Bit of a revelation. Learn what you wished you had not?"

A movement across the road caught Pearl's attention. A silhouette backlit by the tavern. Still. Watchful. Obscurely familiar.

"Oh," said Pearl, remembering, "I have something of yours." And she slid the earring from her little finger, placed it in Cassidy's hand and then ran.

She ran until there were no houses, only forest on either side and the sea before her. She looked back but there was no one so she slowed to a stumbling walk, wondering why it could not have been Osmo offering her hot rum and a hot bath? What would they do to poor Mr. Mirza Ghulam Ahmad who thought he was Jesus Christ? Put him in a room and lock the door? Had he reached this conclusion in the day or the night, in a blinding flash or a slow evolution? Where had he come from, Mr. Mirza Ghulam Ahmad, what had his childhood been like? Pearl should have liked to meet him and have a chat, because perhaps he really was the Second Coming of Jesus Christ. Why not? Someone, somewhere, sometime had to be, unless

Miranda was right and it all really was just a lot of bunkum. But fate was taking Mirza Ghulam Ahmad in one direction and Miranda in another and Pearl in a third, and she felt like the proverbial bird that has flown from the stormy night into the torchlit mead hall and was now about to exit once more out into the dark. How brief her flight. Alive then dead. She glanced back again but there was no sign of Cassidy or anyone else. She sobbed once then sniffed and squared her shoulders for what, after all, did any of it really matter? Maybe there was Heaven and maybe there was Hell and if the Catholics were right a place called Limbo, and if Carpy was right a brighter version of Limbo called the Bardo, or else there was nothing at all, only dreamless sleep, which did not seem such a very bad thing at this particular moment.

She reached the sea. The waves were not as dramatic as she might have hoped, certainly they did not match her mood, but the onshore breeze was strong and the spray spattered her face. She set her feet wide, shut her eyes and inhaled the cold wet salt air, and thought that if an assassin took her, closed his gloved hand over her mouth and nose, or a cougar bit her on the throat, so be it. Her tears merged with the spray—salt water with salt water—which seemed right and proper, and she laughed and she cried and then, gulping the air and maintaining her balance in the face of the wind, she opened her arms hoping to be borne off to some distant place where she could begin again, knowing what she knew now, and therefore wiser. But she was not lifted up and carried away, she remained right where she was with her feet in the sand, and when she opened her eyes she saw, far out to sea, a small light, no, many lights, a cluster of lights, and understood that it was a ship, perhaps heading for China, and she mourned for she had missed it, missed her boat, which was typical, yes, typical, and so she stepped toward the water and felt the waves rushing up over her feet and then up her shins to her knees, each wave encircling her legs and then pulling her deeper, like so many groping hands, the hands, perhaps, of the mermaids Carpy had spoken of, souls captured in bottles then set free in the sea. Would Pearl swim with them? Would they escort her down to their palaces of coral? Or would they drown her like the fool she was?

"Hey." A woman stood there wrapped in a blanket that whipped about her legs. "What're you doing?"

Pearl did not have the strength to shout over the roar of the wind and the waves that she was going to kill herself, so go away and leave her alone.

"Come on." The woman waded in and caught her hand and led her out of the surf and then along the beach and around a point to a circle of people seated about a fire. Songhees. The woman pointed to an opening in the circle and Pearl, cold and wet, miserable and yet relieved, sat and looked at the faces intent upon the flames as though listening to a storyteller. They formed a tight enclosure protecting the fire whose flames nonetheless ran horizontal when the gusts rushed raw and fierce then stood straight and calm when the wind relented. The coals seethed incandescent. The woman added branches and the flames embraced them, coiling possessively, flowing hungrily over and around them then running flat as the wind accelerated again.

Sitting cross-legged, Pearl's knees and hands and face were hot while her back was ice. She studied the others. Their eyes reflected the flames, as if the flames lived in their eyes. No one spoke. There was no meat grilling, no dancing or singing. Pearl asked the woman, "What is this? What's going on?"

The woman appeared to be about forty, wore a wool toque and geometrically patterned blanket snugged to her cheekbones. She cupped her hand to her ear meaning: Listen.

Pearl listened and heard the fire and the wind and the waves. Her tears had dried tight to her cheeks, she shivered and was hot. "I don't understand."

The woman patted Pearl's knee reassuringly. "We're staying warm."

"Then why don't you go home?"

The woman gazed at her a long moment. "We are home. This is home."

Pearl considered this. Did they live on the beach? Were they creatures of fire?

"Why don't *you* go home?" said the woman, in a tone that was both a question and a suggestion, and not without a burr of anger, as if to remind Pearl that she was the interloper.

Home as in house? Home as in land? Some women in the circle cradled infants. Would they adopt her? Would these people take her in if she were to ask? Would they accept her? Pearl thought of Eunice Williams, a New Englander kidnapped by Mohawks in 1703 at the age of seventeen, the very same age as Pearl. Within two years Eunice Williams had forgotten English, married a Mohawk, and, refusing to return to her birth family when given the opportunity, lived to be eighty-nine. Pearl regularly saw Songhees out and about in Victoria, and she knew that they had their villages, that all Victoria, all Vancouver Island, had been theirs. How they must resent her. But at the moment, no one even seemed to notice her presence, at the moment it was only fire and wind, spatters of rain, and the slow drum beat of the ocean pulsing through her body.

Now the woman next to Pearl pointed and she saw a woman on a horse pushing down through the salal. She rode the horse around the circle then stopped behind Pearl and the horse lowered its head to Pearl's shoulder and she stroked its cool, damp nose.

"This is Johnny," said the rider.

His mane luffed in the wind and the woman on his back looked from the fire to the night and said she'd been thinking about flowers.

She said, "Isn't it odd that there are so few green petalled flowers. There are white flowers, blue flowers, red, yellow, black, and of course the chocolate lily, but only a few that are green, which is the colour of life."

No one seemed to find these observations or her presence odd. Perhaps only Pearl could hear her above the wind.

"She's lost," said the woman next to Pearl, who did not know whether it was her or the woman on the horse to whom she referred.

"Come up and I will give you a ride home."

Home, thought Pearl, home, comb, dome, foam, loam, gnome, poem, tome, tomb, womb. A half rhyme is as good as a wink to a blind beggar. "Oh God," she said to the fire. "I am so tired."

Before struggling to her feet, Pearl thanked the woman next to her in the circle, and the woman looked at Pearl as though from a great distance and Pearl endured a powerful urge to sob. She thought of her mother and the photograph of her father, she thought of Cassidy and she thought of poor Mr. Mirza Ghulam Ahmad who thought he was Jesus Christ. It was as if she were looking in a mirror and yet instead of seeing herself, she saw everyone everywhere who had ever lived and who ever would live, their eyes wide and wondering. Then she stood and the woman on the horse pulled her own foot from the stirrup and extended her hand and Pearl stepped up into the stirrup and onto the horse's rump and they circled the fire and proceeded back up through the salal. Pearl put her arms around the woman's waist and wept against her back all the way home.

Chapter Nine

THREE DAYS PEARL STAYED IN bed tended by her mother and Carpy, with visits from Doctor Meadows who prescribed ginger infusions and camphor compresses. Pearl was dimly aware of these ministrations and largely indifferent, doing her best, if anything, to remain submerged in the delirium in which she floated like a specimen in a jar in an apothecary's shop. She wondered whether this was what it had been like in her mother's womb and if there was any way to return to that innocent and primordial pond.

Yet all too soon she surfaced. She found Doctor Meadows smiling down upon her with his short grey teeth, triumphantly announcing that youth would out, that the organism strove for life like the flower of the garden and the tree of the forest aspiring to the sunlight. The elfin doctor fairly hovered in the air with wings of gossamer aflutter. Pearl could not share this enthusiasm, for her crisis waited as loyally as a dog: she was still pregnant. Added to this was the fact that as soon as Pearl was up and about, her mother fell ill, having apparently contracted some sickness of her own, or more likely whatever ague Pearl had brought in from the night.

More than a little too fond of Florence, Doctor Meadows became an almost permanent fixture in the house as he redoubled his attentions upon his new patient. He had a vast and idiosyncratic pharmacopoeia to call upon, and he vibrated with the conviction of one ever eager to advance medical theory and practice. So committed was he to medical progress that he routinely tried out new treatments on himself, and if these resulted in rashes or fevers or convulsions, as did his experiments with strychnine and mercury, it was merely the price of science. He took medicine seriously, the Hippocratic oath was Holy Writ, and having studied in London and Montpellier and spent one winter in Padua, no physician in the city was held in higher esteem. He could have enjoyed a successful practice in London or New York, and yet for an undisclosed reason he had chosen tiny, obscure Victoria.

During her mother's illness, Pearl became mistress of the house. Sorting through the mail one morning she recognized Mr. Gloster's handwriting, and she took it upon herself to read the letter—an invitation to tea—and responded by the midday post, informing him of her mother's condition. He came that evening, breathing hard as if he'd run the entire way. Pearl could not picture Mr. Gloster running, or rather she could but it was not flattering. When she opened the door to let him in, she saw his buggy by the gate. His pale brow and frantic eyes shouted that he was a man in love. And so Pearl promptly showed him into her mother's room, an indiscretion perhaps but he was so distraught she couldn't bear keeping him alone in the parlour much less turning him away at the door. After all, had they not taken Christmas dinner with him, had he not proposed marriage, was he not all but her mother's fiancé and Pearl's stepfather?

Gloster was not ten minutes with Florence when Pearl responded to a second knock and admitted Doctor Meadows.

"Doctor."

"Young lady." Meadows was smiling and eager even as he was grave and professional. He asked who belonged to the other buggy at the gate and, when he learned it was Gloster's, his smile died and he became severe. "She should not be receiving visitors."

Florence soon found herself being attended by two men, neither of whom welcomed the other's presence.

Gloster would have been blind not to have detected Meadows's interest in Florence at the Dunsmuirs' party. The fellow had contrived to wedge himself between them both physically and conversationally. It had gotten so bad that Gloster had been ready to pick the doctor up and carry him down the slope and shove him head foremost into the shrubbery. Few would expect it, but he had boxed as a boy in England and studied Indian wrestling in Benares.

Meadows, for his part, had been monitoring the progress, or more importantly the lack of progress, that Gloster was making with Florence. Rating it nil, he had seen fit to make advances. His time in Montpellier and Padua having not been devoted solely to medical studies, he believed he had learned a great deal from his fellow students, French and Italian, in the *Ars Amatoria*.

Florence had been all too aware of the doctor's excessive concern for his new patient, and had Giles Meadows been the keen observer he imagined himself to be, he would have noted her expression of dry-eyed fatigue each time he came sailing in all breezy with cheer and a new remedy to hand. That Meadows was scarcely five feet tall in his French boots made Florence feel she was being courted by a dwarf. This was uncharitable, she knew, but there it was.

Now there were two of them, each admirable in his way, each at the moment utterly too much.

Meadows wasted no time in playing his trump. He was a physician with his patient and therefore must insist... Gloster saw no alternative but to withdraw, though as he did, he attempted significant eye contact with Florence who did her best to reciprocate, reaching out to take his hand and giving it a squeeze. Meadows nearly whimpered in agony at the sight of them touching. Nonetheless, when Gloster was gone, Meadows gave Florence a look to imply their shared relief at being rid of the pestiferous fellow. He then set about erecting a canvas canopy painted robin's egg blue overtop of her and set a mix of peppermint and salt water to simmer for her to inhale. Pocket watch in one hand he frowned and put his forefinger to her inner wrist—so pale, so smooth, the arteries and tendons so intimate—trying not to be diverted by the sheer thrill of touching her and, counting her pulse, was pleased to announce that it was slow and deep and steady. "We want you up and about before the weather turns so that you face November in full strength."

"I feel better already," she lied.

He smiled and nodded and took her at her word. "That is the spirit." Bold, he took her hand and pressed it and she returned the pressure. Why not? She was tired and confused and only wished he would leave.

Elated, he asked if there was anything he could do.

"You've done so much," she assured him.

"There are patients and there are patients," he said, his tone rich with innuendo.

"I will sleep now."

"Excellent, excellent."

When he was gone, Florence directed Carpy to get rid of the canopy and bring her a whiskey. When she had glugged it down, she turned over and shut her eyes. She wished that she was Alice and could go through the eyes of the photograph and find the only man she'd truly loved. But that was a fantasy. Soon the whiskey did its work and she slept and dreamed that she was the woman in the bottle she'd given Gloster for Christmas. In the dream she was emerging up onto the deck, breathing the sea air and feeling the freedom of travelling far from land.

✦

WHEN GLOSTER HAD EMERGED FROM Florence's room, exiled by the doctor, Carpy had been waiting. She put her hand to her hair as though to check that it was in order and then placed it on Mr. Gloster's forearm and leaned close and spoke to him. Gloster appeared alarmed and then intrigued and finally nodded his agreement. Pearl had watched this from down the corridor and when she joined them, Carpy pointedly ignored her and then went off to attend to her duties. Gloster seemed distracted and Pearl asked if he was feeling unwell and he said that he was worried about her mother.

"As am I," Pearl assured him.

"Of course."

"Meadows..." he began, though did not continue.

"I'm afraid you have a rival." Pearl offered a sympathetic expression.

"So it would appear."

"Do not give up."

Gloster regarded her, his eyes seeking, and receiving, solace and assurance.

"Please," she insisted. "She will come around."

He was heartened and asked after her studies.

"I am not attending school."

He frowned uncomprehendingly.

Pearl had been about to indicate the missing rugs and vases but realized that Gloster had never been inside their house and therefore could not mark the changes. "Reduced circumstances." She shrugged in what she intended to be a display of dignified stoicism.

Gloster was about to express his pain that they had not turned to him for help, but he held back for he understood that Florence was proud. He admired that. Still, it could also mean that she was determined to keep him at a distance and that was not a welcome sign.

"And how then are you occupying your time?" he asked.

Squaring her shoulders and holding in her stomach, she said she was reading widely in history, literature, and the more speculative arts, hoping that the latter might engage his interest, but he seemed distracted. "How is Cleopatra?" she asked.

For a moment he did not comprehend. "Ah. Passable. I'm afraid the climate here is hard on her. I fear it was selfish of me to take her out of her natural environment."

"Perhaps if she had a companion."

"I had considered that. The logistics are not simple. And perhaps not wise."

"Another trip to Egypt," suggested Pearl with sincerity. "For Cleopatra's sake and Mother's. I would think that the dry climate would be most beneficial to her chest."

He smiled gratefully. "Perhaps I shall suggest it."

"Do."

"Well," he said, about to depart.

Seeing an opportunity passing, Pearl put her hand on his arm to halt him, glanced around, saw that the corridor was clear, and asked if she could tell him something.

He lowered his voice. "Of course."

As Pearl told him about Cassidy, Gloster was silent, blinking and frowning, and finally nodded as if to say he understood. When he was gone, Pearl turned from the door and found Carpy at the far end of the corridor, watching.

✦

THE FOLLOWING DAY FLORENCE GOT out of bed and Cassidy, with impeccable timing, made her third visit.

"I do hope you are recovered, Sinead."

"I thought we agreed."

"And so we did. I can only plead the press of unexpected complications. How is Pearl? Time not weighing too heavily, I hope."

"More heavily than it weighs upon your conscience."

"Ah, you are one to lecture on the topic of conscience."

"What can I do for you?"

"Ever to business, Sinead. Always your way. I have a proposition."

"Of what nature?"

"Information transfer."

"Pray explain."

"I would keep you informed."

Florence thought she heard a shuffling in the corridor and knew that Pearl or Carpy or both were listening. Cassidy noted the shift in Florence's attention and observed that in this day and age of newspapers and telegraphs everyone was hungry for data.

"It is a thirst we all share," said Cassidy. "Satisfying on so many levels and ever the more necessary."

Florence would have argued the opposite; all too often the less she knew the less she worried and, hence, the more serene she felt. "And upon what topics would I require data?"

"Family."

"You refer to Pearl."

"She is at a fragile age."

Florence waited.

"And about friends."

Florence did not know that she had any friends.

"You have admirers in Charles Gloster and the good Doctor Meadows."

"I hardly need you to tell me that."

"Men are not always what they seem."

"Nor women," said Florence.

Cassidy let that slide. "Certain men you know have secrets."

Florence said nothing.

Cassidy smiled, sphinx-like. In contrast to her previous visits, she was clean and well dressed, hair neat and complexion clear.

The clock on the mantel ticked and the fire in the grate hissed. Florence was in no way surprised that Cassidy was busy digging dirt yet would on no account appear interested even if, in truth, she was frightened and desperate to know more. Had Cassidy unearthed something about Charles? That he was a fraud, a murderer?

"That is a fine locket," said Florence.

"It contains a miniature of one I once knew."

"Surely you have known far too many to fit such a small device."

Cassidy smiled, immune to the implications. "There are people and there are people, just as there is knowledge and there is knowledge, Sinead. You know that." She went to the parlour door where she turned and stated that she would be back in two days.

When she was gone both Pearl and Carpy came in, Pearl speechless at what she'd heard and Carpy sucking her teeth and regarding Florence with a stern-eyed expression meant to remind her of what she'd said about there being people who did things.

"Yes," said Florence, acknowledging Carpy's look. "I rather think it is time for strong coffee."

Pearl and her mother had coffee in the parlour and watched the wind shred leaves from the trees.

"Mother."

"Don't be naïve, Pearl. Each of us has a past. Surely you've worked that out by now."

But it was the future that concerned Pearl. She looked around the parlour and her gaze halted at the photograph of her father. She glanced at her mother and began to speak but stopped herself. She slipped her palm to her belly—how round and hard and hot it felt—then quickly withdrew it. She looked at the mantel above the glowing coals in the fireplace. A profile of the Queen, a few ceramic figurines, a vase containing pampas grass. She thought of the sphinx at the Dunsmuirs', she thought of Mr. Gloster and imagined he and her mother and herself sailing away on one of the ships in the harbour, the *Queen of Yokohama* perhaps, or was it the *Queen of Hong Kong*? She tried to imagine Yokohama and Hong Kong, and thought of the streets here in Victoria's Chinatown, narrow, spiced, strange. Oh, to simply sail away.

Her mother's hand settled upon hers, cool and dry and almost but not quite reassuring. The wind intensified and began shrieking in the attic and more leaves sped past the window followed by a spatter of rain.

"I have an idea," announced Pearl.

"Do go on."

"We move to New Zealand. It is just coming on spring there."

"New Zealand."

"Or Hong Kong or Australia or Cape Town. I have had very good reports about Cape Town."

"I have heard rumours of war," said her mother.

"Then New Zealand it is."

"Pearl, I am not going anywhere."

"We can escape Cassidy."

"She is inescapable. But don't trouble yourself. She's my concern. Trust me, I can handle her." And again, she patted Pearl's hand.

"Why don't you marry Mr. Gloster?"

"Why, why, why. You sound like a bird."

"Mother! He loves you, he would be an ally."

"Ah, enlist him in our little war. I'm sure that is exactly what he desires in a marriage."

Chapter Ten

HER MOTHER'S CALM WAS SO baffling that Pearl suspected she must have some plan. Pearl's plans were a mess. She was now almost five months pregnant and it also should be her time of the month, meaning that she had to sneak into the pantry and secure some blood from the meat chest and wipe it on her pads. She'd been doing this on schedule from the start, all too aware that if she forgot it was just the sort of thing Carpy would notice and thus Pearl would be exposed. Only this morning there was no meat in the cooler. Carpy was off at the market. Panicking, Pearl took a knife from the rack and returned to her room and arranged her pads then clenching her teeth was about to slice into her finger but halted. Perhaps some spot on her leg would be more strategic? But there would be stains. Bite her lip or tongue? She cringed at the thought. She positioned the point of the knife on the inside of her thumb, then changed to the ring finger on her left hand, deciding it was more poetic, and with a whimper cut in and then hurriedly smeared her pads and put them in the hamper.

She had also been strategic about making a point of eating more. Whether or not she was hungry, and often she was not, she forced herself to second helpings and then vomited later in the outhouse.

"You're very calm," said Pearl that evening at supper. "Cassidy is coming back to destroy us and there you sit, a veritable buddha."

"Destruction, instruction, construction, deduction. Do you know the difference between *deduction* and *induction*?"

"You're mad, Mother. I'm going to send for Doctor Meadows."

"Perhaps you should go for one of your walks."

Pearl's gaze wavered and she fought not to blink her teary eyes.

The next day passed without incident. The day after, however, Pearl and Florence found themselves acutely aware of every bump and knock in the house, dreading Cassidy's predicted return. Carpy baked oat and corn biscuits to go with a roast venison stew but no one had much appetite for lunch. The long journey across the afternoon stretched before them.

"You would do well to practice your French," said her mother.

Pearl was about to be sarcastic but instead her heart leapt. "Are we going to France?"

"No."

"Montreal?"

"No."

"Haiti?"

"Hardly."

"Then why should I practice my French?"

"There may come a time—"

"I think we should go to Montreal. Or Quebec City. Or Paris. Do let us go to France, Mother. Please. It would—"

Then came the knock. They looked toward the door and Pearl very nearly sobbed while Florence clenched her napkin in her fist and stood.

"I'll go!" Pearl grabbed up her fork like a dagger.

"Sit."

Pearl glared, threw down the fork, but did not sit. She straightened her shawl, crossed her arms over her chest, felt that this was exposing the shape of her belly so uncrossed them, then turned and marched out of the nook of a dining room toward the front door.

"Pearl Greyland-Smith!"

Pearl defied her. Hair long and loose and flowing she strode to the door, determined to shove Cassidy off the porch and down the stairs. She swung it open.

"Good afternoon to you, ma'am. I am Inspector Osmo Beattie."

Pearl very nearly fell over backward. Drawing in her belly, she struggled to be calm and splendid and alluring and poised and intriguing rather than a galumphing hulk of a pug-nosed girl. "And good afternoon to you, Inspector," she said, gauging her tone and judging it adequately mature.

"I hope I've not caught you at an awkward hour," he said.

"Not at all, not at all." She willed him to recognize her, for surely he couldn't fail—here, now, in the full light of day, even if it was an overcast November afternoon—to remember her, to know her from having *known* her, to at the very least recognize her voice. He was, after all, a detective, it was his job to recognize people and unwind secrets. And yet there wasn't a flicker. Was she so bland, so inconsequential? Was he such a cad? Were men like roosters, and a hen but a hen but a hen? She quelled these thoughts and, heart beating fast, stepped back and ushered him toward the parlour where she indicated the chairs. He preferred to stand. He was nattily dressed, a gloss to his hair, tie fresh and collar starched and a shine on his boots. He held his bowler behind him and compressed his lips in a grave expression and for a moment Pearl saw him as if for the first time: he did not look like her notion of a policeman, certainly not the sort of bruiser generally seen plodding a beat, gripping a billy in one fist and knocking it against his thigh, impatient for a tasty target.

"You are the lady of the house?"

Did she look so old? Or was it a compliment on her maturity? She pitched her voice deeper and swelled her chest. "No. My mother has been ill."

"I'm sorry."

"Nothing serious," Florence reassured him as she entered and shook his hand.

"I'm very glad to hear it."

So here he was, thought Pearl, the Man from the Sphinx, Inspector Osmo Beattie, the man who'd walked past her in the street without a glance, the reputable, dutiful Inspector Osmo Beattie who, Pearl did not doubt, was also a bit of a lad and a philanderer and who knew what else.

He became solemn and informed them that there had been a death, at which Pearl and Florence made appropriately concerned sounds. "The corpse of a woman was discovered yesterday, in the water in James Bay. And this was in her pocket." From his coat he withdrew a wallet and from it produced an opened envelope, which he presented to Florence. It was dry but showed water damage, the ink blurred but readable. "As you see it is addressed to this house."

It was true. Not only did it bear her name, Florence Greyland-Smith, it had the stamp of the Provincial Seal, Office of the Registry, rearing stags flanking an escutcheon. Pearl stepped close to see for herself and knew that Cassidy must be behind it, that Cassidy was the dead woman, and was relieved and could feel that her mother was relieved as well.

"So she drowned?" asked Pearl.

The Inspector inhaled and shook his head. "Difficult to say. She may have been dead beforehand. Poison is a possibility, but it usually leaves discolouration or swelling. The time in the water has compromised the evidence. We must wait for the coroner's report."

Pearl studied him. He frowned as he spoke and turned his hat in his square strong hands. He was physical yet cerebral—what a ringing word, *cerebral*, bell-like and clear—and Pearl envisioned him swimming miles out to sea at night, like Lord Byron, and then floating on his back and naming the constellations: Orion's Belt, Ursa Major, Ursa Minor, and there, a comet, or was it a meteor, and knowing the difference between the two...

What a grave existence. Pearl imagined his life immersed in such grisly events and wondered if he brooded upon them in the evening as he fell asleep and then dreamed of them through the night and thought of them when he woke. Did he dwell on them Sunday afternoons, or while taking his exercise or eating his meals? Did he discuss these crimes with his wife or think it best to keep her innocent, except of course there was no wife—or was that only Pearl's hopeful, desperate naïveté? Surely a married man did not live in a boarding house. She glanced furtively at his finger but saw no ring. Did policemen perhaps not wear wedding rings in case they got in the way of apprehending criminals? Certainly, she would be more than ready to talk him through his dilemmas or simply be there in silent sympathy, day in, day out, and in the long hours of the night. Yes, she would read his manner and expression and do what was best, it being the least a wife could do, for he was too young to shoulder such burdens as murder on his own.

"Dreadful," said Florence. "Can you tell her age?"

"Forty. Thirty-five. Perhaps younger."

"Tragic," said Florence. "A woman with so many years yet before her."

He gathered himself, shifted his hat from one hand to the other, held it behind him then in front, and asked, "And so you've no idea who the woman could be or how she came to be in possession of your mail?"

Pearl was about to mention Cassidy—unable to resist the temptation to offer him something and thereby deepen his interest and draw them closer—but her mother, sensing the direction she was about to take, cut her off.

"None at all, none at all."

"You've had no...visitors?"

"We live a quiet life. Truly, I find this all very upsetting," she added.

Inspector Beattie was prompt to offer his arm and guide her to a chair while Pearl watched and found herself jealous. "Mother, you should return to bed."

Her mother ignored her. Once settled in the chair she studied the envelope, turning it over and over until, looking up, she declared it a mystery.

"So, you've no—"

"As I say, none." How genuinely bewildered and innocent she appeared; Pearl had to admire her acting.

Osmo Beattie compressed his lips and contemplated. "This letter, may I enquire as to its nature?"

"I lost my birth certificate." Florence looked at him though she seemed to speak to Pearl.

He considered this. "And you've had no unusual visitors?"

"Not that I am aware." She looked enquiringly at Pearl and then to Carpy who had emerged from the kitchen and now stood in the doorway of the parlour.

"Then it must have been purloined en route." He frowned and looked down at his hat. "Well then." With an apologetic smile and a slight bow, he thanked them and said that he would see himself out.

Pearl nonetheless accompanied him to the door and onto the porch and down the steps and along the shell-lined walk. Her mind sped. It felt as though they were proceeding down a tunnel. She had to say something intelligent about the case that would impress herself upon his mind. Or should she lay some hint about their night in the sphinx, an inadvertent hint, or a blatant one? "What a mystery," she said. "Like the sphinx."

They had reached the gate. Beattie regarded the young woman, his thick eyebrows arched, admirable head tilted in an attitude of professional interest.

"What will you do now?" she asked.

"As I said, await the coroner's report."

"Of course." She cursed her stupidity. "Was she well dressed?"

"Yes, as a matter of fact."

"Perhaps a concerned family member is even now at the station."

"Possibly."

Pearl was aware of her mother watching from the window. A crow launched itself cawing from a branch of the arbutus. Would he think more or less of her if she told him that her mother had lied; would he have greater respect for an adherence to principle or loyalty to family?

"Thank you for bringing the letter," Pearl said. "I'm sorry we couldn't be of more help. If I think of anything I shall most certainly let you know."

He thanked her. Perhaps it was the habit of a man in his profession, but he studied her as though to describe her later to a police artist, and she was afraid, because she didn't want to be in any police log and because she was not beautiful and his scrutiny might find yet more flaws; then again maybe it wasn't so much what he saw but what he heard—her voice, reminding him of that summer night—but his conclusions, if any, remained hidden. Now he turned from her and considered the cold grey overcast. In the distance, on the American side of the strait, stood the mountains. "My suspicion is that this is a murder," he said slowly, as if the thought was coming to him only now. "And the killer." He paused. "The killer may well be a woman."

The air abraded Pearl's throat and it hurt to swallow. "How do you know?"

"I don't. It is a theory. One develops a sense."

"How subtle."

"As I say, one develops an instinct."

"Intriguing. And terrible. Sphinx-like," she added.

"Just so," he said. "Odd thing," he continued. "Perhaps nothing. But the dead woman had a snake earring, a green serpent devouring its own tail. Well." He presented his card and touched the brim of his hat and then went out of the gate.

Inspector Osmo L. Beattie
Victoria Metropolitan Police
City Hall

When Osmo was out of sight Pearl turned back to the house and was relieved to see that her mother was no longer in the window. She went over every word and look and pause between herself and Osmo and could scarcely keep from weeping. Had he realized who she was but kept it to himself? Was such self-control part of an inspector's repertoire? Surely it behooved a man such as he to be strategic and keep his own counsel. But in his private life as well? Or did the one spill into the other? These were large questions. They so preoccupied Pearl as she went back inside that when she found her mother unconscious on the parlour rug, she could only stare. Then she shouted and Carpy came running. She knelt by Florence then directed Pearl to get the doctor. An instant later Pearl was in the street and found a boy with a brace of ducks dangling from his belt and begged him to go for help. She returned to the parlour where she and Carpy helped her mother, groggy but awake, to bed.

Meadows was there in twenty minutes, bounding from his gig, which he left swaying before the gate, his two mares steaming.

"Florence!"

"Doctor."

Stung by such formality, he said, "Giles, please."

She smiled apologetically. "Giles. Shameless of me to bother you again. I fear that Pearl and Carpy have overreacted."

"You've had a relapse."

"Not at all. We had some distressing news. I merely stood too quickly." She was sitting up in bed and smiled easily.

He was taking no chances. Lifting her wrist as though it were a rare lily he took her pulse, his chin disappearing into his red cravat as he frowned at his gold watch. Clearing his throat, he said, "If I may." And placed the end of his stethoscope on her chest and listened to the heart he so wished to win. What he heard worried him.

"Do I have a dicky ticker?" asked Florence, trying to be lighthearted.

"An erratic pulse." He exhaled heavily.

"Meaning?"

"You need calm. What is this news you mentioned?"

"A policeman," said Pearl. "Inspector Osmo Beattie."

"A policeman. Here?" Alarmed, Meadows looked at Pearl then back at Florence. "What did he want?"

Florence explained.

"He thinks it was murder," said Pearl.

"Well, that is distressing," agreed Meadows. After a moment's grave reflection, he turned again to Florence. "Headaches?"

"No more than usual," said Florence.

"Cough?"

"No."

He asked if her dreams were disordered and she smiled and said she did not believe they'd ever had any order at all, that that was the nature of dreams.

He was severe. "The mind and the body," he said, cautioning.

"You are admirably progressive."

"Her colour is actually quite good," offered Pearl, for her mother was, as a matter of fact, looking radiant, her cheeks pink, brow smooth, eyes clear, and her hair, loose about her shoulders, lustrous.

Meadows, however, was unimpressed. He instructed Carpy to pack her mistress's pillow with lemon rind and ginger, burn sticks of cinnamon of which he had a ready supply, and take one glass of stout at breakfast and red wine with supper. He took Pearl aside.

In his considered opinion something grave was on her mother's mind. "I suspect a trauma," he said. "And it has lodged in her blood. I have seen it in women her age. Does she drink coffee?"

"We all drink coffee, and tea."

"Tobacco?"

"She does not smoke."

"I recommend iron wine before bed. She must have iron."

Instructing Carpy in the simmering of nails in port, he also showed her some powder, tasteless but effective, guaranteed to make her sleep.

"A Chinese remedy," he explained, having been in Peking during the Second Opium War in the medical service. Then to Florence he added, "I've been meaning to ask, but I seem to recall a Major Edward Greyland-Smith." He gazed enquiringly at her.

Florence grew vague and let her eyelids sink as though she must sleep.

"Good," said Meadows, as if they were in absolute agreement. "Rest."

When Meadows had gone Carpy said, "He'd marry you tomorrow."

"I do not wish to marry him tomorrow or any day."

"It's Gloster then, is it?" asked Carpy, with the grim expression of one reaffirming bad news.

Florence thought of the woman in the ship-in-a-bottle she'd given Gloster. "What I desire at the moment is a bottle of sunshine in which I can curl up and sleep. That or a coffee." She smiled and stretched her arms out then threw aside the bedcovers, got up and stretched her arms high over her head.

✦

AT SUPPER PEARL REMARKED UPON her mother's impressive recovery and excellent appetite then asked if she had any theories.

"I suspect that our dear Cassidy had an assortment of victims and therefore a wide circle of enemies."

"Will we get our carpets back?"

"They're probably in a brothel."

"Mother!"

Florence helped herself to more wine.

"You don't seem very sad."

"Are you?"

"She's where she belongs," stated Carpy, entering with the rice pudding.

"In the Bardo?"

"Ha. She'll be lucky to be reborn as a snake."

Being the first Wednesday of the month, Carpy was off to her meeting of the Theosophical Society. Over the years, Pearl had become less intrigued and more troubled by Carpy's theosophical business. As a child Pearl had accepted it; as an adult she was judgemental. Carpy? Pearl could see her in the Catholic church on her knees but theosophy, as far as Pearl knew, was a much more refined and elevated business. There was a side Carpy kept hidden, maybe many sides, and this frankly shocked Pearl. The very idea that this stumpy, pie-faced drudge had a life apart from scrubbing and cooking and complaining, a side that was, of all things, mystical, was almost an affront, and hence even more intriguing.

"Do you see Mr. Gloster at your meetings?" she asked Carpy.

"As a matter of fact." She spoke in a studiously neutral tone as she pulled on her gloves.

Pearl looked from Carpy to her mother, who paged through a copy of *Punch*.

When Carpy was gone, Pearl asked her mother what she knew about theosophy. Florence regarded her daughter as if to say there you go again, asking questions, putting your nose in.

"What Carpenter does on her own time—"

"But you don't find it odd? I mean...*Carpy*." Pearl heard her tone of condescension and thought what a smug and scornful beast she had become, for there was a time not so very long ago when she earnestly wished for Carpy to take her to a meeting of the theosophists. "And what of Mr. Gloster's interest in it? If you marry him, won't you be obliged to go along as well? Won't you at least be curious?"

Her mother held out her mug with its gold trim and Pearl refilled it from the decanter of iron wine. "You might try some of this yourself," Florence said.

"It's too early to sleep."

"It might keep you out of trouble."

Pearl blanched. Trouble, what did she mean by trouble, what was she implying? Holding her stomach in and fluffing her blouse, she put the decanter back on the shelf.

Her mother drank down her wine then returned to her magazine, on the cover of which a wreath of comic grotesque characters like something out of Hieronymus Bosch encircled a painter in a clown outfit who was rendering a dog into a lion.

"We should go to England," said Pearl.

"We should go to bed," said Florence. She closed her magazine and stood. At the parlour door she turned. "Divine wisdom."

"Excuse me?"

"Theosophy. It means divine wisdom."

"So, you have taken an interest," said Pearl.

"No midnight snacking," said her mother. "You're gaining weight."

"Of course I'm gaining weight," said Pearl, brazen. "I'm bored, idle, and depressed. I should be at school."

Florence considered this. Yes, sad girls ate, got fat, became sadder, ate more, and it became a vicious circle.

"If you married Mr. Gloster he would pay my tuition and buy us a new rug."

"Good night."

Alone, Pearl stared into the fire. What possessed the flames to such fury? Some ravenous obsession, or mere blind chemistry? Carpy claimed that there were cases of people combusting, one moment going about their business and the next, poof, up in flames. At one time Pearl would have enjoyed seeing Carpy combust, spontaneously or any which way. It would have added excitement to her life, but that was then; at the moment she had all the excitement she needed. Cassidy—dead. Her mother—two suitors. Herself—pregnant. Osmo—right here in their parlour and yet he might as well have been on the moon.

Chapter Eleven

AT EIGHT THE FOLLOWING MORNING, Doctor Meadows was back. He was still there at ten when a boy delivered a bouquet that consisted of cedar boughs, azalea, and hibiscus flowers. It was accompanied by a note from Charles Gloster who had heard from Carpy at the meeting of the Theosophical Society the previous evening that Florence had suffered a relapse. The doctor appeared alarmed and unhappy at these flowers. He insisted they be exiled to the parlour. Florence, Pearl, and Carpy were not a little shocked even after Meadows explained that the cedar would conflict with the diffusion of mint and lemon balm he had prepared.

Meadows seemed excessively anxious, especially given that Florence was feeling so much better. She'd been up and about since seven and had even hummed various tunes as she went about her toilet. The normally impeccable Meadows had egg stains on his tie and wore a collar that was not crisp.

"Really, Doctor—"

"Giles, *Giles!*"

"Giles. But I'm on the mend."

"You're pale."

"It is November. Most everyone is pale."

He wasn't amused. He tested her pulse. Hands like a raccoon, thought Florence. He shook his head. "Your heartbeat is weak."

"Well, a weak beat is better than no beat, wouldn't you agree?" Meadows's lip twitched. He hated not being taken seriously. "I will have chamomile tea," said Florence to placate him. He frowned. "You need strong coffee. Something to invigorate."

"Then coffee it is," she said and even managed a smile. When he was gone at last, Florence read Gloster's note.

> *My Dearest Florence,*
> *It was with the deepest regret that I learned of your relapse. Permit me to express my concerns. If there is anything at all that I can do, anything at all, please let me know. My time is yours. My carriage is yours. I beg you, do not hesitate to call upon me, and, when you are recovered, which I hope will be very soon, I hope that I might come and pay my respects.*
> *The flowers, I trust, are not overly clumsy.*
>
> *I remain,*
>
> *Yours,*
> *Charles Gloster*

When she had finished rereading the letter, Florence called Carpy to bring the bouquet back in and place it on the table beside her bed. Florence translated, pointing to the cedar boughs as symbolic of devotion, the azaleas as a plea to take care of oneself, and the hibiscus as meaning that the sender lived but for she who received the bouquet.

Carpy looked as glum as a toad and left the room without a word.

A moody stump of a creature, thought Florence. What good was all her theosophy? It was too bad that Doctor Meadows wouldn't set his cap for her, but a doctor and a drudge, it was out of the question. Cupping one of the five azalea blossoms in her hand, she smiled then frowned, which was how Pearl found her.

"Mr. Gloster?"

"Yes."

"Do you love him?"

"No."

"But you like and admire and respect him."

"It's a lovely bouquet."

"And Doctor Meadows?

"Hardly."

"They both love you."

Florence gazed off through her bedroom window, which looked onto the laurel hedge separating them from the Livingstones' next door. She observed that Pearl and the inspector had been all tête-à-tête the previous day.

"He thinks Cassidy was murdered. By a woman."

"He's a handsome fellow. You all but threw yourself at him."

"It's good that she's dead."

"They don't respect that."

"I only wanted more information," said Pearl. "Did you kill her?"

"Yes, I strangled her. It was most satisfying. I might take it up as a hobby. Though it is rather hard on the fingernails. And of course, there's all the blood."

"There'd be no blood if you strangled her."

"Quite the expert, are you?"

"I want the truth!"

"An overrated commodity. Apt to cause nothing but pain. Someday you will know that. What a drizzly morning it is."

"It's always drizzling. Victoria is wretched. It drizzles ten months a year. And if it's not rain there's fog or snow. We should move to Australia."

Florence held out her cup and saucer for Pearl to fetch her more coffee. Alone, she thought that perhaps she did love Charles Gloster. Certainly, she was impressed—frightened and impressed. That is if he did indeed kill Cassidy, if not with his own hands, then having had someone else do it. Did this put them on an equal footing, each of them now having done the dread deed? Or was this an ill-fated way to start a marriage?

Pearl found Carpy smoking a cheroot and reading an article in the *Colonist* about members of Clan na Gael sentenced to life in Millbank Prison for attempting to blow up the Tower of London. Pearl thought of the women in the lives of these men—mothers, sisters, lovers. Did they visit them? Were Irish Dynamiters allowed visitors? It seemed darkly glamorous, and she envied them their strange and tragic destinies. She asked Carpy if she was a Fenian, at which Carpy raised a frying pan as if to give her a clap on the side of the skull.

"Do you speak Gaelic?"

"Your mother doesn't like garlic."

"I'm serious."

"This is the New World."

"Not to the Songhees," said Pearl. "They're going to rise up and stab us in our sleep," she said with grim triumph. "If I was a Songhees it's what I'd do. I'd creep in and stab each and every one of us in our sleep, right through the heart, so there."

"If you were my daughter, I'd beat you blue."

"Well, I'm not your daughter, thank you very much, so you're out of luck."

"Luck." She snorted.

"Why do they say the luck of the Irish?" Pearl asked, suddenly troubled. "They seem a very unlucky people."

"Maybe it wasn't an Irishman who said it. The Irish are a wounded people. There's a difference. In Dublin they go to Grangegorman. For the sick of soul."

Pearl thought about that: the sick of soul. She stared around the kitchen. The door to Carpy's alcove was open. "What's that?"

"What's what?"

Pearl pointed to the hose-and-funnel contraption on her window ledge with those strange bottles. It was the thing Carpy had used on Grandfather Snead's old dog, Medusa. Carpy regarded Pearl with suspicion and then said that it was a siphon, for sucking. "I've told you."

"A siphon for sucking what?"

Carpy said nothing. She mashed the stub of her cheroot into a clam shell ashtray then refilled her mistress's cup with coffee and presented it to Pearl.

As Pearl carried the coffee to her mother, she thought of dropping it on purpose to shatter the cup and saucer. It seemed an inspired idea. She halted in the corridor and raised the saucer and cup as high as she could reach and was about to let it fall when she changed her mind, not because it was such a beautiful bit of china that her mother valued so absurdly but because she had rather more pressing business to which she must attend.

Chapter Twelve

AS SHE DID EVERY MORNING now, Pearl stood before the mirror in her room gauging the state of her abdomen. Round, full, warm, and yet not obvious beneath her jumper—or not overly obvious, certainly not glaringly obvious. Well, she cautioned herself, her mother had noticed but not reached the dread conclusion. She turned to the right and evaluated her profile. Frowning, she exhaled then inhaled, squared her shoulders, and stood taller. Better. If nothing else, it was a goad to improve her posture. Standing straight and tall and inflating her chest with her ever more fulsome breasts, her belly was of little note—or of lesser note. Not that anyone noted her anyway what with her pug nose and wide jaw and indifferent hair. She turned her back to the mirror and looked over her shoulder. There was no doubt that her rear end had widened. The word *buttocks* took on new meaning. What a tangible term: *buttocks*. Butt ox. It was all she could do not to sob.

Seeing Osmo's card on her desk, she picked it up. It felt scandalous to hold it while naked. *Inspector Osmo L. Beattie*. What did the *l* stand for? Langston? Lawrence? Lazarus? Lemuel? Leonard? Leopold? Lowell? Logan? Lupo? Lyndon? Lucky? No, she could not see him called Lucky. Lucky was a name for a dog or an American. What did it matter, except that everything about him mattered, that perhaps the key she sought was buried in one seemingly insignificant detail? The letter *l*. Love. The key was not how to make him fall in love with her, for love, she had decided, was a ludicrous delusion, but the letter *d*, how to make him do his duty by her. Was he not a dutiful man? Meaning what? Simply tell him? Resulting in marriage and then motherhood, thus preserving the family dignity and maintaining, or winning, her mother's respect and keeping Carpy's mouth shut. Yes, this was the only route to pursue. Except that she wondered if there had been others before her, others who had confronted him. How had that gone for them? And what of the fact that she'd worn her veil? He might well doubt her word. No. It was too close to blackmail. She envisioned a grim and tedious scene. How chilly the room was in spite of the fire murmuring in the grate. She drew on her robe. Sitting at her desk, she put her fists to her temples and urged her brain to work harder. Was his showing up at their door after her many failed attempts to meet him not a gift, a sign, a godsend? She had to capitalize on it. If love and duty were out of the question, was there some other approach, some other reason to contact him? She got up and began to pace, analyzing everything about Cassidy and her visits. It would have to be something good, for she could not waste his time and make herself look silly. She had to be profound and insightful and mature, not some ridiculous girl who had got herself up-the-spout of a summer night. On a sheet of paper, she listed everything about Cassidy's clothes, manner, speech, any detail she might have let slip that could be a clue, and kept returning to the singular fact that Cassidy had quite plainly pinched a piece of their mail while in the parlour. Yet why a letter pertaining to her mother's identity? Or had it merely been the most convenient, the one lying at the top of the pile?

At the same time, she worried that if she did discover a clue it might lead to her mother's arrest, which implied that she'd actually done it. Had she? Her mother? Was it possible? No.

Never. Then again . . . Pearl knew she had to consider every possibility, that this was too grave a matter for slipshod thinking, much less sentiment. Clear, cold, implacable logic was essential. It became a tic in her brain. Over the following days every time she looked at her mother she evaluated her, trying to spot the potential for murder. She had a temper and a quick hand and good reason to fear Cassidy. But murder?

Perhaps she'd suborned Carpy into serving as her accomplice? Pearl began watching Carpy as well.

"Carpy," she asked, "what do you think happened to Cassidy?" She was standing beside her in the kitchen. Above them the suspended rack of newly washed laundry dripped *hiss-spat* onto the hot stove, the copper kettle was beginning to tremble as it approached a boil, and a slushy rain slid past the window. It was a day so cold and clammy that Pearl might well have crawled into the oven itself. As it was, she stood so close her thighs were scorched, though she did not step away. She extended hands, palms riding the rising heat like birds on the wing.

Carpy sucked her teeth and shrugged. This was unusual. Carpy, no theory? In spite of her low beginnings, she read widely in the gazettes and even books from the lending library and relished trotting out nuggets of information. *Soon they'll heat the world from volcanoes. Soon the doctors'll do away with pain. In Germany they're breeding birds that will drop bombs on the French* . . . But as for the fate of Cassidy, she was suddenly mute. Pearl was suspicious and wondered if Carpy was covering up. She wanted to suggest that she consult her onions but feared she'd think Pearl was mocking her, which, in a way, she was, for Carpy did indeed see mystical properties in onions, handling them with reverence, separating their layers one by one, and studying them in the morning light spilling through the kitchen window.

"So you don't have a theory?"

"I might have many things."

"The inspector thinks she was murdered. By a woman."

"So you said."

The kettle began to vibrate faster as if some trapped sprite was growing frantic to escape.

"Mother had a motive."

Carpy bunched her lips as if biting them in order to stay silent.

Pearl lowered her hands over the stove; the heat intensified and the skin on her palms tightened. "I'd be tempted to kill her. She was blackmailing us." The skin of her palms began to burn.

"Your mother's almost an invalid with a dicky heart."

"She's big, and she's not so very old."

"Mine pegged out at twenty-seven."

"The money," said Pearl. "Mother poisoned the blackmail money."

"Or the spoons," said Carpy. "Poisoned the silver spoons so that when Cassidy slurped her soup it'd do her in. Or learned some of that Japanese jiu-jitsu. Or hit her with one of those Aborigine death shouts. My cousin Gerald wrote me a letter from Wollongong saying how he got nicked in the ear by a shout at forty paces." Her voice had remained so sincere that for a few moments Pearl was almost taken in. She envied men, who could simply punch each other to vent their rage.

As she had Carpy talking, she pressed on and asked about Osmo, the inspector, as she was careful to say. Carpy claimed never to have spoken to the man and Pearl said, but you've heard rumours. Carpy shrugged and said, maybe, maybe not, and Pearl said she was surprised, implying that Carpy's sources weren't so very good after all. Pearl turned to leave the kitchen and, as hoped, Carpy, unable to resist, relented and said she'd heard that the inspector had been a tile setter and a typesetter and a paint maker. Then out of the blue, at the age of seventeen, he up and solves a murder. It was the case of the ghost ship

Venture out of Valparaíso. Every hand, including the captain, found dead, lying on their backs in their cabins and hammocks, clad in clean white robes belted with tasselled lengths of white rope, each corpse looking peaceful, each clasping a page on their chests on which was handwritten a sentence from the Book of Revelations: "Blessed are those who wash their robes, that they may have the right to the tree of life and may go through the gates into the city." The only creatures alive were the ship's three male orange Manx cats. Every sort of theory was put forward—plague, murder, divine retribution, punishment from on high, nefarious influences from Luciferian forces below. Some suspected that the robes themselves were tainted with the smallpox, and yet no evidence was found. The corpses were fresh, as if newly embalmed. The first on the scene even claimed that the bodies smelled of clover, that the entire ship smelled like a flower garden in spring. It was Beattie who saw that it was a mass suicide by men brainwashed into believing they were taking a shortcut to the Hereafter. The question was who had led them and how? Was he one of the corpses, or had he fled once the ship arrived in Victoria? The answer came in the form of an itinerant preacher a few miles up-island, attempting to compel a crew of Cumberland coal miners to divest themselves of all their worldlies in favour of riches incomparably finer in the World to Come. Young Osmo had heard the rumour and on his own initiative investigated. Authorities soon discovered one Thomas Jepps in possession of Spanish and Portuguese coins, as well as dozens of gold and silver watches and rings, many of them personalized, corresponding to the names on the crew list of the *Venture*.

The kettle began to shrill. Carpy wrapped her hand in her apron and gripped the wire handle and slopped water into the teapot and gave it a swirl.

"Well, something happened."

"Happened to who?"

"Cassidy."

"Got what she deserved and amen to that. You'd do well to keep your snoot out of it. Where there's one murder there's often another."

"So you do think it was murder!" triumphed Pearl.

Carpy faced her. "Don't be a bobstick. There's no more meat on the bone so leave off gnawing, you'll only wear out your chompers."

Pearl waited for her to go on but Carpy busied herself sliding the hot cobbler onto a blue plate, then set it and the teapot and cups on the black lacquered tray along with napkins and spoons and a pot of marmalade. Pearl followed her along the corridor to the parlour where Florence sat with her knees against the peacock-patterned fire screen. Carpy set the tray on the brass table and, pursing her lips and sucking her teeth, awaited some sort of acknowledgement. When it did not come, she sniffed and left.

"Is fire not a fine thing?" said Florence. "It punishes and it purifies and it illuminates."

Pearl studied her mother then looked about the room at the Victoriana. When her gaze passed over the photo of her father, she asked, "Do you miss him?"

Florence did not look at Pearl but continued staring into the fire. "Of course I miss him. Every day I miss him. He had no business going off like that."

"He was a Servant of Empire," said Pearl, frowning, confused. "The British Empire."

"Tell it to the American Indians. Tell it to the East Indians. Tell it to the enslaved Africans." She watched the coals in the grate hiss and collapse.

Ah, her mother was in a mood. The relief and buoyancy at Cassidy's death had passed and she'd gone into a despond. Guilt? What she needed was protection. It seemed to Pearl that the rich might kill, insult, thieve, be as blithely cruel and brutal as they pleased and never be held to account, but the poor, especially poor women, were vulnerable. "You should marry Mr. Gloster."

"Yes, so you've said, and said, and said again. Perhaps you are right for once."

✦

FLORENCE AND GLOSTER SAT IN the Tipperary Tea Room which was decorated in Himalayan motif. Photographs included mountain vistas and of course the famed tea estates, with close views of tea plants and pickers, handsome, healthy, smiling, dark-skinned alpine women with baskets full of leaves on their backs, held by a tumpline across their brows. Even the china followed this theme.

Gloster was describing the ride up in the toy steam train, so-called due to the narrow gauge of the rails, the change in the air as one rose higher into the hills, and the enormous rhododendrons that reached the size of fully grown maples.

He wore a beige wool suit with brass buttons, his fringe of dark brown hair and beard with hints of grey newly trimmed. It was so impressively thick, his beard, that the term *pelt* came to Florence's mind. He wore a red carnation in his lapel, which matched his tie. His eyes were grey and his ears small and his nails neat. He looked comfortable if not quite handsome, though where these two qualities met or diverged, she was not quite certain. His temples were damp with perspiration, for despite the chill overcast November afternoon it was hot indoors. She imagined him in Africa and India under blazing suns and monsoon rains. He was in a hearty mood, and appeared to be enjoying his tea immensely, having had three cups with plenty of milk and lots of sugar. After all, they were celebrating.

Earlier, they had walked on Beacon Hill beneath the Garry oaks. He had proceeded with his hands clasped behind his back, though when he judged that the path grew treacherous he offered his support by touching Florence's elbow. He knew the Latin names of a great many plants. She found this endearing and for some reason reassuring. At one point they passed a wild rose bush, its flowers long gone but the rosehips bright and fat and he described the herb markets of Isfahan where, depending upon their complaint, Persians sit before select shrubs breathing in their curative properties.

"And is it effective?"

"Well, yes, I think it helps." He smiled and admitted that at any rate it was a pleasant way to pass a half hour.

"Isfahan," said Florence. "Such an elegant name."

"It is an elegant city. I should like to take you there."

Florence focused on her breathing in order to calm herself. Long breath in, long breath out. She thought of the ambiguity of the word *take*. She said, "The sun must be very bright in Persia. Radiant."

"Marry me."

There were others on the paths on the hill but none within earshot. Tears started to Florence's eyes and one escaped to explore its solitary path down her lower lid and onto her cheek, then travelled in toward her nose, then alongside her nostril. She looked off and covertly gave it a wipe with the tip of her forefinger.

"I've upset you."

"Not at all."

They walked in silence. The path was not muddy but hard in the stiff air. The grass was yet green in places, some of the leaves on the ground retaining their gold.

"You cannot be surprised."

"No."

As yellowed as they were, his eyes were soothing. Could they really be the eyes of a killer? Did he kill Cassidy to protect her? She was impressed and grateful and terrified. Was this the measure of true love? But how did he come to know of Cassidy? Pearl must have said something. Yes, it must have been, the girl could not keep her little yap shut. Well, it was done. Perhaps she should thank her.

"Of course you would come and live in my house," he said, "you and Pearl."

She nodded mutely. She did not wish to disappoint him, nor did she wish to lose him. She had her secrets and now he had his. Did she feel safer? Certainly she felt that they were now equal, and if there was a glass wall between them, perhaps that was good, even inevitable, he on his side keeping his own counsel and she on hers doing the same. She thought of the woman on the deck of the ship-in-a-bottle, she thought of the man in the photo on her wall. "I should be happy to marry you."

"Splendid." Laughing, he very nearly skipped. He glanced about as if wishing to share the good news.

Florence took his hand and they walked along like children, swinging their clasped hands forward and back. No, he was no murderer. At the very worst he was but a man who had defended his love. What man worthy of his woman would do less?

Now in the Tipperary Tea Room, Gloster asked if she preferred an autumn or a spring wedding.

"Spring."

"Or autumn," he said, "for then we could escape for the winter on our honeymoon. We could see the butterflies of Angangueo. There are millions."

"Spring or autumn. It doesn't matter," said Florence. Then she said, "Angangueo. What wonderful places you have visited. Is the sun very bright?"

"Luminous."

"And the sky?"

"Sapphire."

"Darjeeling, Isfahan, Angangueo," recited Florence, cautiously, uncharacteristically optimistic.

Chapter Thirteen

PEARL WAS SINCERELY JOYFUL AT her mother's news and wondered if there was any way of turning it to her own advantage. Perhaps she could simply vanish into the depths of her new stepfather's vast house, with its many rooms and floors, put the baby up for adoption when the time came, and then reappear, face saved, reputations intact all around? And the baby? *Her* baby? With strangers? She put her palms upon her belly and felt its heat. Or perhaps she could accompany the bride and groom on their honeymoon—not conventional to be sure, but not unheard of—and return with the infant and a story about a tragically brief marriage. Or, better yet, if the honeymoon went on long enough, they could say that the baby was her mother's. Yes, yes . . . This of course meant telling her mother, and meant Carpy would know as well. But Carpy wouldn't come on the honeymoon, no. Still, telling her mother would be awkward, but better than the alternative. Not yet, however, not yet. First let her mother enjoy her moment in the sun, especially as it was almost winter.

✦

THAT MOMENT, HOWEVER, DID NOT last long. The clouds hung as low and heavy as sacks of wet sand on the morning Pearl opened the front door to find Inspector Osmo Beattie folding his broad black umbrella and leaning it against the doorframe.

"Inspector!"

"I'm afraid so."

Pearl suppressed her panic at the thought that he had bad news, that he'd come to arrest her mother. She led him into the parlour then stood aside while he bowed to Florence. Pearl went and stood with her back to the fire, holding her stomach in and drawing her shoulders back and elevating her chin while turning her head just a few degrees to the right after the manner of a Venetian lady in a painting she had seen in a book.

Florence was as suspicious as Pearl about Beattie's visit. "Do please sit down, Inspector."

"Thank you." He took the wing chair matching hers. The round brass table between held a bowl of walnuts and raisins along with the morning post.

"You are looking very serious, perhaps too serious for such a young man. My husband was a serious young man. That is his portrait."

He dutifully spent some moments looking at the photo of the uniformed hussar with the moustache. Pearl followed Osmo's gaze and saw the picture from a fresh angle. It was an impressive moustache. Such a strange thing to have under your nose. What monkeys were men and women alike, sprouting hair all over to no other purpose than to shave it and trim it and curl it. She wondered what their Lord and Maker was thinking, unless it really was true that they were the cousins of apes. Did it follow, therefore, that tens of thousands of years from now, Man would be utterly bald? How closely Osmo had shaved. Pearl could see that he was scraped raw about the chin and even bore a spot of blood on his throat. What a chore attacking oneself with a blade each day. Or did he visit the barber? She imagined his morning rituals. Would he bring her tea in bed when they were married? Or would they have a maid to bring them both tea in bed? How much was a police inspector's salary?

"He is passed?"

"Sadly so," said Florence. "A Servant of Empire, like yourself." Florence hoped that no trace of irony infected her voice. Her comment occasioned a moment of silence as they contemplated the awesome obligations and sacrifices necessary to the glory that was Britain.

"But to your business," she said, brisking up. "To what do we owe the pleasure?" She folded her hands in her lap and raised her chin, signalling that she was ready to listen to whatever it was that had brought such a stalwart as he to her humble door.

Pearl was so impressed by her mother's complete immersion in her character of an innocent woman that she had to assume that Cassidy had been killed by someone else. Or was her mother setting herself up for an even greater fall? And if it was Mr. Gloster who had done it, was Osmo here to inform her of his arrest, or arrest her as well for conspiracy? Pearl put her hand on the warm bricks to steady herself.

The inspector was direct. "It seems that the woman who was found with the letter intended for you had a friend. Patricia Curtin. She is newly arrived from Australia. Cassidy Brennan had been lodging at the Inverness Rooms. When Miss Curtin went there, management informed her of what had happened."

Florence remained the picture of composure. She could have been modelling for a portrait. Keen to hear what her mother would say, and how she would say it, Pearl watched and listened as though an aspiring actress eager to learn from a master.

"Fascinating," said Florence. "Truly, you inhabit a most compelling world, Inspector. You are in the midst of the maelstrom. But I fail to understand how it involves us." She glanced to include Pearl. "Unless this other woman also had some of my post."

"A reasonable question. And no, she did not, or if she did, she declined to say so. However, she did mention that Cassidy

Brennan had described a woman named Sinead Molloy, and that she was tall. Very tall. Uniquely tall."

Florence merely elevated both her eyebrows while the rest of her face remained perfectly still, as if waiting for the inspector to get to the point. As he clearly believed that his point had already been made, he said nothing more and a silence spread, during which Osmo and Florence seemed to be waiting each other out to see who would speak first. As the silence threatened to grow awkward, it occurred to Pearl to say something. But what? That her mother was not really so very tall, certainly not *uniquely* tall? She herself was not uniquely tall. Biggish, perhaps, even strapping, a horse of a girl according to some, but far from uniquely tall; Miranda Robinson at school was nearly the same height, if of more elegant figure.

The embodiment of composure, Florence wielded a masterful command of silence. Pearl did not doubt that, if she so wished, she could go the rest of her life without uttering another word. What mettle. Her respect for her grew. In the game of silence Osmo had met his match, and at last he conceded victory and stood, bowed, thanked her, nodded to Pearl, and let himself out, treading softly as if to preserve the floor wax. Pearl moved to follow him—to say what she had no idea—but her mother cautioned her.

"Pearl," she said with quiet command.

Yet Pearl could not be stopped. She hurried out the door. Too late, however, for he had vanished into the rain. She remained a few moments on the porch mourning another opportunity lost. She almost began to laugh. Nihilism was the branch of philosophy that concluded nothing mattered. Was there a branch of philosophy that concluded that everything was ludicrous?

Standing on the porch walled in by the hammering rain, she was not so frantic as to be blind to Osmo's shortcomings. That the fellow did not recognize her voice said all too much about him and none of it good, while it made Pearl feel small.

Did there not exist some bond between a man and a woman who had *known* each other? Unless the inspector was the sort who frequented brothels and had thus dulled his sensibilities. How could she be happy with such a man? Or was he merely distracted by the murders? Would this not always be the case, Osmo absorbed to distraction by his work and ignoring Pearl, his wife? Then again perhaps the birth of the child would bring them together. Unless the child was choleric. How many mothers had Pearl seen shoving prams that held shrieking infants? The punished expressions on their faces! And often these women were already big with yet another child. Once again she had to face the plain fact that she did not know if she even liked, much less loved, Osmo Beattie. How could she know? It was absurd. It occurred to her that she had more in common with Mr. Gloster. The pyramids and cobras and the sphinx were magical to her while meaningless to her mother. She returned to the parlour.

"You are smitten," said her mother.

Chilled, Pearl went to the fire and stared into the writhing flames.

"He is handsome," acknowledged her mother, "and not without significance. Still."

"Still what?"

"You are being clumsy. And you scarcely know him."

The heat scorched her belly. She stepped back a pace. Should she ask her mother's advice on how to go about snagging her prey? "It's all very well for you."

"For us, Pearl, for us. I have good news."

"Yes, you are to be married. You told me already. Congratulations."

"What I was going to say is that you will be able to return to school in January."

Pearl turned from the fire.

"Well, I would have expected a somewhat happier expression than that. Come and sit down."

"I do not wish to sit down."

"Then please yourself and stand. Why are you not happy? Cassidy is gone, you can return to school, and we will know the security of Mr. Gloster's house."

"I'm too old for school."

"It's your final year. You're lucky. I never—" But she halted.

"Exactly," said Pearl. "You never. You never tell me the truth, about our Irish origins or your sordid past. Did you have a sordid past, Mother? Is the man in the photograph really my father? Who are you, Mother? Who am I?"

"You? You're hysterical."

Pearl managed to control herself and even smile thinly. "And you are deceitful."

"In the fullness of time—"

But Pearl walked out.

That evening Gloster sent his carriage for Florence who joined him for a meal, leaving Pearl alone. Pearl was jealous and hurt and thought *good riddance* as she stared into the fire. It occurred to her that she must read *Faust*. She needed to know how to contact Mephistopheles. Yes, she understood that it was a tale; all the same, it was an abiding one that had been written and rewritten by various authors in various centuries in various countries and hence bore some weight. She wanted to see how Faust went about the deed, for such persistent stories were often based in reality or so she decided. She knew about reciting the Lord's Prayer in reverse. She began writing it down and then carefully started transcribing it backward. Superstitious, Pearl halted after the first five words. She would read *Faust* as a start, and yet searching the bookshelves she could not find it. Certainly Mr. Gloster had it, of that she had no doubt. Pop on over? Sorry to barge, but . . . What she knew was that Faust barters his soul in exchange for worldly power, or something like that, she wasn't quite sure, but it was for something he wished. What did Pearl wish? To not be pregnant?

For Osmo to marry her? For some better man to marry her? She didn't even know if she wanted to be married, she didn't know anything, other than she wished that everything would go back to the way it was on the day before the Dunsmuir fete, only with her knowing what she knew now.

When Florence returned some hours later, she announced to Pearl that she and Charles had settled upon a spring wedding.

"Congratulations."

"Thank you."

"Will we now be Greyland-Smith-Gloster? Gloster-Greyland-Smith. Greyland-Gloster . . ."

Florence regarded her daughter. "You will of course be maid of honour."

"I'm too fat."

"Then you must start exercising. Perhaps we should get you a bicycle, it is all the rage now. You could be the next Louise Armaindo."

Pearl ignored that. "And where will you honeymoon?"

"I don't know. Perhaps Mexico. Or Hawaii."

"I am sure you will have a lovely time." A dreadful thought struck Pearl: her mother and Mr. Gloster might have sex. Was it possible? And if they had sex, her mother might possibly become pregnant. Queen Victoria had had her last child, Beatrice, at thirty-eight. Worse, and even more unnatural, was that her mother's child would be younger than Pearl's, and that Pearl's would be older than her mother's, that is to say Pearl's, half-sister!

"Ah," said Florence when Carpy appeared. "Perhaps a glass of brandy is in order. Join us."

Carpy looked dour as she went to the sideboard and decanted three measures into gold-fringed glasses.

"To Mother and Mr. Gloster," said Pearl.

"Yes," said Carpy, her eyes like prune pits. "Will you be joining us at the monthly meetings?" she asked. "Or will Mr. G. be withdrawing?"

"Oh," said Florence, savouring the bite of the brandy, "who can say what the future holds."

✦

TWO DAYS LATER the *Colonist* headline read: "Second Woman Dead in James Bay: has the Ripper come to Victoria?" Harry Hearne was in full flood.

The death grip of murder drags us deeper into malign winter. A woman very much like the first in very much the same spot: the outfall by the Knox Fish Plant, as undignified a final resting place as one could devise, and one no doubt chosen with grim intent.

Touring the site with the inimitable Dr. Giles Meadows and the redoubtable Inspector Osmo Beattie, we crossed the cordon and waded down onto the muddy sand and knelt by the wreckage of what was once a human being. Judging by her condition the good doctor concluded that she was not twelve hours dead. The inspector concurred. No detail escaped either of them. The fair hair, the sun-browned face, the tattoo of the green snake around her wrist. Yes, Inspector Beattie knew this woman! She had presented herself to him only days before, seeking information on a friend—the other murderee.

And so a pattern begins to emerge. It reveals itself like a figure from the mist. Two women dead in the same place, both bearing emblems of a green snake.

The inspector signalled to the mortuary attendants to bring the stretcher. He gazed around

*the site, at the bridge, the woolen mill, the fish
plant, and then off into the distance, perhaps
wondering what strange fate had brought him
to such a calling . . .*

*As we crossed the sand and reclaimed solid
ground I asked for his conclusions, and he,
wise, wary, stated that it was too early to say.*

*But with certainty we can say this: the New
World has many advantages, not least being the
opportunity of a new start. Yet it is the woe of
Man that he will bring with him the burden of
his animosities, his grudges and vendettas, the
rivalries of clan and tribe, and naught but blame
and excuses for failure. We see it all too often
in the aging wretch who fritters his final days
lamenting the past. And it is not just old men but
young and, I am forced to say, young women,
who have fetched up upon our fair shores here in
Victoria, bearing their antique rages.*

*I have spoken in these pages of the
Irish-Egyptian Alliance, which hearkens back to
the antediluvian days when the snakes did not
merely thrive in Ireland but were worshipped
there just as they are to this very day in Egypt.
And just as the snake is poisonous and violent its
cult is poisonous and violent. We have now seen
two murders, both corpses bearing the emblem of
the green serpent. Who but the willfully blind can
fail to make the connection? Who but the willfully naïve can fail to accept the need to restrict
immigration?*

✦

"YOU LOOK AS THOUGH YOU have not slept, Inspector."

He admitted that he hadn't, adding that he did not sleep much at the best of times, and that it had been a longer night than usual. Florence was sympathetic and said that it must weigh upon his spirit and colour his view of humankind, to which the inspector responded that man was indeed a dark and extraordinary animal.

"You are level-headed," said Florence.

"Do please sit down," said Pearl.

"Yes, do sit," said Florence. Seated in one of the wing chairs, she tilted her head back the better to study him. "Are you sure you won't take tea? Or coffee? Or perhaps a glass of iron wine? My physician recommends it."

"Perhaps another time. Are those kumquats? I will take a kumquat."

Florence slid the bowl across the brass table. "Take two. They are Chinese. Are you interested in things Chinese?"

"I'm afraid I've never given much thought to China," he admitted. His hair was uncombed, which lent him an air of distraction. Pearl thought of photographs she'd seen of German composers and French painters, men obsessed to distraction by their muses. "Perhaps I should develop an interest," he admitted. He selected two of the tiny bitter oranges and slipped them into his breast pocket. "And you, Madam, are you interested in things Chinese?"

Here Florence regarded him with a slight smile as if he were trying to turn the tables and catch her out.

"I enjoy walking in Chinatown," offered Pearl.

The inspector looked at her but whether he was seeing her was another matter.

"And pagodas," she added, bold, reckless, her throat tightening. "The Widow Dunsmuir has a pagoda. I was inside it at her gala last summer."

"Ah."

Was that it? Was that all? Pearl studied his eyes and saw no flicker of realization, no recognition, nothing.

Florence said, "My dear, will you take this tray, please? Don't make me ask you again, child."

Child? Scalded, Pearl stared aghast at her and then slowly, with dignity, took the tray and went to the door, all too aware of the swing of her widening hips. In the kitchen she slapped the tray on the counter.

Carpy said, "Dear oh dear, look at you. Big girls don't stand much chance, do ye. Your plod don't see you even if you are as wide as a door."

Whacking Carpy across the skull with the tray would be satisfying, as would ploughing her in the gob with her fist, then again, she might pin her down and grind her thumbs into her piglet eyes, but these pleasures would have to wait. Pearl slipped back along the corridor and halted out of sight by the door—Osmo was still in his chair but leaning toward her mother in such a state of agitation that Pearl thought of a besotted swain. Good God, she thought, is he making love to my mother? The idea was as absurd as it was terrifying and yet there it was, impossible to ignore. A thousand other thoughts raced through her mind in the single second that she stood watching. Osmo is betraying me. Mother is betraying me. Betraying her own fiancé, Mr. Gloster. Or is Osmo begging her to confess her crimes, vowing to stand by her side, beguiling her with a scheme via which together they'd flee the city, for who better than he to protect her? They would enjoy better lives, glorious lives in some distant place . . .

She crept closer.

"I will solve this," he vowed to Florence. "I will find the murderer," he assured her, though his inward tone suggested that it was himself he was trying to convince. He trembled as he spoke, his body taut and gaze adamant, a study in conviction. Then he lapsed back in the chair, his hands sprawled forgotten on his thighs as he confessed that he dreamed of the case, that it consumed him. "It's happened before," he said. "I lose myself. Lose perspective. Become obsessed." Head falling to one side and then the other, he closed his eyes and raised a hand and massaged his temples.

Florence admired his performance. Perhaps there was a measure of truth to it, the very ingredient that lent it so much pathos. Was he begging her to confess, to take mercy upon him and relieve his suffering? What notions this foolish fellow entertained about the sensibilities of women. She wondered if she should tell Charles about this, describe the scene and how the inspector was hot on her scent, determined to frame her for the two murders, the two crimes of passion committed by Charles. How would he react? Would he be compelled to do the honourable thing? Yet she did not wish him to do the honourable thing if it meant seeing him on the scaffold. Should she convince him that they must flee immediately? And Pearl? Where was Pearl in all of this? Florence leaned forward now and caught Osmo Beattie's hand and held it tight as if she would save him from his headlong tumble into the abyss. "You are all too alone, sir. How is it that you are not married?"

Panic stung Pearl's heart . . . Or hope. Perhaps her mother was about to propose Pearl as the solution to his isolation? It would certainly get her out of her hair. And yet at the mention of marriage, Osmo recovered himself and sat up and straightened his coat and tugged his sleeves and retrieved his hat from the floor. He stood while Florence remained seated with her hands in her lap, a benignly querying expression on her face.

"I've taken too much of your time," he said. "I'm sorry, I shouldn't have come. I've been overworked." He bowed to Florence then hurried out, not noticing Pearl in the corridor.

When the door had shut and the gate clapped to, Florence, not turning her head, perfectly aware that Pearl had been listening, said, "Oh dear, I do believe that our inspector is in love."

Pearl entered. "In love? With whom? You?"

"Me? Don't be absurd."

"Me, then? He's scarcely aware of my existence," said Pearl, desperately hoping that her mother would disagree and explain exactly why.

"You? No, no, Pearl, sadly no. He is in love with the case, in love with the murder, with the murderer."

"But . . . I thought you killed them?"

"Yes, I daresay the inspector has entertained the same suspicion. But no, I did not kill those women. The good inspector is besotted with the very mystery of it all."

This struck Pearl with the force of revelation. Osmo was in love with the case, in love with the crime, in love with the murderer, whom, he was convinced, was a woman.

"They're very good," Florence said, popping a kumquat into her mouth peel and all. "Tart but sweet. I do hope the inspector does not forget the ones in his coat pocket. They are apt to stain."

Pearl stepped to the window. The afternoon was deepening toward dusk and scatters of black crows cawed their way west. It was Saturday. What would Osmo do this evening? Supper at some public house with colleagues, then a walk and a cigar as he returned to his room? Did he lock the door to his room, or would that insult the Greer Sisters who ran the boarding house, implying that it was not secure or that they were apt to pry? She imagined his room, his single bed, bookshelves, mirror, closet, saw him sitting in a chair in a corner and removing his boots and rubbing his feet and thinking of the case, the murderer, the murderess, who was still at large, or was he too anxious to sit, perhaps he paced his room and wrung his hands and even talked aloud to himself.

Pearl continued to look out the window, past the barren arbutus to the sky enclosed in clouds of slate.

"Pearl."

"Yes, Mother?"

"You are in a daze."

In fact, she'd never been more lucid. She was having an epiphany: the only way to compete with the case of the two dead Irish women was to become the murderer. Yes, Pearl herself would assume the role of murderess and thereby become the one who dominated Osmo's thoughts and dreams, the criminal who gave meaning to his life, the one whom he could not ignore, the one who cut to his essence, the tantalizing fiend who had insinuated herself into his heart as sweetly and stingingly as a honeyed syringe.

She turned to her mother and smiled the smile of one who has reached the far shore, of one who has emerged from the cold water onto solid ground. This smile disconcerted her mother, which was pleasing to Pearl, like a bonbon on her pillow. "Excuse me, Mother."

She left the parlour and paced her bedroom, bringing the full weight of her intellect to bear upon her plan. It was more of a vision than a plan. She was seeing the expression in Osmo's eyes the first time he beheld her as the murderess. It would be his revelation. Would he hear music? How wide his beautiful dark eyes would grow, riding a wave of awe and bewonderment. Would he smile? Would he weep? Drop to his knees? Call her a fool, a splendid fool? And she? She would open her arms to welcome him home—home to the realm in which he belonged, Odysseus to the isle of Circe ...

Naturally he must place her under arrest, put his palm against her back and guide her solemnly toward the police wagon. If it took place here at home, her mother would watch from the parlour window, step out onto the porch, weep, or who knew, count herself well rid of an insane child. More importantly, Osmo would visit her in gaol. Pearl imagined these visits, the sunlight tilting in through the barred window, Osmo leaning forward with his elbows on the table, his strong, sensitive, dry—but not too dry—hands on hers, looking into her eyes, trying to understand how he could have been such a blind fool. What a lot of delicious lament there would be, how they would weep together, and she would console him, console and forgive.

He would, of course, be there every minute of the trial—she would not trouble Judge Begbie with denials—and Osmo would not be restrained from accompanying her to the scaffold. She would wear a dress of green velvet or robin's egg blue silk, depending upon the season, and his hand would be the last touch she'd know, a reassuring squeeze, a gentle pressure from his fingers, hinting that if only they'd met under more favourable circumstances, and then a few final words followed by a kiss, yes, a kiss. When she was dead, he would sob and redouble his vows to be the most devoted father to their baby, for Pearl's execution would have been delayed until after she gave birth.

But, for all that this was a satisfying scenario, it was madness. Osmo would never allow her to go to gaol much less be hanged, not her, not the mother of his child. When he learned she was the murderer and was carrying his baby he would engineer their escape. That very night, that very hour, they would take a ship to San Francisco and on to Tahiti or New Zealand and thus their new life, their real life, would begin. She envisioned a deep-porched bungalow in a tropical forest that throbbed all night with cicadas. The servants would be noble and silent and of impeccable bearing—though terrible in their vengeance if their honour was sullied. Osmo would wear cream linen suits, Pearl the sheerest silk. She would be carried in a palanquin or be paddled in a long sleek pirogue with a canopy. She would browse barefoot among the orchids and sunflowers with her children, of which, she foresaw, there would be two, a girl and a boy, who would be great favourites with the locals.

Alternatively, they would go to the mountains. Kashmir, Darjeeling, Kalimpong. What air, what vistas! Or an African

savannah. Or a city in the desert, yes, the far desert, with bal-
conied towers and arched walkways of sun-baked mud painted
ochre and blue, with potted cacti that would bloom in the night
but once a year.

Pearl halted her pacing and looked at herself in the oval
mirror with its shell-encrusted frame. Now the work must
begin, she told her reflection, she must plant clues that would
lead Inspector Osmo Beattie to her, for if she were to go to him
and simply confess, he would never believe her and certainly
not value her. No, she must be a worthy adversary, a worthy
prize. She must position the clues so that he did the work of
assembling the puzzle into a convincing picture. He must put
it together piece by enigmatic piece until he beheld Pearl's
face. To achieve this, to enter his heart, to obsess his mind, to
capture his soul, she must slip into his room and lay the clues.
How utterly entranced he would be to know that she had stood
in his room, that she was watching him even as he sought her,
Pearl, his adversary and muse.

Chapter Fourteen

OVER THE FOLLOWING WEEK, PEARL committed three thefts. First, she stole a cobra from a novelty shop called Grimmer's. It was made of silk rope artfully woven and painted, with a hood that expanded and retracted, eyes of yellow-green glass, and genuine, if venom-free, fangs.

Second, she went after a sphinx from a shop in Shanghai Alley where the crone of a proprietor eyed her with such naked suspicion that Pearl was forced to purchase a grinning Buddha to divert her. The loaf-sized sphinx was sandalwood and Pearl hid it up under her now frankly impressive bosom.

That she could easily have purchased the snake and sphinx was irrelevant. Or completely the point. She was now a criminal. These thefts were more than mere fun, she was not only honing her skills but collecting the clues she would plant in Osmo's room. She began looking at the world through the eyes of a robber, which was absolutely necessary, for she must become someone else, perhaps not her best self, or her ideal self, but an exciting self, secret and clever and contained, a being Osmo would obsess over.

The third and most challenging acquisition would be the mummified cat that Osmo himself had mentioned was housed in the collection of the late Sir Robert Dunsmuir in Craigdarroch Castle.

Getting into Craigdarroch would be challenging, though not as challenging as getting into Osmo's room later on. Pearl considered disguising herself as a tradesman, a rather fat tradesman, a delivery boy, or a blind girl seeking alms; she even thought of renewing her acquaintance, such as it was, with Lady Dunsmuir, by writing her a note reminding her of their summer meeting in the gazebo, under the guise of seeking her wise counsel on some topic that would gratify her, such as her august lineage or her secrets of longevity, beauty, grace, and wisdom, but that seemed imprudently risky, as there were rumours that the roots of Lady D's family tree were not deep, that indeed only a little digging could topple it altogether. In the end Pearl opted for simple stealth. This took brass, as well as a few cuts of laudanum-soaked pork for the mastiffs. She arrived at Craigdarroch after midnight, drenched from a late November rain, having twice been forced to hide in bushes to avoid sailors bent on mischief. She forced a window with a butter knife she'd brought along. Once inside, she dried herself on a curtain—not one of her finer moments but she feared catching a chill. Slipping her shoes off she tied their laces together and hung them across her shoulders. Craigdarroch smelled of linseed and furniture wax. She proceeded along the corridor, keeping to the runner so as to pad her footsteps until a shriek halted her. She pressed herself against a wall. A door whacked open upstairs and steps thumped then stopped and another door banged back.

"Bloody hell, Mother! What now?"

There was a muffled response, some sobbing and pleading, a slap followed by more cursing—bugger-sodding, shite-eating—then steps thumping back the way they'd come and a door slammed. Pearl waited; her heart thumped; somewhere a clock ticked with a rich thick tock. She repeated the phrase to calm herself: *a rich thick tock*. Clocks ticked stolidly on even as murders were committed, such was the grim indifference of time. The rain intensified, shrouding the house in deepening gloom. Did she hear a drawer scrape open and then hear the clink of glass upon glass as though someone was pouring themselves a much-needed whiskey?

Eventually she found the Egyptian Room. Along with the knife, she had brought matches and a candle. The scrape of sulphur under her nose nearly made her sneeze. She touched the match to the wick and the flame came to life. As she moved about the room silhouettes reared and loomed—Isis, Osiris, Horus, painted figures half snake and half human, a marble column engraved with hieroglyphics, chunks of stone on a bench, rolls of papyrus in glass-fronted cases, astrological instruments, ancient books, sun-bleached bones, a skull, and, standing upright in a corner, a pair of open coffins, each housing a mummy. The room smelled of blanched dust and bitter herbs. On a shelf stood a small upright clay casket eighteen inches high containing a cloth-wrapped corpse identified by a card as a cat. Pearl put the corpse into a sack, pocketed a gold ankh for good measure, then crept out.

As she was hurrying back to the window through which she'd entered, she heard another set of voices, these ones approaching from an adjoining corridor. She stood behind a potted fern, then darted across to an alcove and pressed her back to a wall behind a half-curtain and held her breath. An elderly couple, snickering and whispering, proceeded past, he clutching an armload of beer bottles and she with a cake on a tray. And though they kept their voices low, Pearl distinctly heard the man—round-shouldered, bald, and white-whiskered—tell the ample-bosomed woman that he wouldn't half enjoy taking a bite out of her bum, which caused her to skip and the cake to nearly slide off the tray. With a yip of panic, she caught the cake while he reached to give her backside a squeeze. One of his beer bottles toppled. The carpet muted the thump. Yet both conspirators stopped right opposite Pearl and cringed, peering at the rooms above, holding this pose a full two minutes by the thick tick of the clock. At length the fellow, sixty years old at the least, retrieved his bottle and they scuttled off around a corner and a door opened then closed.

Pearl was appalled and indignant and considered marching up to Lady D's room right then and there and informing her of the goings-on under her hallowed roof, then decided it would be more prudent to pen a note instead. Seconds later she was making her escape past the drugged and snoring mastiffs.

The three Egyptian thefts were merely the first phase. Next, and most importantly, she had to get into Osmo's room and place the clues.

She reconnoitred Greer's Boarding House. It was a reputable establishment operated by Gwen and Giselle Greer, sisters, devout Baptists, steadfast and upright African American ladies admired for their dignity and decorum. The house had an abundance of fretwork and pillars, a broad balcony framing the front and sides; the paint was bright, the roof free of moss, the mock-brick asphalt siding scrubbed, the fence straight. Laurel hedges separated it from the neighbours, on one side a shop occupied by a maker of wooden limbs and on the other a private residence.

Osmo lived in the top right room with an oriel window looking southwest. Pearl had seen him in that window, hands behind his back, pondering the dusk. In the afternoon light, the glass panes were silver; in the evening, they were copper. Casual questioning revealed that Carpy knew one of the chars, who said that he was a great favourite of the Greer Sisters who were happy to have such a man safeguarding their interests.

But how was Pearl to get in? Climbing a trellis or a ladder or scrambling across a roof in her condition were out of the question. Then there was the fact that Christmas was nearly upon them. Decorations were up, excitement in the air, and activity around the boarding house was escalating. People came and went, exchanging greetings with Ed, the elderly albino who all but lived on the front porch in spite of the cold winter weather. Of nine lodgers, eight were employed and therefore absent most days while Ed spent his days on a wicker throne on the porch. Ed's hair and beard were long and formed an alarming halo of whitish-orange. He'd been a '49er and come north on a ship full of freed slaves, now he devoted himself to silver smithing, buying plate and filigree, and fashioning jewellery, which he sold. He wore two or three rings on each finger and thumb as well as bracelets and earrings. If the angle was right and the sun broke through the clouds, this metal glinted and sparked so that Ed was illuminated in a nimbus of metallic light lending him an even more otherworldly air. Some said he was a dead man come back to life, or a live man not fully deceased. He was a known figure throughout Victoria and as people passed, they called greetings to which he nodded in solemn reply.

How was Pearl to get past Ed into the boarding house and place the cobra, the sphinx, and the mummified cat in Osmo's room? She'd need a disguise. Victoria was a capital city and yet also a small city, and Pearl risked being recognized. She knew the Greer Sisters by face, having often seen them out and about, though whether they knew her was less likely.

Still, she needed a ruse. It was one thing to be hidden in veils on a summer evening, quite another to stand face to face in the plain of day with women of the world. And then her condition had to be factored in. Could a fat girl be made to look like a fat boy? And just how much did the Greer Sisters know of Inspector Osmo Beattie? Dare Pearl pass herself off as a sister or cousin only to be confronted by a pair of perplexed expressions: *But he said he had no sisters or cousins!*

It would be safer to pose as a friend just in from Vancouver or maybe farther afield, Winnipeg or Toronto, eager to see his old chum Osmo. What was his name? Robert? Daniel? Too plain. Lucas Devlin, a combination of Lucifer and the Devil? Too heavy-handed. Alexander Nyle? Alexandria and the Nile. She liked that.

She went to a wigmaker in Chinatown. The shop smelled of oil and powder and was not a little eerie what with all the faceless wooden heads in wigs. She said she was going to a costume party. Mr. Fogarty spoke excellent English. He had come from Canton to pan for gold and then worked on the railroad. Pearl could not resist observing that in her admittedly limited experience, a Chinese person called Fogarty was unusual. He explained that his father had been a fusilier from Donegal who fell off a gunboat in the Yellow River. Presumed drowned, he was left behind and made a new life. Mr. Fogarty was about sixty, had grey eyes and silver streaks in his brown-black hair. He said that along with wigs he did indeed make beards and moustaches, mostly to cover facial scarring due to leprosy and backfiring guns.

Pearl said that she wanted to look convincing.

"Convincing to whom?" he asked, eyes crinkling with amusement.

"Convincing to other women."

He acknowledged that that was a taller order than fooling men and advised rubbing dirt in the beard, blacking out a tooth, and eating raw garlic.

When she said that he sounded experienced he grew wary, as if caught out in a career of deception. They chatted, agreeing that the weather was erratic, balmy one day and frigid the next, what with winter nearly upon them. He recalled December as a boy in Canton as warm and humid. "The bamboo grew so fast you could hear it."

Pearl tried imagining that. "What does bamboo sound like when it grows?"

He thought a moment, eyes rolling up as he cast himself back to his childhood. "Fibrous and crackly."

"Your English is excellent."

"My Cantonese is better, but my Portuguese only so-so and my Gaelic was passable before my father died."

Pearl confessed that she had always been a lazy linguist and asked what else he recalled from China.

"The feral cats hunted snakes, which hunted frogs, which hunted dragonflies, which hunted mosquitoes, which were eaten by bats."

"I don't like bats," admitted Pearl, "though strictly speaking I've never had any direct experience of them, either good or bad, so perhaps I tar them unfairly by reputation alone."

Herbert Fogarty said that he had heard they baked up well in pies.

Three days later the beard was ready. Thick as a pelt, two inches long, a mid-to-light brown to match her hair. Herbert Fogarty also gave her a pot of glue boiled from horse hooves and duck eggs. As Pearl was leaving she hesitated, for she found Mr. Fogarty and his shop intriguing. She asked him if he ate snake, there being a wheel-shaped bamboo cage full of them in the window of the shop next door.

"Oh no," he said. "I'm a pantheist. I don't eat meat at all."

"But you said bat pie was so good."

"I said I'd *heard* that bat pie was good."

"Are you happy here in Canada?" she asked.

"There is happiness and there is happiness."

Pearl bid him explain the distinction and he said that he believed in degrees of illumination.

"And the brighter the better?"

"Not necessarily," he cautioned. "Brightness can blind. Light also comes in many colours; the more muted is sometimes the more revealing."

"Chromatic theory," she said, eager to prove that she was not altogether a dunce. "The rainbow."

"Yes."

"What is the Cantonese word for rainbow?"

"*Choi hung.*"

She was tempted to ask whether rainbows were happy but asked instead if he had a Chinese name as well and he said yes but declined to share it. When she asked why, he only smiled and shrugged and said they scarcely knew each other. Pearl agreed that he was perhaps wise. She said goodbye and went out, thinking they had been engaged in a strange game of conversational chess and unsure who had won or if they had played to a draw.

There was also the problem of timing. She had already observed that Osmo kept to a routine, departing Greer House at 7:25 each morning, though when he returned varied. Greer House was seven blocks from the police station. He went there directly except for a pause at Narne's for a newspaper and a cheroot. He carried the paper folded under his left arm and held the cheroot in his right hand and smoked as he walked. Pearl's dilemma was this: was she better to arrive at the boarding house in the morning or afternoon? Too early and the sisters could snag a boy to run and catch him; too late and Osmo might walk in. What with the perpetual presence of Ed, sneaking in unseen was out of the question. She would have to present herself to the Greer Sisters and somehow get past them into Osmo's room. A tall order. Perhaps too tall. The more she thought about it, the more fearful she became. She listed everything that could go wrong: an unexpected return, the Greer Sisters could get suspicious, Pearl's disguise could come undone, she could lose her nerve, she could even, God forbid, go into labour, something that she had read could be triggered by anxiety.

Her mother remarked on her preoccupation, saying that she was pale and twitchy and that for a large girl she wasn't eating much, to which Pearl responded that she was trying to slim down, adding, "You should have let me return to school."

Her mother also observed that at her age most girls were done with school, and then reminded her that if she wished she would be able to return in January, a mere matter of weeks.

"Most girls?" said Pearl. "Most girls? What and who are these *most* girls to whom you refer, Mother? Am I *most* girls? I thought we Greyland-Smiths aspired to higher things," she added, smirking miserably.

"That expression does you no justice."

"Well, I'm bored and therefore idle."

Her mother said that boredom should inspire her. "Have you no interests?"

"Of course I have interests. I was cultivating them at school," she said, thinking she'd scored a point.

"And pray what are they, these interests?"

"A great many things."

Her mother waited for her to expound. How smug and superior her mother looked. Pearl hated her. She went to her room, stuffed her pockets with all the coins and jewellery she had, then announced that she was going for a walk and sailed out, feeling less like a clipper ship than a lumber barge. At Shaw's Pawnbroker she got three dollars and sixty-five cents, bringing her up to a grand total of four dollars and sixty-eight cents, not including the Peruvian peso.

She visited various rag shops seeking a coat, yet nothing was suitable. If she had been after a bathing costume she would have been in luck; stripes vertical or horizontal or even diagonal to be had for a bargain. She tried the street market on Tree Lane. Nothing. She saw some Russian sailors in fur coats and thought there was the answer, except how was she to afford a fur coat? In a store in an alley, she poked through the racks and bins and found Japanese shoe-socks, a coonskin cap, an embroidered burgundy fez with a gold tassel, a box of masques fit for the Venetian Carnivale, but no coat to disguise herself as a man. No disguise, then? Yet to show up at Greer House blatantly pregnant would be dicey. She would have to rub onion beneath her eyes to sprout tears. She would either be shunned or adopted. *Oh, please, Mrs., I've no one else to turn to!* How this would advance her interests she did not know. Better to find a good thick coat and muffler to go with the beard.

On the way home a sudden rain made her put her head down and squint. She would have missed the small dark shop next to the Lock & Key altogether if not for the twitch of the electric bulb in the window. She stepped in and there, on a mannequin, as if patiently waiting, was the very coat: dark waxed canvas with a matching hat trimmed in elk.

"It's a man's coat, miss."

"It's for my husband."

"It wants some stitching."

"I'm very skilled."

"Very good then. I'll wrap it up."

"And these trousers," she said. "What about boots? Do you have any boots?"

"Boots aplenty, ma'am."

Pearl tried on various pairs, explaining that her husband had small feet. She paid for her purchases.

There were other challenges. She could not very well waltz out of the house in full disguise, meaning there would have to be a change of clothes en route. But where? She decided upon the Tipperary Tea Room because the Ladies' was next to a rear door giving onto a lane.

Finally, which day? Was Monday better than Tuesday, Wednesday more strategic than Thursday? She decided that on Monday Osmo would be at his most diligent to attack the week's work. Then again, he was not a grocer, crime could not be compared to celery, it did not take a break at the weekend. She was impatient and yet fearful and so settled on Monday. As it was now Tuesday, she had a long week to wade through, yet reasoned that this gave her time to rehearse and anticipate the what ifs, for this was a one-time performance and it had to be good. Most daunting of all, there was no script and she would have to improvise.

To soothe herself she envisioned the life she and Osmo would live together. After loving each other they would lie in bed with their limbs entwined and he would examine his criminal cases like pieces of jewellery, sharing them with her, evaluating them from all angles, and they would compare points of view, evolve theories of motive and character, and Pearl would remind him that humans were beasts driven more by emotion than logic. "So you blame the moon," he would say, "the female principle?"

"You are a strangely simple-minded detective, Mr. Beattie. Ask yourself this: who was the logician who engineered our union?" He would concede the point and she would remind him, "*Cherchez la femme*, Mr. Beattie, *cherchez la femme.*" They would laugh and drink wine and love some more. If the baby woke and cried, he would go to little Osmo or little Esmerelda.

There was a kick inside her. The baby... She still had difficulty with the terminology. *Fetus* was too clinical. Our baby, little Osmo or little Esmerelda, almost too optimistic and she feared it might jinx her. Either way, it was the child, her child, their child, yes, *our child*. Howsoever she referred to it, the creature was thrusting and straining more often, showing the outline of a foot or elbow or head. It was alarming. She had moments of panic. Was it a bad omen by having been conceived in a sphinx? Would it be a strange creature? Against her will, she imagined some goblin growing within her. She thought of women who'd had six, seven, ten children, women who'd spent decades pregnant until it became an almost permanent condition, lactating, suckling, breeding, waddling about enduring a permanently aching back and swollen ankles and crabby disposition. How had this happened to her? Yet again she gnawed the question. Her one and only time, her first and only time. Was it a Divine Punishment or a Divine Gift, or was it the Fates, blind and whimsical and cruel? She could easily believe in a pantheon of impish gods: a god of bad luck, a god of good luck, a god of restlessness or sloth, a god who made you prefer blue to green, a god of thieves, of envy, hate, suspicion, and of course Chronos, plucking the hours of your life one by one by one and depositing them in a chest beside his throne. Were there stories of clever men like Odysseus outwitting Chronos and causing him to return some of those hours, or sneaking into his lair while he slumbered and opening that chest—broad and deep and hasped with great leather straps—and reaching in and stealing an armload of time, minutes like pennies, hours like dimes, days like dollars?

She also wondered if there was some bargain she might strike in which God let her relive that one ill-fated hour with Osmo. Or was it Satan, Mephistopheles, to whom she should appeal? Again she thought of Faust. A fly in a web, we are but flies in webs, she thought. And for all her fanciful imaginings, she kept returning to the fact that she scarcely knew Mr. Osmo Beattie, that their lovemaking, if it could be so called, had been disappointing and that to be married to him was in fact a bleak and desperate prospect. Then again, many girls were thrust into arranged unions, often with men twenty or thirty years older. Perhaps she put too much weight on romance. Look at her mother.

How isolated she felt. If only she could tell someone. She could imagine Miranda's reaction should Pearl confide in her. *Oh Pearl, you are now a fallen woman. How exciting. How deliciously tragic. I will always remember you. Of course, we can never see each other again . . .*

As if on cue, a letter from Miranda arrived.

> *Dearest Pearl,*
> *You are cruel and strange to leave us, your intimates, so very much in the dark as to why you have abandoned us, as well as your education. I have seen no notices in the newspaper as to your death so can only wonder at what you are doing with yourself. Indeed, there was talk of mounting an expedition and investigating. What, the troops cried, has become of Miranda's most loyal aide-de-camp? We put it to the vote.*

Only by the narrowest margin was the propo-
sition of visiting your house defeated. Rather
we resolved that I should pen an epistle. You
know womankind, Pearl, data is our manna.
We must have information. (Whether it is true
or accurate is scarcely relevant. What is essen-
tial is that it be interesante, muy interesante.
Capiche?) I do, therefore, beg you dear, dearest
Pearl, not to disappoint.

I remain,

Yours,

Through calamity and triumph,
Miranda Robinson

Pearl reread the letter then slid it into the fire. She had long been expecting something of this sort and had devised various responses that would not merely explain but glorify her situation. Her mother had sold her in marriage to the Sultan of Oran for one hundred and one camels. The Sultan, rumoured to be terrible, was even now sending a galley rowed by naked slaves to fetch her. Her mother was putting Pearl into a nunnery where she would be sealed in a brick wall to facilitate a life of devotion to Jesus. Pearl had gone mad and was bound writhing to her bed. Pearl's true identity as one of Queen Victoria's nieces had come to the fore and she was now residing at Balmoral, awaiting betrothal to some Bavarian duke.

When it came time to put pen to paper, she wrote none of these things. Instead, she put Miranda off by saying that she had fallen ill with what the doctor described as a rare and highly contagious tropical distemper contracted via bananas. Once she had fully recovered, she would be back at school. Miranda wrote back asking for further details. Pearl responded by saying that it was a Peruvian distemper, Peru having been in the news of late for an outbreak of plague in Lima. She re-emphasized the contagious nature of her malady, adding that she had for a time frothed at the mouth. Miranda wrote that she had driven past Pearl's house—lavender-soaked kerchief to her nose—and saw no yellow quarantine flag. Pearl said that it must have been stolen. Miranda responded that they might well consider moving from that low neighbourhood, adding that she herself was in a quandary. *I have a Christmas gift for you, Pearl, indeed many gifts, that must needs be presented in person so that you might appreciate them in all their richness. Shall I give you a hint? A taste? I must! It is this: Beryl Morley has been exposed as a fraud who could not trace her lineage back to a Shoreditch dung collector much less Queen Anne. But more anon . . .*

Pearl writhed with the desire to hear more yet dared not meet Miranda.

Chapter Fifteen

ONE CHALLENGE PEARL KNEW SHE dare not avoid was the need to test her disguise. To simply dress up and appear at the Greers' door would be madness. But practice how? Where? She chose the Lord Nelson tavern after dark, when the smoke was thick and the gentlemen drunk and less discerning.

The next evening, she sat with her mother in the parlour and filled her tumbler to the brim with iron wine that she'd heated over the fire. When she nodded off and began snoring, Pearl slipped out. If Carpy was spying, as she most likely was, she could think what she pleased.

Pearl walked briskly. She passed a trio of men debating the merits of over-under shotguns versus side-by-side barrels. They thrust their cigars at each other like darts as they argued and did not so much as look at Pearl, the bearded young man in the fur-lined cap and dark canvas coat.

The Lord Nelson had a carved and painted sign showing a ship at sea firing a cannon. Pearl smelled smoke and beer and heard shouts and laughter. The Lord Nelson was reputed a seemly establishment. It was said that no less a man than Mr. Begbie himself frequented it, that he had his own bottle of single malt there and, if he was in voice, would sing arias. Pearl walked on past, needing a few more minutes to muster her resolve. As if to goad her in, a rain began to fall. She took three deep breaths and then about-faced. As she neared the pub, two men approached from the opposite direction and bowled right on in as if they owned the place. A man's world indeed. Pearl checked her beard and with a last deep breath pushed the door open. Or tried. It stuck. It wouldn't budge. Then the door flew open—outward—and a man exited, nodding curtly to her as he went on by while she, embarrassed, glimpsed the low lights glinting off the bottles and glasses and mirrors behind the bar and then took the plunge and stepped on in.

A few heads turned but generally she was ignored. It was hot. Her toque and beard and scarf and coat and pants and boots felt like a layer of blubber. Her pulse pounded, her beard itched, and her eyes stung from tobacco smoke so dense that the taller men were all but headless due to the cloud hovering thick about the ceiling. The room smelled of boots and brine and beer and wool. To Pearl's right ran the bar, backed by ranks of bottles; to her left a field of tables held down by hunched and bellowing men. A waiter wheeled past like a circus performer, spinning an empty metal tray on his fingers.

What was the protocol? Did she sit at a table and wait for the fellow with the tray? But there were no tables free. Did that mean she had to leave? She looked around. A scrum of men massed against the bar. Politely but firmly, she pressed her way through and tried catching the barman's eye as he slid side to side like a shooting gallery duck, plucking empties five at a time in each hand and clattering them into a tub of soapy water. He dashed rum into glasses, ran beer into tankards, raked away the foam with a stick then topped them up. At last he halted, fists on hips, looking Pearl four-square in the face and she drew back, fearing he was about to demand what the bloody blue blazes she was doing dressed in that get-up? He did not. He merely raised his eyebrows queryingly.

"Beer."

"Stout or ale?"

She nodded.

"Which?"

Was he insulting her?

"Stout or ale?" he repeated as if she was hard of hearing and slow of mind.

Stout sounded more masculine. "Stout."

He whirled a tankard like a six-shooter and slammed it down beneath the tap in time to catch the brown liquid drooling from the spigot. Pearl repeated the word *spigot* in her mind. *Spigot.* He set the stout on the counter and she set her nickel beside it. She knew that beer cost a nickel from the ads in the *Colonist.* She nodded in response to his nod and turned away, a man among men. Elbow out and fist tight, she gripped her tankard like a shield and surveyed the room. There was a table in a corner occupied by a sot slumped forward with his face on his arm. There was also a free chair. Was she permitted to occupy that seat, or did she need an introduction?

When Pearl sat the sot stirred but did not lift his head, only belched then farted and settled himself more deeply into his stupor, putting Pearl in mind of a frog in mud. The table afforded her a new angle on the room. She saw Harry Hearne. And there was Judge Begbie, regaling his confrères with some tale that set them slapping the table and howling in delight; no doubt it was a yarn about a sorry fool he'd hung. Judge, a position as weighty as the word itself. Judge. I judge you guilty hence you will hang . . . Did Osmo know Begbie, had they met? A spasm of terror jolted through her: what if Osmo was here? She looked around, but saw only the ceiling smoke stretching and lolling like a sentient thing, reacting to every wave of a hand. Pearl set her feet wide and firm and sat back in her chair. So far so good. This business of being a man was not so very complex. She minded her own beeswax and avoided eye contact and sipped her beer—stout—which was a tad weighty to her taste, rather as she imagined brewed bog water, but it gave her something to do and soon enough her tankard was half down.

Her table companion woke. Slowly raising his head off his arm, he stared at Pearl. His eyes narrowed then widened. "Give me a dollar," he said.

Pearl's eyes narrowed and then widened as well—in alarm, for she recognized the man, yes, it was none other than her girlhood love, Desmond Terence Padraich Orlovski-with-an-*i*. She blanched and gripped the table and looked toward the exit. But Desmond Terence Padraich Orlovski-with-an-*i* did not recognize her. Pearl felt a surge of tears and fought the urge to pull off her beard and throw herself into his arms. This, she thought, was fate. This, she thought, must mean something. But what? He was not looking at all well, Padraich. He was pale and unshaven, his eyes were a dirty yellow, he needed a haircut, and he had a scab on his ear. Pearl said that she did not have a dollar.

But he was not listening, he was waving his arm for the waiter. Then he announced that he had been in a despond. Forearms on the table he let his head hang, displaying the sad thatch of his matted hair.

"A despond?" Pearl asked. "Why so?"

"Lost me foot then, didn't I." He extended his right leg which indeed lacked a foot. The pantleg was folded up and tied with a length of twine. On the floor lay a crutch.

It did not escape Pearl that his right foot was the one that had been afflicted with warts. Oh Padraich, she was about to . cry but caught herself. "Did it hurt?"

"Like a bugger."

She asked what had happened.

"Happened? Got bloody stung by a devilfish in the Sea of Cortez is what happened."

It seemed as wonderful as it was terrible. Pearl wanted to ask how he came to be in such a place, and what had happened to his plans to buy Ronald Bench's old bow saw and sell cord wood. The waiter plunked down two ales and took Pearl's two nickels.

"Your health," said Padraich.

"And yours," said Pearl.

They clanked tankards and gulped and belched then drank again. The ale was much more to her taste, lighter, with a hint of bitter berries.

"Desmond Padraich Orlovski." He extended his hand.

"Alexander Nyle." She extended hers and they shook. How thick and calloused was Desmond's mitt, not the slender hand she recalled from their youth.

"You don't look like an Alexander," he said. "I'd've put you down for a Matthew."

"That's my middle name."

"Is it then?"

She nodded then drank more ale, thinking she had committed a strategic blunder by offering too much, but it had just popped out.

"Mine's Terence. Desmond *Terence* Padraich Orlovski, with an *i* at the end."

"An *i*?"

"An *i*. Many Orlovskis are spelt with a *y*."

"But not you."

Desmond winced as if horrified at the notion of having a *y* at the end of his name.

Once again Pearl fought the urge to tear away her beard and identify herself. Had he not been her first love? Had they not discussed and planned their future? Oh Padraich, she wanted to say. He would marry her, and she would hem his pantleg and rub balm on his stump. Instead, she said, "The Sea of Cortez. When?"

"March last. It's taken some time to heal."

They regarded his foot, or rather his absence of foot. The pantleg was tied mid-shin. It occurred to Pearl that it was both strange and a shame that salamanders and squid could regrow limbs but not men, who had been created in God's likeness.

"A devilfish?"

"Hurt like fuck," he said.

"What were you doing?"

"Wading ashore. I'd been tossed over the wall. Would you like to see the stump?"

"Perhaps another time," said Pearl.

He nodded as if agreeing that the tavern was perhaps not the place for such business. He finished his tankard then belched. "Gad, but I've a thirst."

Pearl searched her pockets and set two more nickels on the tabletop.

"By God if you're not sweating like a Turkish whore," said Padraich.

She trowelled her forehead then loosened her scarf and wondered if Padraich, her sweet, innocent young Padraich, knew first-hand of what he spoke when he talked of Turkish whores, or was this only the manner of sailors? It pained her to think of him lying with trollops. Then again who was she to talk? Perhaps trollophood was a complex affair. More importantly she wondered if, in his heart of hearts, he still loved her, and were she to reveal her identity and her condition if he would still marry her. Would they live such a bad life? Could he not still get a saw and cut cord wood in spite of his foot, or lack of foot? Of course, her mother must utterly disown her and Carpy mock her, and Miranda never speak to her again. Yet here he was, dear Desmond Padraich, Desmond *Terence* Padraich. Surely it must be fate. Pearl Orlovski. It did not sound so very bad at all. How hot she was. Her armpits were swamps and the toque and beard itched while Desmond looked comfortable. The ale had revivified him. He wore a Russian peasant blouse buttoned down the left side. The fresh ales arrived. They drank and Pearl comprehended the attraction of beer. Cooled, she belched like an old hand at beer swilling.

But Desmond's expression suddenly altered. Mug halfway to his mouth he frowned and lowered it to the table and stared at her. Pearl panicked. Had she spoken her thoughts out loud? Then Padraich reached across the table. But he did not grab her throat or punch her face, no, he put his fingers in her tankard and came up with her beard. He squeezed it dry and then he offered the sodden thing to Pearl who tried to stick it back in place. Finding that it would not hold, she put it in her pocket and thanked him.

"You've a fine complexion," he observed, seeming to sober.

She touched her bare cheek and chin. The moustache was still in place on her upper lip. She thanked him again. Then she grew very still and waited for Padraich to recognize her. But he did not recognize her. He was too drunk. Or perhaps the devilfish sting had affected his memory. Or—and this was a devilfish sting of its own—he had forgotten her. Was it possible? Had Turkish whores driven her, his first love, from his head and heart?

He asked, "Are you a castrato?"

At that moment Judge Begbie burst forth in song. His voice rang across the taproom silencing every man, including Desmond. All heads turned. Even the smoke seemed to wheel about and pay attention. Judge Begbie sang in Italian, his voice rejoicing and lamenting at the same time. Standing, one arm aloft, his hat and forearm lost in the smoke, he made the last note hover like an eagle soaring on high, an eagle noble and solitary, terrible and remote until, at last, it descended in a long, slow spiral and came to rest, and then he sat.

"Plaintive and exalting," said Harry Hearne, breaking the silence that had followed.

Applause erupted. The waiter spun his serving tray on the end of his finger, lowered it down under his arm and then under his raised knee before he tossed it still spinning to the tip of his other finger. The judge said they were all too, too kind.

"Your skin and your eyes," continued Desmond, returning his attention to Pearl.

"I am not a castrato," said Pearl, in the deepest voice she could manage.

"No offence intended. Do you have another nickel?"

She banged down two dimes and said they would move on to whiskey.

"As you wish," said the long-suffering Desmond.

"As I wish," said Pearl, low in her throat. She finished her beer and Desmond did the same. Pearl was not sure whether she was feeling triumphant or crushed.

"I saw a castrato in Venice two years ago. Month of June. We'd put in with a load of sand for the glassworks. I was coming out of a church and there was this carriage, no horses, no wheels, just a big lad at each corner, a palanquin they call it."

Pearl struggled to envision Desmond in Venice.

"Blond fellows. Tall. Well made." Desmond sat back to let the waiter set down the whiskeys. With a wink and a grin, he raised his and they clinked and he decanted his in one slow go into his mouth.

Pearl gulped and coughed then wiped the tears from her eyes. "A palanquin," she prompted, her voice simultaneously a squeak and a croak.

"And out of it steps this fellow. Shape of a pear. Crimson wig. Indigo coat. Tight yellow trousers. Rather lank of shank, as if he did not walk much. Tiny white seashells sewn to his red shoes," said Desmond. "More like slippers than shoes actually, as if he rarely ventured out of doors. Hanky tucked up his sleeve. A pair of long-haired white cats on red silk leashes. And by God the rings on his fingers!" Desmond paused for emphasis, wide eyes inviting Pearl to gasp.

But she did not gasp. What she did shocked even her. Gripping the arms of her seat she offered Desmond her fiercest glare and said, "Are you saying I remind you of this creature?"

"Well . . ." Desmond saw where he had landed himself.

Pearl saw that she too had put herself in a corner. All around them men shouted and swore and laughed and threatened, and this supposedly one of the more genteel establishments. How to proceed? She was lost. What she did know was that she was riding a wave of whiskey and beer and had no idea what she was going to do or say next. It also occurred to her that this was how she had ended up in bed in a plaster sphinx. "I warn you," she said, horrified at the words escaping her mouth, "that I have killed." She pressed her right hand to her hip as if a knife or pistol was hidden there.

"They say Billy the Kid had a very fine complexion."

"There you are."

"Here I am," agreed Desmond. And added, "As ever I was. Or rather, not as I once was."

Pearl revised her opinion of the subtlety of Desmond's intelligence and thought it best, after this show of manliness, to be magnanimous. "One more whiskey?"

"I'm at your service."

She signalled to the waiter. He nodded then did a double take. Had he noted the change in her appearance? If so, it was apparently nothing odder than he saw each night for he made no remark.

"Killed what?" asked Desmond. And then added, "Where and when and why?"

Their gazes touched like sword tips and for a moment Pearl feared he had recognized her at last.

"Baltimore."

"I've had oysters at Kelley's in Eutaw Street."

Pearl had never heard of Kelley's in Eutaw Street and she did not like oysters. The waiter arrived. This time the whiskey went down like tame fire. She was feeling quite the lad. Leaning forward, belly cut by the table edge, she set her right elbow on top signalling that they should arm wrestle. Is that not what men did? Desmond seemed beleaguered but he put up his arm and gripped Pearl's hand. Through the fog of booze, she dimly perceived that she was out of control and must escape as soon as possible.

"What business did you say you were in?"

Pearl tried to think of something that would account for her smooth hand and slim fingers. Cobbling and carpentry and bricklaying were out. Would she pass for an accountant? She thought of saying that she made dentures. "Actor."

"Actor? Is that why you were wearing a beard then?"

"Exactly," she said.

"So you are rehearsing a role then are you?"

"Begin!" she said.

They heaved to. For a moment Pearl held her own. Then with the slow and mechanical inevitability of a steam lever, Desmond's arm drove hers down flat to the table.

"Two out of three?" he offered.

The tendons in her elbow shrieked and her bicep felt ruptured and tears started to her eyes. She looked away and made a show of shrugging indifferently even as she fought not to sob at the pain throbbing in her arm. Standing, she mustered her huskiest voice and wished him a good evening.

"Do you not wish to know why they threw me off the ship that led me to be wading ashore and getting stung by a devilfish?"

She had forgotten the question entirely. Waving vaguely, she stumbled toward the door and made her way home. If her vanity was injured at Desmond Terence Padraich Orlovski-with-an-*i* having forgotten her, she nonetheless rated it a valuable evening, for she'd had a lesson in humility, had learned the necessity of better glue for her beard, and most importantly, she now felt ready to proceed with her plan to infiltrate Greer House and place the taunting clues that must lead Osmo directly to her. The game, once begun, must be played out. Fate's hand was at her back giving her a shove.

Chapter Sixteen

BUT FATE'S HAND, IT TURNED out, shoved her down the stairs. It happened on the very Monday Pearl chose to visit Greer House and place the clues that would lure Osmo to her and, consequently, bring about her salvation. The weather had turned. Frost crystalized the grass, glazed the remnants of the garden, and rendered the front steps treacherous, a discovery Pearl made all too late when she was briefly, but vividly, airborne, having slipped on the first stair and sailed out, arms flung wide, satchel containing her disguise thumping ahead of her down the steps. In that momentary flight Pearl knew many things. She knew that she had failed to take due care on the icy step, knew that this would not end well, knew that gravity was ever lurking, after the fashion of an assassin awaiting its opportunity to strike, and above all she knew that inexorable fate and her own foolishness were a combination that toyed with her like a cat with a mouse.

She landed hard. But before she landed, she reached out to break her fall and as a result broke her right wrist, bruised her right hip, and sprained her right ankle. How long she lay there at the foot of the steps panting in the frozen air she did not know, but it took the combined efforts of her mother, Carpy, and Mr. Livingstone from next door to carry her to her bed. Doctor Meadows arrived to find Pearl pale and cold and trembling and moaning. He tried to examine her, but she fought him off with feral strength. He convinced her to drink laudanum and her moaning eased and her colour returned and she allowed the doctor to palp her ankle and her wrist but on no account permitted him to expose her hip. Gathering her quilts and pillows about her she insisted that her pelvic region was undamaged. Meadows reminded her that he was a doctor. Floating now above the pain, she stated that she was well aware of his position and assured him that she had a bit of bruising and nothing worse. The doctor and her mother retired to the parlour to confer. When they returned, Meadows bound Pearl's ankle, set her wrist, and gave her another dose of laudanum. Arranging her bedding like a barricade, Pearl slept.

Christmas and New Year passed in an opiated mist. The world became slow and syrupy. Mr. Gloster paid regular visits, as did Meadows. Once, Pearl thought she overheard Meadows in the corridor begging her mother to marry him and not Gloster.

✦

WHILE PEARL RECUPERATED, FLORENCE WORRIED even more than usual. Often, while Pearl slept, Florence entered her room and studied her. Yes, Pearl had been eating a lot, yet the weight gain was solely on her belly, not around her neck or face or arms. Good God, was it possible? And if she was, when had it happened? Pearl was all but a hermit. True, she went for walks, but even so. If she had a man in her life, it would be apparent in her manner, unless he was some low sort of fellow and she was ashamed and of course, if she was pregnant, she was most definitely ashamed. Florence inevitably recalled her own pregnancy, and just as inevitably recalled the shame and the fear and the rage, and the feel of the rolling pin in her fist and that of wood striking skull. First his skull and then his wife's. Such an expression of outrage on her face—outrage and blame—for it was clear that Florence had lured her good husband into her bed, that sorry mattress stuffed with wood chips and straw in the back of that pawnbroker's shop. Had the woman but overheard her good husband as he'd lied and groped, begged and drooled and threatened.

One morning Florence mustered her resolve and, taking the breakfast tray from Carpy, delivered it to Pearl. This alone was enough to put Pearl on her guard.

"Pearl," she asked as she poured the girl's tea, "is there something I should know?"

Pearl, far ahead of her, said, "Yes, yes there is."

Florence stifled a sob and waited.

Pearl made a show of turning over her toast with disgust then shoving the kipper aside and stating that she hated fish for it tasted fishy and would prefer eggs and bacon and perhaps a piece of roast pork.

"You know, you can tell me anything."

Pearl made a glum face and said thank you. She reached out and gripped her mother's wrist and gave it a squeeze, then with her other hand plucked a piece of toast, took a bite, and then shoved the whole thing into her mouth. "Ask Carpy for more butter," she said, chewing.

✟

FLORENCE HAD BY NOW SPENT many evenings at her fiancé's house. Conversation flowed. Charles spoke in a mellow monotone rich with anecdote. Never did he admit to killing the two women, never did he so much as mention them. And so, while the mood was easy on the surface, underneath, in the depths, Florence suspected shadows swam like sharks. She often felt that she was dreaming, that some tidal wave or typhoon was rolling toward her while she helplessly watched. Was it possible that he had not killed them? How else could he seem so easy with his crime, unless, that is, he was psychotic? Then again, if he had killed the two women, why would he confess, or was it a confession he would make only upon his deathbed, or did it require Florence to come forth and disclose her own secrets? She had said nothing about the man and woman she had killed, why therefore should he speak of the women he had killed? Or did it behoove them to start their life together with a clear slate?

"Charles, how do you suppose those two ladies died?"

He seemed genuinely perplexed. "Ladies?"

"The women found in the water, by the fish plant," she reminded him. She held his gaze as he regarded her, and she thought of two adversaries deciding whether to throw down their arms or continue the fight.

"Ah, yes," he said, "the Irish ladies." Drawing in a deep breath he frowned and considered. "It has always seemed to me that a woman's lot in the world is a precarious one."

Was he placating her? Blowing smoke? How kind his eyes were.

Their visits were always decorous. Once, though, he tried to kiss her and she flinched. She quickly apologized and he asked her pardon. She caught his hand and squeezed it. He smiled and drove her home in his carriage sharing a bear skin across their laps. It was a cold but clear evening and to compensate for her rebuff she asked if he would mind very much driving around for a little while and, as she'd hoped, he was pleased, and so they proceeded to the clop of Benjamin's hooves, the rolling clatter of the wheels, the creaking of the springs, the occasional shout from a house or corner, the call of an owl filling the night making conversation superfluous, and she felt full and happy and safe with this man who knew how to keep his own counsel and demanded so little of her. When they had completed a large circuit of the streets and came to a halt before Florence's gate, she put her hand upon his knee

and leaned and kissed his cheek through his beard and then
waited as he got down and came around and offered his hand.

✦

BY MID-JANUARY PEARL WAS HOBBLING about on crutches
and the cast had been cut from her wrist. One of the first journeys she made was into the pantry to the meat cooler for some
blood to stain her pads. Still, she spent most of her time in bed,
hiding her ever expanding belly beneath the eiderdown. Often,
she had conversations with her baby. He appeared to her as a
little gentleman in a three-piece suit of Donegal tweed, spats,
hat, and cane and advised her on the subjects of coat hangers
and shoe trees, or alternately her baby was a girl of twelve who,
as Pearl herself had once done, possessed absolute certainty
about everything under the sun.

One morning her mother brought her a cup of tea in bed.
"Pearl, I've been meaning to ask."

"Ask what?"

"Forgive me, but the satchel you were carrying when you
fell."

"Satchel?" Pearl fought to mask her terror.

When her mother held up the false beard in one hand and
waxed canvas coat in the other, Pearl said that she was joining
a group of travelling players.

Florence would not put such a whim past her. Then again,
she knew that Pearl was lying. Once again, her worst fear came
to the fore, Pearl's breathless manner around Osmo Beattie not
having escaped her. "Are you pregnant?"

Pearl did not miss a beat. "If only. It would give me something to look forward to."

"Then what is the meaning of this?" Again, she held up
the beard.

"I want to know how the other half lives."

"You are a singular girl."

To which Pearl responded with a rhyme: "A singular girl was Pearl, a singular girl was she, give her a rope to twirl, and she would hang herself one, two, three."

✦

THEN, ONE MORNING IN FEBRUARY, Pearl woke to the sound of a fly battering itself against the window glass. Sunlight set the far wall ablaze with the sort of illumination that she was convinced preceded visits from angels. She waited for the glowing patch on the wall to coalesce into a beatific face, golden-haired and serene, and begin imparting wisdom. It did not. The fly lifted off from the window and came ploughing across the room and landed on Pearl's stomach where it proceeded to violin its forelegs in a most nefarious fashion. Pearl stared. Did it have a face? She blinked, squeezed her eyes tight, opened them. The fly ploughed off and became snarled in a spiderweb high in the corner. Now the sunlight on the wall had shifted and set the silken filaments of the web aglow, the light skating up and down these fine lines as the fly struggled. Pearl felt remorseful but also rekindled. For the hatching of flies was an early sign of spring, a foretaste of the waning of winter. How glorious was that light, how happy the spider. She sat up and her mind was clear, her spirits were quickened, and she knew that she must proceed with her plan as soon as possible. It was Sunday. Tomorrow, Monday, she would go to Greer House; surely fate could not be so cruel as to throw any more obstacles in her path. Had she not suffered enough? Bundling herself in jumpers and shawls, she tapped at her mother's bedroom door.

"Come."

Pearl opened it and peeked around the frame and announced that what with the turn in the weather and the improvement in her condition, she was going for a bit of air. Her mother was reading the *Ladies' Home Journal*. Pearl asked if she wished her to have Carpy prepare breakfast. Florence replied that Carpy was out but that she was well able to fend for herself, thank you, adding that, come spring, she should very much like to take up polo or, failing that, extend the back porch and glass it in and grow sunflowers. Pearl wondered if she'd been at the iron wine. Her mother turned a page and Pearl understood that polo and glassed-in porches were very likely being featured in the magazine.

"But are you, *are we*, not moving in with Mr. Gloster?"

"Of course, but I have no intention of selling my house." She raised her eyes from her magazine and gazed at Pearl.

Pearl was shocked. "Do you not have faith in the marriage?"

"My dear daughter, I have faith in myself."

"What about me?"

"I love you more than anyone on earth, but you are young and erratic."

Pearl said nothing. Then muttered that she would not be gone long.

In fact, she meant to march herself into exhaustion. Otherwise, she would never sleep that night. She headed to Chinatown and then along Wharf Street. She passed the Songhees beauty who stood every day behind a stack of baskets looking like a Venus on a half shell wearing a Hudson's Bay Company blanket around her and playing slow, sad music on a violin while people tossed coins. She was said to be a princess and said to be very sad and said to be wise and said not to be Songhees at all but the love child of a Frenchman and a Laotian courtesan borne in Vientiane and sent into exile.

As Pearl walked, she imitated a fat girl rather than a pregnant woman. She'd noted that fat girls slumped along, slope-shouldered and glum with their palms turned back, while pregnant women moved with hips thrust forward and were always caressing their bellies. Then again there were women

with child and there were women with child, just as there were
fat girls and there were fat girls, and their manner could as
easily be proud and upright as defeated and forlorn; it was all
determined by where they came from, some cultures apparently prizing a Rubenesque figure whereas the style of late, at
least according to the London and Paris gazettes, was tending
more toward the wasp-waisted and willowy. For a moment
Pearl nearly lost heart. If only Desmond Terence Padraich
Orlovski-with-an-*i* had recognized her. If only he had begged
her to marry him then and there. But why would he do that,
why would he want to marry a woman pregnant with another
man's child? She gave herself a shake, commanded herself to
buck up, reminded herself that she was a Greyland-Smith,
and even if that was hollow and meaningless, asked herself to,
pray, list her alternatives. She had no choice but to march on.

She began the long plod toward the beaches. In spite of the
unseasonable warmth of the sun, mist still hung over the sea.
Or perhaps it was because of it. She didn't know. She didn't
know anything. What was that line in *A Christmas Carol*?
Scrooge, buoyant with his epiphany, dancing about his rooms,
singing: "I don't know anything!" But one was a tale; this was
life. She thought of the circle of people she had sat with the
evening she'd decided to end it all. What had become of them?
And the woman on the horse who had given her a ride home?

Across the Strait, on the Yankee side, the mountains stood
capped with snow, their western slopes brilliant and eastern
faces solemn. Her feet and ankles and knees hurt while her
now perpetual backache worsened. The potholed road was
mud and slush and she stepped in a puddle and got soaked.
Carriages and riders passed, as well as bicycles and an open cart
stacked with tables and chairs and half a dozen mongrels, one
balanced atop the uppermost stool yapping to beat the band.

Pearl might have missed Carpy altogether if the woman with
Carpy had not barked back at the dogs. Pearl's first thought was

that Carpy's companion believed herself to be a dog, especially given that she was on a leash. Her bark was thoroughly convincing, ending in a yip and a howl. Pearl wasn't the only one to turn and stare. Carpy's friend's head was shaved to stubble, she was short and thick, with a face as round as a pie pan, wore a quilted coat of black and red checks, and plimsolls. Carpy was not at all pleased to see Pearl, in fact she was horrified, and her expression dared Pearl to mock. Pearl did not have any inclination to mock; she did, however, expect an explanation.

Scowling, Carpy said, "This is Dot. Say hello, Dot."

Dot crossed her arms over her chest and frowned deeply in refusal, causing Carpy to tug her leash which was fitted like a belt around her ample middle.

"H'lo."

Through clenched teeth, Carpy grumbled, "Dot's me sister."

Pearl was delighted. Knowing Carpy's name to be Desiree, she said, "Dot and Des."

Carpy glared from under her brow then wound the leash tighter around her wrist as though fearing Dot might get fractious and nip.

"Is she older or younger?" Pearl asked.

Now Carpy's red face verged on purple.

"We're twins!" said Dot, suddenly beaming. "Des took her sweet time and blocked the door and I come out feet first head last. Would you like me to lift you up? I can do it with one arm."

"That's enough, Dot."

"I can do twenty prone presses with Fern LaRue sitting on me back. Twenty. I can count them out loud in French."

"Not here, thank you, Dot," hissed Carpy under her breath. "We don't want to stop the young miss on her perambulation, do we. There's a good girl."

"Will you come to tea?" Dot asked. Then to Carpy, "I want her to come to tea. We've got tea in a big tin box. It's very good tea. It came from Ceylon on a ship."

"Is Fern LaRue very heavy, then?" asked Pearl.

"Well, not really," admitted Dot. "She's only four foot and eats the feathers in her pillow. But I reckon I could do ten with Des on me back and maybe five with you. Are you very far along?"

"Along?" Pearl struggled not to look at Carpy but even so could see that her humiliation had become glee.

"Oh, now, Dot. Miss Pearl's just portly is all. Don't you see, there's no ring on her finger. No ring at all. She's got no man in her life, no, no, she's just her lonesome self."

"Half the girls in the home are knocked up and no ring," said Dot, picking her nose and studying the gup.

"Well," said Pearl, battling the tremor in her voice and the urge to vomit, "that's why I'm out walking. For exercise and air."

"Me 'n Des walk at night sometimes on account of I'm a daftie."

Carpy gave the leash another tug but Dot scarcely noticed; it was like hauling at a stump with a thread.

"I've had ever so many lads try it on with me, but I put the choke hold on them. I don't like to. Honest, I don't. I don't like to hurt anyone. Though Des says sometimes it's necessary. Isn't it, Des?"

"Thank you, Dot. That's quite enough of the chitter-chat."

"My full name is Dorothea," she said airily, giving her head a bit of a toss as though in recollection of when she had long flowing locks.

"Dorothea. That's a lovely name."

"As is Desiree," Dot added quickly, lest Carpy be jealous.

"It is," agreed Pearl. "It is. You must come to our house for tea some afternoon."

At this Dot descended again into gloom. She shrugged and hung her head and spoke to the ground. "I'm not allowed. I knock things over." She began kneading her hands.

"And where do you go on your nighttime walks?" asked Pearl while studiously avoiding Carpy's eyes.

"Hard to say because it's dark then, isn't it."

"Of course," agreed Pearl. "Of course."

The pale sun had gone behind the clouds and the wind was kicking up off the sea. They were all shivering so said their goodbyes. Pearl shook Dot's hand, thick as a man's. She'd have given Desmond a match in arm wrestling for sure. There was a look in her eyes that made Pearl think of a fish surfacing and hovering a moment to observe the world of people before sinking back down. On the walk home Pearl wondered how Carpy had managed to keep her sister a secret for so long. She also wondered why it was Dot instead of Carpy who got the short end of the stick at birth. It was bewildering. You could be born first or second, rich or poor, male or female, a Spanish princess or a one-eyed hunchback, all without rhyme or reason, just as you could turn left or right, say no, say yes, make one teeny misstep on a summer's eve in the belly of a sphinx and your life was arse up in the mud.

Chapter Seventeen

THAT EVENING PEARL KNUCKLED HER eyes and with a loud yawn left the parlour, saying good night. A touch theatrical perhaps but her mother was absorbed in an article on the Queen's theories on chromatics as pertaining to watercolours and she scarcely seemed to notice. How her back ached. Weren't doting hubbies supposed to rub your back? Would Osmo prove a doting hubby? She fought down a sob. Soon enough Osmo would spirit her away, soon enough he would be rubbing Cleptopatra's back.

The clock read 9:10 PM. An interminable night stretched ahead. Her mind was all cats and squirrels. Had her mother convinced Carpy to make Dot throttle Cassidy and the Brennan woman? It made sense. Dot would never be hung, merely put in a room with a lock on the door. Perhaps her mother was using Pearl's tuition fees to pay Carpy off? That too made sense. Set Dot on Cassidy and then, when the other showed up asking questions, set Dot on her. But that meant another payment. Between the blackmail and the bribery no wonder her mother was skint.

Pearl lay in bed wondering if her scheme was mad. Why should a silk cobra, a sandalwood sphinx, and a mummified cat lead Osmo to her? What had she been thinking? What *was* she thinking? She was not Cleptopatra but Clodhopperpatra.

She re-evaluated her options and saw three courses of action.

One. Go through with her scheme.

Two. Leave Victoria for Winnipeg or Toronto or Montreal where, when her time came, she would present herself at a hospital or convent, some sort of Sisters of Charity affair, and give birth and pursue a life of obscure enigmatic dignity, just her and her child, and perhaps write poetry or novels.

Three. Confess to her mother and give birth here with the aid of Doctor Meadows while Carpy looked smugly on, thereby destroying her mother's world as well as ruining any future either might have had, for surely Mr. Gloster would withdraw his marriage proposal. Or would he? Perhaps, doting and loyal, he'd spirit them abroad, her mother, herself, little Osmo, all under his calm, wise, protective guidance to live in a villa in Italy or a mansion on the banks of the Nile.

Pressing her palms to her eyes she rolled her head side to side and tried not to moan. Perhaps if she joined some religious community? Were there not utopian communities scattered about North America? Was there not a Russian outpost up near Alaska? Could she become a Mormon or Mennonite? Did they not have two and three wives and scads of kids? Then again, she seemed to recall some Chinese emperor who, deciding that it was time for him to leave this world, ate gold leaf to pave his way to Heaven. Yet she did not own any gold leaf or believe in Heaven, even if she did feel as though she were in Purgatory.

She woke late. Her mother was in the breakfast nook off the kitchen. The sun shone through the panes and there were snowdrops poking up around the base of the fir in the backyard and even the shoots of daffodils and crocuses. Good omens? Pearl joined her mother who set her teacup down with a rap and levelled her gaze upon her.

"Pearl," she said. "Do you not think it time we had a talk?"

She felt her eyes widen with alarm and her face stiffen.

"What," her mother said, enunciating each word as though Pearl were hard of hearing and slow of wit, "do, you, intend, to, do?"

So Carpy had peached. Pearl glared at her but Carpy feigned preoccupation with that strange collection of jars and tubes on the shelf in her room off the pantry.

"How long have you known?"

"Not long enough. Why didn't you come to me?"

"Seriously, Mother? And say what? Please Mummy make it go away?"

Tears magnified her mother's eyes. "You've been so very alone."

Now Pearl was weeping as well. She shrugged and looked out at the snowdrops and envied them their beautiful if brief existence. How did something so pure grow in dirt?

Her mother spoke quietly. "What were your plans?"

Shrugging pathetically, Pearl said that she did not honestly know.

"Is he the father?"

She was about to say who, but of course her mother guessed, so she merely nodded.

"Is he aware?"

"No." She stared into her tea, at the cream that had broken into tadpole-like clumps with curling tails. How innocent those little white tadpoles. How innocent the red and white checked tablecloth. How optimistic those snowdrops. Again, she envied flowers their brief glory, the joy they brought, the rooms and gardens they brightened, and the poetry they inspired. Would she ever inspire poetry? She shivered around her hot stomach and thought what a disappointment she was and how her mother must regret having had her; and now here she was about to be a mother herself and she'd scarcely given a thought, a realistic thought, as to what that truly entailed, much less how or where she intended to live.

"He has no idea?"

"None."

Florence sucked her teeth and then nodded. "Right." She set her hands firmly upon the table. "You will pack immediately."

Pearl was shocked and hopeful. "For what?"

"To leave. To go wherever you wish. Australia. New Zealand. Cape Town. Or perhaps America. San Francisco. Though I do not recommend it. I think Toronto. We could be there in a week. That should be more than enough time to compose your biography. Of course, you will need a ring." Pearl watched her mother stride down the corridor and into her bedroom. Pearl looked at Carpy but she was still pretending to be busy. Her mother returned with a small jewellery box, set it on the table, opened it, and spilled the contents. Why had Pearl never found it on her numerous snoops through her mother's room? There were brooches, bracelets, pins, buttons, clips, and rings, many rings, even a copper-coloured jewel beetle that her mother carefully picked up and returned to the box, after which she began pushing various possibilities forward for Pearl's perusal. There were silver bands and gold bands, some plain, some set with stones ranging from a single pearl to multiple rubies. Carpy, unable to resist, joined them.

"Many are paste or glass," cautioned her mother. "But there are a few authentic stones. This is Bohemian crystal, these are Burmese rubies, here is a sapphire, that is a topaz, and this is a Cape diamond set in Kolar gold. Very handsome. Choose two."

Pearl asked her what she was talking about.

"Honestly, Pearl. You are a bewildering combination of cleverness and stupidity. Your engagement ring and your wedding ring. You are a widow, all the more tragic for being so young. How did he die?"

Something heroic, of course, some noble if doomed cavalry charge, or was that too easily researched and contradicted? Then again, was that not the story behind her so-called father?

"Well," said her mother, unruffled, "we have a week on the train to come up with a story. Here. What about this emerald. Set in Potosí silver. I think it looks very well with your eyes."

Pearl turned the ring in the light and then slipped it on her finger. Perfect. She began to blub. "Thank you, Mother. You are being most understanding, far more than I deserve." She stood. "Excuse me. I need some air to compose myself."

Her mother said not to hurry, that there were arrangements to be made. She would see about the schedules and the tickets, and that they would very likely take the boat to Vancouver tomorrow morning or evening. Pearl threw her arms around her neck and hugged her. Then Pearl stood back, aghast, and said, "What about Mr. Gloster?"

"If he truly loves me, he will surely understand and all will be well."

Chapter Eighteen

THE HOSTESS AT THE TIPPERARY was a girl not much older than Pearl, with a pale complexion and most of her teeth and a pink and blue bonnet that partially hid the smallpox scars along her hairline. Carrying a black leather satchel, Pearl followed as gracefully as she could manage toward the empty table, studiously avoiding eye contact with anyone. She thanked the hostess who curtsied. Instead of sitting down, however, Pearl carried on toward the Ladies' intending to change into her disguise. If they were leaving Victoria tomorrow, then the clues had to be set today so that Osmo could get to work and find her. As grateful as she was to her mother—and Pearl had never loved her more dearly—there was no reason she should lose Osmo or that little Osmo or Esmerelda should lose their father. How many times had Pearl wished for her own father? And what must her mother have felt raising her alone all these many years? Yes, Pearl could pass herself off as a noble widow and save face, but then what? Decades of loneliness was a high price for the facade of decorum. And besides, did Osmo not deserve at least the chance to do the right thing? It was a gamble to be sure, but the stakes were too high not to risk all. And if Osmo failed, then Pearl would depart in quiet dignity.

Approaching the Ladies', Pearl recalled the many Saturday afternoons that she and Miranda had been allowed to come here on their own for tea. It had been the highlight of the week. What freedom! What liberty! Would she ever return here in triumph? Not if she was a widow. No, only if she carried through with her plan.

The Ladies' Room was discreetly located behind a partition. As Pearl stepped around it the door opened and a young woman emerged. Miranda. Both halted. For a moment neither could speak. How splendid Miranda looked in robin's egg blue with her slim waist and sandy blond hair piled high, showcasing the long and graceful curve of her neck and sapphire earrings. A stunner and no mistake. What doors must be opening for her. What offers of marriage must be piling up. What power and what glory were in wait. In the half a second it took for these thoughts to spin through Pearl's mind she saw the expression in Miranda's eyes, or rather *expressions*, for they were many and they splashed about in those blue pools like frolicking swimmers: genuine pleasure at seeing Pearl was submerged by utter delight in the dawning suspicion that she was pregnant, which sank under the sincere wish to help, which in turn sank under the need to gloat and tell someone what she had seen, and yet all of these were shoved under by Miranda's desperation to know every detail, the who and the where and the when. For an instant Pearl considered taking her aside and telling her. What a story it was. An escapade as romantic as it was tragic. Miranda would almost be jealous.

Miranda said, "Pearl."

Pearl said, "Miranda. I've so much to tell you."

Miranda nearly swooned at the prospect.

Pearl leaned close. "Just let me use the facilities and I'll join you." She squeezed Miranda's shoulder and slipped on past into the lavatory. Once inside, Pearl sank back against the door and shut her eyes and fought for composure. What was Miranda doing here on a Monday? Spring break already? She groaned and recognized the scent of citrus oil that served to suppress everything else in the room. She opened her eyes and discovered that two of the three stalls were occupied, leaving no option but the middle one. The lid was down so that she was not forced to look into the bowl. From previous visits she knew that it was glazed with a pastoral scene of shepherds and sheep in a field. It had always struck her as abominable. What did the artisans think about their work being put to such use?

From the next stall came the sounds of weeping. Or was it muffled laughter? She put her ear to the wooden partition. No, most definitely weeping. From the other stall there was only silence. Were they, too, listening? Pearl got down to work, swapping dress for trousers and her coat for a still bulkier coat, and then fiddled with the glue pot and brush and applied her beard thinking of Herbert Fogarty in Shanghai Alley. Had his father returned to Ireland or did he still live in Canton? She pictured an aging Irishman, lean, distinguished, in a Chinese coat and goatee. Did he consider himself Irish or Chinese? In which language did he dream? She must someday return to his shop and ask. Before departing the stall she stuffed her dress and coat into the satchel, tugged at her beard to test the glue— felt it threaten to peel away, so daubed on extra and pressed it more firmly into place—and a moment later stepped from the stall not as Pearl Greyland-Smith—if that was indeed her real name—but as Alexander Nyle. She moved quickly to the door. This was a sticky bit: a man emerging from the Ladies'. As she stepped out a man was leaving the Gents' at the very same moment. The timing would have been impeccable if they had been going on stage in some opéra bouffe. Fortunately, he was still busy with his buttons, and when he looked up and their eyes met, Pearl nodded confidently—hale fellow well met—and did the only thing she could, which was to go on past him and enter the Gents'. Two men stood urinating at either end of a long wooden trough that angled downward to a hole in the wall. Pearl's eyes stung and her nostrils burned at the pong of ammonia. Both men kept their eyes firmly on their business. She turned and went back out in time to see a woman emerging from the Ladies', her eyes red and lips trembling. What calamity had befallen her? Was she, too, with child out of wedlock? The woman hurried past. It seemed to Pearl that a better partition between the two facilities was needed. Perhaps she would write a note. Now, however, she must step around the partition and for a moment be in full view of the tearoom proper. As she did, she couldn't keep from glancing in—and saw Miranda at a table with three other girls, all leaning in like gluttons to gorge on scandal. Pearl stared. Sensing that they were being studied, all four girls turned and looked and for a moment they gazed at Pearl even as she gazed at them. Did they recognize her? Pearl felt the widening distance between them, as if she were on a boat drifting away from the dock on a voyage from which she could never return. She fled past the kitchen that was all aclamour with clanging pans and rich with the odours of coffee and yeast. The back door stood wide open. She staggered down the steps into the alley. How free she felt, as if escaping prison. She thought again of the weeping girl in the next stall, and she thought of the word *wedlock*. *Wed—lock*. Safety or imprisonment? Osmo Beattie, gaoler or companion?

The February sun was shining and the air fresh. Why could she not simply spend the afternoon walking, and when the sun began to decline and the chill set in, stop by the Lord Nelson and have a mulled wine or a hot whiskey? Such were the freedoms of men. Men did not get pregnant, men merely went on their way, whistling and laughing. She shifted her satchel to her other hand, rolled her shoulders, and, armoured by her disguise of boots and pants and coat and beard and hat, she clenched her teeth and swung her legs in a longer and more manly stride thinking of gents and their tackle. Until last summer she had known little of such business, only what Miranda had told her, she who was more informed about everything high and low, wide and narrow.

With all the detail of an engineer, she once sketched the hydraulic nature of male "equipage" in the various stages of excitation. Pearl had been as terrified as she was aghast. She could well imagine what Miranda was on about now back in the Tipperary. Yes, Pearl was fallen, she was a disgrace, a calamity, a tramp, a trollop.

Well, she would see about that.

She spotted Greer House. On the porch sat Ed, eyes closed and his face raised to the hard light of the winter sun. Pearl told herself that she should not disturb him, that it was inauspicious, and that she should continue on past. Yet she had known he would be there, he was always there on the porch, and besides she could not be going back and forth, it would be suspect. Or did it make sense? Her ruse was that she was new to town and seeking her old chum, Osmo. She walked on another block to regather herself, and then another. If she kept going, she'd reach the sea, abode of mermaids and disembodied souls if Carpy was to be believed. She turned around. As Greer House came into view again her insides felt like pudding, her back ached and the boots rubbed and the beard had begun to itch. Yes, a double whiskey at the Lord Nelson and a jaw with the lads, maybe run into her drinking buddy Desmond Terence Padraich Orlovski-with-an-*i* and learn why he'd been thrown overboard and forced to swim ashore only to be stung by a devilfish and lose his foot. The Lord Nelson was not so very far away, only a few blocks. But here was Greer House. What was the adage? Faint heart never won fair lady. Did it work both ways? She pushed through the gate as if leaping from a cliff.

Heavy-eyed and otherworldly, Ed observed her approach. Pearl thought of his life, a white-skinned black man. But there was no time for such speculation.

Pearl called, "Hello, sir!" and cringed at the squeak in her tone. Coughing, she said it again, in a lower register, "Hello. A fine day. Considering the season." She climbed the wooden steps and saw that he was in fact an extraordinary colour, whitish-yellow verging on pale orange. His eyes, too, were pale. She thought of a ghost in the daylight. In his lap sat a tray with silver wire and assorted bits and in his hand he gripped a pair of pliers. On a table beside him was a hinged box lined in black velvet containing earrings and bracelets. "You are an artisan!"

He said nothing.

Was he mute as well as albino?

"House is full," he said after having given her a thorough sizing up.

Pearl looked from him to the door where there was indeed a NO VACANCY sign. She shifted her bag to her other hand. There was still time to thank him and wish him good day. Was he eyeing her strangely? Did he see through her disguise? Were albinos keener of sight? Did they see in the dark? She turned and looked at the street. Across the way was a furniture concern and next to it a haberdasher. She found herself repeating the word *haberdasher*.

"In fact, I'm not looking for a room," she announced even as she saw, even as she knew, that this was the moment of proverbial truth, that after this there was no going back, she was crossing the Rubicon. She took a breath. "I'm looking for my old friend Osmo Beattie."

"Police station."

She feigned concern. "Is he in trouble?"

Ed frowned. "No, he's a police."

"Osmo?"

The man nodded once, up then down, like a pump.

"Osmo a policeman," she mused.

"An inspector," he said.

"An inspector?" Her rising tone said this was still greater news. "Are you the proprietor?"

His pale eyes narrowed as if studying her for mockery; she maintained an openly innocent expression. "You want the sisters," he said.

She put a hand on the doorknob and gave him a querying

look. He nodded and she, committed, took yet another deep breath and, just like that, went in.

And found herself in a hall of glass. Three gold-framed mirrors to her left, three gold-framed mirrors to her right, each tall, each reflecting the other and everything between, and everything between was made of glass. On a glass-topped table sat glass vases and jugs and decanters, swan-necked, tulip-shaped, as well as flutes, dolphins, cupped hands, nymphs of rose glass and gods of green glass. Pearl would have reached out to steady herself, so dizzying was the spectacle, but feared toppling the glass figurines, maidens and lambs, elegant ladies in pensive poses, cavaliers and noblemen, birds on branches, goats on crags. She looked down. The hexagonal black and white tile floor was disorienting. She looked up. The ceiling was inlaid with stamped copper so bright, so gleaming, so luminous that it mirrored everything while the light of the lamps flowed like rippling water over the translucent surfaces.

Of course, Pearl had been expecting this. Or should have been, for the spectacle of the Greers' foyer was well known in Victoria. But she had never experienced it first-hand. A visual nausea overtook her. Backing up against the door, she fumbled behind herself for the handle and would have escaped but a woman appeared—it was as if she had stepped straight from the wallpaper, for no door was visible. And then there were two of them, or the same one twice, reflected. Pearl shut her eyes and shook her head, fearing she was seeing double. Opening her eyes, she saw that they were not big women but had a large presence that verged on the formidable, silver-grey hair straightened and swept up and held by pins, thick necks, jowly faces, staring dark eyes. They did not seem surprised to see her—him—as if errant strangers were forever stumbling into the phantasmagoria that was their glass decorated foyer.

"Not an uncommon reaction," said one. "I suppose it's time for a thinning out. Would you like a glass elephant? Or a crystal goblet?" Before Pearl could respond the woman began to explain that Victoria was so grey compared to Missouri that, in winter especially, they were starved for light and the glass magnified and multiplied it.

The other woman, heavier in face and manner, advanced like a man bearing down upon a foe. "I'm afraid we have no vacancies, as the sign outside plainly states," she added with a hint of impatience, as if the illiteracy of the age was an ongoing irritation. Her voice was thick with fatigue or beleaguerment. She looked to be about sixty.

Apologizing, Pearl said that she understood. And then said, "In fact, I'm not after a room."

This brought Gwendolyn Greer up short. She regarded her—him—with eyes like those of a formidable raven and Pearl said she was looking for her friend Osmo, Osmo Beattie. As she spoke, she became overly conscious of her beard, which itched her nostrils and lips and neck. Was Gwendolyn looking at it? Could she see through this sorry disguise? Pearl imagined the lady slapping her face and berating her, imagined her contacting her mother, and then her mother confronting Pearl, with the mocking Carpy looking smugly on, two humiliations in one day. But now Gwendolyn turned to Giselle, who had approached as well. How completely their expressions had changed. Osmo Beattie's name had altered everything as though a magical phrase, and Giselle was now smiling and Gwendolyn less fearsome, indeed Gwendolyn was indicating the door to the parlour on Pearl's left.

The parlour was mercifully subdued, shell wainscotting below plain powder-blue paper, a lightbulb in a red shade suspended on a cord from the rosette in the ceiling. The fire was banked, the heat screen embroidered with a sunset over a tropical isle, the chairs tan, a few landscapes on the wall, the window looking onto the porch and the back of Ed's orange head. Pearl was invited to sit. She obeyed, placing her satchel on the floor, conscious of keeping her knees wide and feet set solid after the manly fashion.

"You must be hot," said Gwendolyn. "Giselle, take the young man's coat."

Pearl was perspiring but insisted that she was fine and went so far as to snug her collar. "I like to be warm," she said.

"You have a very fine skin," said Gwendolyn, peering.

"A lot of men do," said Giselle. "Daddy. He had an immaculate complexion until the day he died. Finer than Mother's."

The dour Gwendolyn did not dispute this.

"And Rabbit Martin," added Giselle.

"The less said about Rabbit Martin the better," stated Gwendolyn severely.

Pearl said that her name was Alexander Nyle and that Osmo had been a childhood friend. Their expressions softened further; they even seemed to breathe differently, as if they'd heard reassuring news of long-lost loved ones. Giselle offered tea, saying that they had black tea, green tea, blackberry leaf tea, raspberry leaf tea, lemon tea, mint tea as well as Lapsang Oolong. Pearl said she was fine, though as she spoke, she wondered if it was a tactical error to decline, for she did not dare make them think she disdained their tea. Giselle then offered hot chocolate, she could have the girl heat some up, very fortifying on a cold afternoon. Pearl said that hot chocolate would be wonderful. Giselle went to the door and called along the corridor, "Celine . . . Celine!" After a moment an accented voice came back and Giselle directed her to bring a tot of hot chocolate. "Tout suite, s'il vous plait!"

"Of course, the inspector won't be back for hours," Gwendolyn was saying. "You do know that he is a police inspector." A hint of challenge and suspicion, a habitual wariness, edged her eye as she gauged how this registered. Pearl nodded quickly, admitting that she'd just learned this from the gent on the porch.

"If you want to see him straight away," said Giselle, "you had best go on down to the police station. It's not far. They'd know where he was."

"Then again he may be on a case," cautioned Gwendolyn. "You wouldn't want to disturb him. Likely they wouldn't tell you."

"Of course," said Pearl. "I wouldn't want to get underfoot." A silence now opened. Pearl found the ladies regarding her anew. A clock ticked on the mantel. Two twenty-nine. She needed to get upstairs into Osmo's room, which suddenly seemed an insurmountable hurdle. She asked how long they'd been in business here in Victoria and for the next half hour Giselle recounted their lives, first in Missouri and then in California and finally their migration north, Gwendolyn offering the occasional correction. Pearl didn't ask about husbands or children, fearing to touch upon tragedy. Both women wore numerous rings and bracelets, and Giselle a gold brooch above her left breast. Gwendolyn wore a gold choker set with blue stones. They had positioned themselves opposite her on a scroll arm couch, upright and attentive, models of decorum.

"But we want to hear about young Osmo," said Giselle.

"And about yourself," said Gwendolyn, eyes narrowing.

"Osmo's so private," Giselle added.

"It does not do for a man in his position to be talky," cautioned Gwendolyn.

Pearl had devised a backlog of anecdotes about Osmo. She'd rehearsed their delivery, chuckling fondly as she recounted boyhood adventures involving high-spirited shenanigans. Only now, in the parlour, facing these two formidable women, she forgot them, while what she did remember sounded forced and artificial, and she fought not to wipe the droplets of perspiration travelling down her temples into the monstrously itching beard, which she feared would loosen and drop away even as she sat there. It was plain that they were not going to allow her access to Osmo's room, and why should they, that should have been obvious.

"You're pale," said Gwendolyn, with a hint of accusation.

"Where *is* that chocolate?" Giselle frowned. "Honestly, these French maids. Give me a German any day." She went to the door and called out to Celine.

Pearl stood. "Well, I thank you ever so much, but I've taken up too much of your time. I'll just go down to the station like you said." She was dizzy and nauseous, hot and clammy. Her hand went to her collar to loosen it, but she stopped herself.

"That coat," said Giselle, stepping toward her as if she would unbutton it herself.

"I'm fine, I'm—"

She woke on the floor.

It felt good down there, the polished planks cool and flat and solid. Giselle had the collar of her coat open and was fanning her with a gazette while Gwendolyn stood behind her frowning as if Pearl were faulty goods. Giselle was saying something. Pearl saw her lips moving. She smelled of some sort of balm. Pearl would have liked to stay right there and sleep with her fanning her like that. How reassuring the floor was, as if she was in the arms of Mother Earth, but Giselle stopped fanning and started undoing more buttons and in a moment would have the coat off, so Pearl rolled away and struggled to her feet. Catching hold of her satchel she declared herself fine.

"Air," she said a little too loudly. "Cool air. And a stroll." She tried to laugh and lighten the mood. "Thank you, thank you ever so much. You have been more than kind." Turning she made to leave but wavered and lost her balance again. Shutting her eyes, she dropped back into the chair. The satchel fell with a thud. Gwendolyn said she'd get that chocolate herself and directed Giselle to fetch a cool cloth. As their footsteps receded Pearl opened her eyes then shut them again and almost gave in to a deep sleep, a complete capitulation; how sweet that would be, how soothing to give in and forget everything, yet in an instant she woke and got to her feet and went to the door. There was the chaos of glass in the foyer, and beyond that an open door and a corridor leading to the kitchen. As she turned and fetched her satchel, she saw Ed's pale orange head through the window. By the angle she could tell that he was dozing, chin on chest.

In the foyer again she looked around. There was the door ... And there were the stairs leading to Osmo's room. She could go out the door or up the stairs. Another wave of dizziness threatened to throw her over. The door or the stairs. In or out. All or nothing. Win or lose. Faint heart or bold. Would she seize the day or not? She looked around once more, then opened her mouth but no sound came. Trying again, she succeeded in calling to the Greers, who were out of sight, announcing that she was leaving and thank you ever so very much! She reached for the door and gripped the knob—cold round copper. Then she let go, let go and crept up the stairs, keeping to the wall because stairs creak less at the edges even though there was a runner in the middle. How had she learned this? Miranda? It was just the sort of detail she'd know even if she'd never be so mad as to do anything like this.

At the first floor she paused and listened. Only the muted sounds of a few birds outside. Satchel in left hand, her right on the railing, she looked back down the stairs. There was still time to escape. She could simply retreat and go out the door. She gripped the railing tighter, shut her eyes then opened them. Her mother knew and was taking care of everything. Why not simply go home? But it was a rhetorical question. Up here there were two rooms on one side of the corridor and two on the other, the doors tall and narrow with a window at the top canted open for ventilation. At one end of the corridor were the facilities and at the other a window propped by a brick, the pearly curtains groping inward on a breeze so that for an instant she thought of ghost hands reaching to drag her off to some Perdition. Then she heard the Greer sisters and she hurried on up to the next floor. The air grew closer and more confined, a smell of wax and wood and vinegar, the light muted. Three doors. One on either side and one at the end. She fought a moment of panic. She hadn't anticipated three. Which was Osmo's? Where was the street in relation to where she stood? The staircase had come up parallel to the side of the house and then done a quarter turn. His was the southwest. She'd noted that, which made it the door at the end, which had a line of light beneath it. The Greers were now at the foot of the stairs. Had they seen her? Had they heard? The front door opened and there was conversation with Ed, Gwendolyn interrogating him; this was followed by footsteps on the porch, then Giselle and Gwendolyn came back inside and the door closed and they decided that Osmo's friend was indeed an odd duck.

"He reminded me of Rabbit Martin," said Giselle.

"How many times must I tell you that I don't want to hear that name," said Gwendolyn, voice rising.

"Are you going to drink that chocolate?"

"I'm fat enough, thank you," said Gwendolyn.

"Yet you were eager to feed it to our visitor who was fatter than either of us," said Giselle. She then added that Gwendolyn was not really so very fat, that they were neither of them fat at all. "We have substance."

Gwendolyn muttered that Rabbit Martin had thought she was fat, to which Giselle responded that Rabbit Martin was an oaf and a fool, adding that this time it was she, Gwendolyn, who had mentioned him. By the direction of their footsteps Pearl judged they'd gone into the parlour.

She reached Osmo's door. Cautiously, she took hold of the knob and turned it slowly clockwise. It stuck. Then advanced. Pearl felt as much as heard the mechanism trip over and the door drifted inward an inch, offering her a peek. Forgetting that doors creak loudest when pushed slowest, the hinges squawked as she pushed it wider. Wincing, she halted and listened. Had the conversation downstairs hesitated? Were the Greers frowning upward, exchanging glances and moving to the foot of the stairs? As Pearl edged sideways through the opening, her belly shoved the door farther, but now it went in perfect silence. She pressed it shut.

Maps. The far wall was covered in maps. Of Victoria, of the British Columbia coast, of North America, South America, Australia, Britain, the world. There was the standard photo of the Queen, in profile, a dour, glum, jowly, foreboding, forbidding, unforgiving, and altogether lugubrious looking little brute of a creature in Pearl's opinion. Her mother's veneration of such a lump had always been bewildering. Looking around, she thought Osmo's room was disappointingly plain. A chest of drawers, a mirror, a clothes press, a hat rack with no hats, a rather small bookshelf. There were volumes on the criminal code, a dictionary, a text on phrenology, two on handwriting analysis, Abbe Jean Hippolyte Michon's *Les Mystères de L'écriture* and Rosa Baughan's *Character Indicated by Handwriting*, as well as Baedeker's *Egypt*. Osmo? Egypt? The sphinx... Mere coincidence? She had a vision of him standing in the desert by the sphinx with the sandy wind swirling about him and a red sun burning at the horizon. She flipped through the pages. She performed an experiment and held the book spine down and let it fall open where it may, where it had been most often studied, which was not the sphinx but the Temple of Kings, Luxor. Pearl was vaguely disappointed. She slotted the book back onto the shelf and faced the room.

His bed was austere. High, narrow, with a plain wood frame, the blankets tucked tight. The maid's work or Osmo's own, the precision of a police inspector, the habit of perfection and attention to detail essential to his work? The cream curtains over the window sieved the light. The room was cool. Sweating so recently, Pearl was now chilly. Stepping closer to the window, she noted a flower box on the outside and some small green shoots and imagined him studying them each morning and evening, perhaps leaning to inhale their scent when they flowered, perhaps even murmuring to them, doting upon an innocence standing in such contrast to his daily work. She turned back to the bed. There was a small red cushion with tassels at each corner and, in the middle, *Paris Exhibition 1889* stitched in gold.

In a move that felt as outrageous as if she had stripped off all her clothes and danced naked, she lay down on the bed, taking care that her boots did not soil the cover. The ceiling was thin strips of slatwood, glossy with shellac. From the centre dangled a bulb on a cord. Pearl shut her eyes and noted the smells of tobacco, wool, leather, and something else, something mineral, compressed, as if the force of focused thought had hardened the very air. It put her in mind of river rock. She rolled onto her side and found herself looking at a closet door. She frowned, for she hadn't noticed it and, of all things, recalled a morning years ago when she went mushrooming with Carpy who'd lectured her to pay attention but not look too hard, otherwise she wouldn't see them. Pearl hadn't understood.

"They'll hide from you," Carpy had explained.

"What," she'd said, "mushrooms, hide?"

"A'course they hide."

"How?"

"They pretend to be asleep."

She'd narrowed her eyes and thrust her jaw in suspicion, sure that Carpy was having her on. But it worked. By adopting an offhand attitude, by seeming to look the other way, Pearl had found that the mushrooms grew bold and all but called out to her, and soon she had gathered a basket full. Now, in Osmo's room, she approached the closet at an angle, hands clasped innocently behind her back, gaze averted, as though approaching a strange cat, and then reached out very slowly to turn the knob.

Had the proverbial skeleton toppled out she would not have been surprised. Had she found Osmo himself crouched within, alone or with a woman, dressed or naked, she'd have been less surprised than finding what she did, for somehow it was both empty and not empty, that is to say it was full of light, in fact it was radiant, and for an instant she thought it was on fire, and she stepped back, raising her arm to shield her face, except that there was no fire, and no lightbulb that had been left burning, for no lightbulb, no chandelier, no oil lamp burned as intensely as the light in that closet. What, then, was she looking at, Mr. Franklin's lightning in a bottle? No, for while it was luminous it was also diffuse, penetrating and yet expansive. She leaned and saw that there was a window in the wall, a square of yellow glass through which sunlight poured, magnified and intensified. She passed her hand through it and the light seemed to cling then fall away like phosphorescence, golden phosphorescence. Pearl thought of a spirit, a figure of radiance, a genie in a bottle, a small god in a high temple. An urge to step inside and curl up overcame her. She would lie like a cat in the sun and when Osmo found her, he would lie next to her and they'd remain there, together, in that closet that was bigger than the world, that closet that contained the world, or all of the world that was necessary. And yet as she was about to enter, she felt a chill, a foreboding chill, and she halted. What was it? Perhaps the house was haunted by the previous tenant, or the one before? Stepping back, she pushed the door shut and thought of the tick of a clock marking its final hour.

Turning, she saw, on the desk, a notebook of plain brown suede. Had it been there before? She shut then opened her eyes, gave her head a shake, stepped closer. Picking the book up she noted its weight. It was perhaps six by ten inches, the stitched spine pliable and worn to a gloss by Osmo's hands. A scent of calf and oil. Seating herself on the ladder-back chair she opened it at random. November 10, 1891.

Dourest month. Little to recommend it. One
thinks of a convict at the start of his sentence.
Oct. gone, and with it the remnants of summer,
that sphinx of a season, so seemingly open and
yet hiding so much beneath the glare...

She proceeded to open the desk drawers, seeking the volume
that included June and their night together. Shirts, socks, pen
and ink, shoelaces, handkerchiefs, a tin of Merryman's Mints,
a knife. But no other journals. She went to the bookshelf. She
knelt and looked under the bed. Stood in the middle of the
room, fists on hips, frowning, went to the closet and looked in
once more and found it less luminous and more ashen because
the angle of the sun had changed. Returning to the notebook
she found case notes of a robbery in December, progress of a
thumb sprained in an arrest, but no more about the sphinx,
no more about last summer or the Dunsmuirs'. She found the
date corresponding to the death of Cassidy and a dry notational
account of his visit to the Greyland-Smith residence. Then a
longer passage.

Corpses forever fascinating. There she was in
the intertidal morass, entwined in bull kelp and
popweed, pale, bloated, bruised, hair snarled,
brow gouged, eyes gone to the fish, mouth, when
we rolled her, debouching sea water and small
red crabs. Truly I begin to believe in the exis-
tence of an animating spirit that absents itself
at the death of the body like a transient lodger,
a restless spirit that is sometimes all too eager
to move on. Do they then wander until they re-
incarnate or become permanent aspects of some
greater spirit, some over-soul, galvanic, electric,
magnetic, alternately intrusive and absent,

fuelling thunder and lightning? Tired. Late.
Rambling on and talking nonsense.

The second visit to their house: *The mother continues to play the invalid. Char? Untrustworthy. Daughter? Troubling. Voice and manner somehow familiar. Gloster apparently enamoured of the lady of the house.*

Somehow familiar?

Osmo's handwriting was bold, angular, and leaned steeply to the right. His *o*'s and *a*'s and *u*'s and *q*'s were perfect, and his *l*'s and *k*'s and *w*'s and *v*'s looked like they'd been cut with a stylus. A mark of confidence and clarity, or rigidity and dogmatism? Pearl consulted Rosa Baughan's book, which had samples from Lord Palmerston and Florence Nightingale, but found that she was unable to concentrate, not now, not there.

Trawling the journal for more references to herself, the sphinx, anything, an envelope dropped out and skated across the floor and came to rest half underneath the door to that strange closet. She stared. She looked around as though to see if anyone else—some grinning ghost, some elf, some gnome—had witnessed this. Crossing the room, she reached down and drew the envelope from beneath the closet door. Standing upright, she felt compelled to open the door yet again. The radiance had dulled, the sun having declined farther or a cloud having passed before it or perhaps the spirit in the closet had curled itself fetal on the floor, weeping. Pearl shook the absurdity from her head. Truly it was as though a stream of nonsense flowed from some other dimension and pooled in her brain.

After a few breaths she pressed the closet door shut and rediscovered the envelope in her hand. If she had been frightened before it was nothing compared to discovering her name on it. It was not Osmo's script. That she could see immediately, for the letters were thin and leaned to the left, like little soldiers unable to make headway against a wind. Pearl recalled Miss

Pinkrose telling them to make their letters bold, to make them march upright like good Englishmen! Turning it over she saw that the envelope was unsealed. Fingers trembling, she tweezed the page out. It was not a letter but a newspaper clipping, old, yellowed, cracked along the creases. She unfolded it with care and yet her hands shook so badly that she had to lay it on the bureau to read.

Pawnbrokers Dead

Mr. and Mrs. Davis Milton, owners and proprietors of King's Park Pawnbrokers, have been found dead. RCMP Sergeant Mannering reports that the pair were discovered by a neighbour who heard the spaniel howling all day and night. The spectacle was gruesome. The neighbour, one Amelia Jackson, fled the scene and fell on the ice and sustained a head injury. Bleeding, she made it to another neighbour who, sturdier of stomach and surer of foot, investigated and contacted the police.

The City Coroner reports that the Miltons were bludgeoned with a rolling pin. The weapon was found nearby. Not found was the maid, one Sinead Molloy. Police are asking for information regarding her whereabouts. She is said to be sixteen, tall, fair complexion, auburn hair, Irish accent.

The motive is not yet known though robbery suspected.

Toronto Globe.

Pearl heard voices on the porch. Thrusting the clipping back into the envelope, she crammed it into her pocket. Standing to one side of the window she peered out and saw men returning from work. The light had changed; the afternoon was waning; the sky had clouded over. She pulled the snake, the sphinx, and the mummified cat from her satchel and arranged them on the bureau. Then she decided to leave the snake and the sphinx on the bureau but put the cat in the closet. Then, inspired, she moved the sphinx to the bed.

Footsteps in the rooms below. A heavy tread mounting the stairs. Pearl hid in the closet where it felt as though she was standing inside a ghost that was as frightened as she was. The steps passed on by and she emerged from the closet. Simply go down the stairs and on out, nodding good evening to anyone she met? And if she met the Greers? Run? *Her? Nearly eight months pregnant?* Maybe if she changed into her own clothes and went downstairs banking on male gallantry to let her pass unmolested...And if she met Osmo? The closet seemed the better option. But she could never last the night and besides she was suddenly bursting for a pee.

Now the house resounded with bumps and clumps and voices and footsteps up and down the stairs and back and forth along the corridors. Everything was racing ahead. The smell of stew reached her; the aroma of potatoes and meat stirring her insides so that she needed the loo more than ever. She went to the window. Day was turning to evening. Lights glowed in the shops opposite. She paced the room then returned to the window and, even as she watched the street, Osmo appeared, yes, there he was, Osmo, her Osmo, moving briskly, crossing the street, approaching the gate, reaching the gate. Now he was coming up the walk. Pearl ran to the door and put her ear to it—the noise of Greer House had become concentrated down in the dining room—she opened the door a crack. The scents and sounds were stronger and the electric bulb in the corridor burned brightly.

Perhaps it was the change of air from room to hallway, but all of a sudden she sneezed. Not a small one; her nose exploded. She put her hand to her face, fearing she was bleeding. She was not but she heard, or thought she heard—or maybe it was the ringing of her skull—all conversation downstairs halt. She remained still. It was as if she could hear them listening. She waited, imagining the men around the dining table with their heads turned toward the door, mouths open, faces frowning upward, which meant only one thing: they were all present and accounted for, every one of them, including Osmo. Another sneeze threatened to erupt but she clamped her nostrils shut and, when that was going to fail, she buried her face in the crook of her elbow and sneezed again, muted, but a sneeze nonetheless. Eventually she heard a chair scrape. Then laughter. Then chatter. Stepping to the top of the stairs, Pearl listened, for she thought she'd heard a familiar voice, not Osmo's but another, lost and then resurfacing in a sea of banter. Was it? Yes. Desmond Terence Padraich Orlovski-with-an-*i*! He was talking about his foot, or rather his absence of foot, explaining why he had been thrown over the wall. There was a hush and then came his voice, solemn, plaintive, perhaps a little theatrical: "Because I'd told the truth," he said.

"And pray, young Desmond, what was this truth of which you spake?" queried another voice, rich with mockery.

"That God's an Irishman."

Gales of laughter erupted.

"If He is an Irishman," came another voice, none other than Osmo's, soft spoken and sincere, "then He is equally an Englishman, a German, a Greek, a Turk, a Chinese, and a Peruvian, and so on and so forth."

This was greeted with silence. Desmond Terence Padraich Orlovski-with-an-*i* said, "Of course. You're right. But they never let me get to that part, did they? It was over the wall with me."

There were sober murmurs and after some suitable silence the conversation moved on.

Pearl hurried to the water closet at the end of the hallway and slipped inside and locked the door. She found the toggle for the electric light and flipped it. The illumination woke slowly, like a sleepy eye reluctantly opening, the coiled filament in the glass beginning to glow blue then red then yellow then almost white. She did what was necessary, and yet even as she enjoyed the blessed relief, she heard footsteps and then Osmo's door open and shut. Silence. One minute. Then another. She imagined him discovering the cobra and then the sphinx—could it fail to bring back that night? Now he was studying each in its place, not daring to touch either for their positioning were clues. How long before he found the mummified cat? How long before he stepped into the corridor and saw the light on in the wc? She switched it off; it died with tormenting sluggishness. No doubt he would question the Greers, unless they had already told him of his visitor, which was the reason for him leaving the dinner table and coming upstairs, no, that made no sense, for it implied that the Greers knew she—he—was up there . . .

Raising the lavatory window, Pearl leaned out. A wall of chill air damp and metallic. The roof slanted steeply upward to her left. The fire ladder was missing, or never existed, and the drop was thirty feet. She returned to the door and listened. No, she'd never make it past the dining room. At the window again, she set her satchel on the roof and climbed out after it, lowering the window behind her. Nudging her bag ahead, she began crawling on all fours up the cedar shakes. Or tried, for they were slick with damp and she kept slipping, one knee skating back and then the other, her fingers unable to grip— then her hands and knees lost all purchase at once and she slid on her belly down and down until her boot tips caught the eavestrough, which strained under her weight. Arms out, cheek pressed to the moss-grouted shingles, she groped for a hold, fearful of putting any more pressure on the gutter, all too aware of her belly and her child, their child, hers and Osmo's. Satchel resting against the top of her head, she dug her fingernails into the wood and slowly resumed clawing her way up the slope. As she reached the apex, the satchel balanced on the ridge then tumbled down the far side. She peered over. The bag had come to rest in a valley between two roof planes.

It began to snow.

In an instant the air was filled with whirling white flakes like a plague of moths.

The baby shifted inside her belly like a massive meal that wouldn't digest, and with dread vividness she recalled once seeing a deer butchered, the carcass slung from a tree and the hunter slice open the stomach, releasing a flop of guts in the midst of which was a sac that the dogs tore into exposing the fetus within, a being almost aquatic, a seahorse, a creature not yet of this world, as yet angelic.

With a heave Pearl straddled the ridge and clenched her thighs as if on horseback. She had in fact never been on a horse and for a time had counted this a great mark against her mother, especially inasmuch as her father was an hussar. She looked up and snowflakes settled on her face and on her eyes cooling her tears. She should have fled to Australia. She should be there now, in a lounge chair on the deep porch of some sheep farm in the outback, the cicadas throbbing under the Southern Cross. Or she might have gone to Africa and been adopted by Bedouin. Or north to live with the people of the Arctic if they would have her. Shoulda, coulda, woulda, one of Carpy's old saws about missed opportunities real or imagined. She began to laugh then cried more and pressed her palms to her face and after some minutes mastered herself. In spite of her coat and scarf and hat she shivered. The snow intensified. Looking around she saw the mirage-like tremor of smoke rising from the various chimneys of Greer House. Crawling and sliding she managed to lodge herself against the thickest chimney, the bricks blessedly warm, and, shuddering, shut her eyes.

By the time the house was silent, the snow had stopped as abruptly as it had begun. A steady breeze blew and she heard a solitary tree frog, which reminded her that the snow notwithstanding, spring was not so very far off.

Perhaps she slept and perhaps she didn't; either way, before dawn a horse cart clopped past and dogs began to bark and roosters crow. Pearl left the lingering warmth of the chimney and crawled crabwise down the roof to the window leading into the water closet, intending to steal along the corridor and down the stairs and out. But the window was stuck. Or locked. Either way, it wouldn't budge. She groped her way back up to the chimney and warmed herself as much as possible on the brick, which had cooled considerably, and then she ventured along to the rear of the house. There was only the faintest gleam of light to the east. In the yard below, far, far below it seemed, stood a tree and a shed.

She sat on the ridge, clutching her satchel like some gloomy goblin on a cathedral. No doubt her mother was worried. Or vindicated. Maybe she thought Pearl, spurning her magnanimous offer, had taken herself off to some obscure corner like a stray cat to have her litter. She and Mr. Gloster could settle into a comfortable routine while unbeknownst to them Pearl would spend her last days here on the Greers' roof and then be picked apart by vultures like a Parsee atop the Towers of Silence. Yet mostly she thought of the envelope with the old clipping inside. There was no stamp so it must have been handed to Osmo, but why him when her name was on it? No, he found it, likely on Cassidy or the other woman, and kept it for evidence, meaning he knew that Sinead Molloy—Pearl's mother—as a young woman, a domestic, had murdered her employers. Clearly Cassidy had intended to use the article as leverage. Was Pearl's real father this Mr. Davis Milton? Had he forced himself on her mother, had he been in denial about the baby, had he been threatening to throw her out? Or perhaps Mrs. Milton had learned the truth and killed her husband in a jealous rage and then attacked Pearl's mother who had fought her off and then fled, taking a cache of valuables to begin a new life under a new identity?

Another cart clattered along the road. Pearl got to her hands and knees, intending to give the wc window another go and, failing that, simply break the glass and make a run, or rather a waddle, but as she began moving, she slipped and her satchel slid down the slope. Foolishly, without thinking, she reached for it and in so doing lost her balance and, to her horror, began sliding. She rolled awkwardly, like a log with a large lump in the middle. How swiftly it was happening. How swiftly one's life turned a corner. This was the second time. First in the sphinx and now here on the roof, some strange mad momentum carrying her away. It was almost bemusing, as though she was watching it all unfold from afar. She slid faster. Yes, she was going to fall. She thought: Pearl, that foolish girl, is going to fall. No, she corrected herself: she *is* falling, and she managed to swivel so that when she went over the edge she did so feet first and then she was in the air.

For a moment it was exhilarating and she nearly whooped as she flew but she was not flying, she was plunging and exhilaration turned to panic as she pedalled her legs and paddled her arms and, dull girl that she was, took on board the fact that there was nothing to grab and she was plummeting to her death. Images flew through her mind: the strangely luminous closet in Osmo's room, French balloonists in top hats crossing the Arabian desert, her mother bearing up bravely under the ignominy of her wayward daughter's strange and singular end. Now everything slowed and became fluid, and she seemed to roll weightless and float warm and relaxed and she wondered if she was already dead and in Heaven or some other equally benign Afterworld such as the Bardo wherein she was free to reflect and meditate upon the birds of the air and the fish of the sea and the flowers of the forest and perhaps meet her father except that if her father was this Davis Milton creature rather than the hussar in the picture she did not wish to meet him—and then she struck.

But kept falling.

Or sliding.

For she'd hit the roof of the shed and was skidding down its slope, groping for a handhold but there were only moss-slick shingles and then she was off this second roof, airborne again, recalling sledding *whoosh!* down Beacon Hill, only now it was rather different for there was no hot chocolate waiting before a roaring fire and no cheery voices and then she struck a second time only this time she did not keep going but halted.

Chapter Nineteen

THE ROARING IN HER EARS abated though the dark remained. Had she cracked her skull? Had she lost her sight? Only after some time did she realize that her eyes were shut. She did not open them for she smelled earth and was afraid that she was in a grave, that she had died and been buried and now had awakened in her coffin, a horror that she had read stories about. There was supposed to be a bell for her to ring to signal that a terrible mistake had been made for she was alive and must be rescued. But they had forgotten her bell. They had forgotten. Clenching her eyes tighter she wept hot tears that itched and, without thinking, she wiped them away and by reflex opened her eyes and saw leaves and mulch and the shed and understood that she was not in a coffin or in the Bardo—though she didn't know what the Bardo looked like—but had landed in the Greers' compost heap. She was lying on her side and her heart was beating and dawn was breaking and she breathed in and she breathed out and she was shivering with cold for there was a thin glaze of snow on the ground. Then she swallowed and after sobbing awhile longer and shivering some more she began to take the measure of her injuries. Was she in pain? No, she was too stunned to be in pain. Was she broken? She couldn't say. She twitched her fingers and toes, opened and closed her hands, tentatively moved her wrist, still weak from the fall on the stairs, shifted an arm, a leg, then slowly rolled onto her back and looked up at the clouds red and gold in the dawn sky.

The clanging of pots and pans reached her from the scullery. Turning her head, Pearl saw lights in the window and silhouettes gliding like puppets. The boarding house was awake. She placed her hands upon her belly, so round, so taut. Eventually she got to her hands and knees in the rich rank mulch. How soft and fertile it was and in fact it held some moist heat. In that position, on all fours, her belly hung and her back hurt and she saw herself as a beast in a field about to calve. She waited a moment, trembling, blinking, inhaling the pungent earthy compost of leaves and peelings and coffee grounds and then stood, wobbled as if her knees were India rubber, saw her satchel, and stumbled toward it. Gripping the bag, she stared around and then staggered inside the Greers' shed and dropped to a round of wood in the dank and stony dark still too shaken to think clearly. Her pulse was pounding and her head reeling and her stomach sick. A part of her brain monitored the clamour coming from the boarding house while another part monitored the roiling of her insides. Eventually the men went off to work. Pearl's trembling settled and she fumblingly changed her clothes, peeled off her beard, and then staggered off up the alley. Nauseous, she was twice forced to turn aside and vomit. But she was relieved. She was exhilarated. She was astounded. Not only had she accomplished her task and escaped but had survived a fall from the roof, even if her ankles and knees and pelvis ached and her stomach churned and her thoughts sloshed like water in a pail. A third and fourth time she had to stop and heave. None of that mattered. What mattered was that Osmo was thinking of her at this moment, that she was uppermost in his mind, that she now dominated his every thought, her, Pearl.

✦

AS PEARL CAME AROUND THE corner, she was halted by the sight of Doctor Meadows's gig. The horse was not steaming, which meant the doctor had been there some time. Pearl estimated it to be eight o'clock, far too early for him to be dropping in unless something had happened. She also estimated that the chances of her slipping into her room and then pretending to have overslept were low, and besides she was in no condition for subterfuge, she'd used up her stores of deception for one night—perhaps the rest of her life—and needed a bath and a sleep.

She cradled her stomach fearfully. What a start for little Osmo or Esmerelda! Entering through the front door she smelled the familiar scent of beeswax and lemon balm, except that this morning there were other elements to it, ammonia and some sort of salts. She was hesitating in the foyer when Carpy burst from the kitchen with a tray on which sat towels and a bowl of water. Glaring she hissed what a fine piece of work Pearl was, buggering off like that all night and terrifying her mother into a fit. She knifed past her into Florence's room. Before Pearl could speak much less follow, Carpy barged back out and caught Pearl's elbow and towed her down the corridor, growling that she'd finally done it, she'd finally killed her. Wrenching free, Pearl ran to her mother's room and found her in bed, Doctor Meadows arranging a damp cloth on her brow. He put up a warning hand.

"A stroke."

Her face was ash and her breath hoarse and she'd aged twenty years. Pearl sat on the side of her bed and gripped her cold hand and thought she felt her squeeze hers in response. Sobbing, Pearl looked pleadingly to Meadows. "She'll recover though," she said, not as a question but as a statement.

His pale blue eyes were wet. "She needs rest."

"I'll save her."

Pearl and the doctor looked at Carpy.

"She's beyond anything you lot can do," said Carpy with authority. "It's her soul."

Doctor Meadows had always treated Carpy with due respect but he could not countenance this bold tone that verged upon belligerence. "I rather doubt that the state of your mistress's soul is ours to diagnose or indeed our foremost concern at the moment."

"It's her," said Carpy, tossing a nod in Pearl's direction.

"She's right," said Pearl. "It is my fault. I have made bad worse. I am erratic and wayward and . . . and eight months pregnant. There is no one to blame but me and me alone." She put her hands to her face and wept. Then a cramp seized her and she folded over, hugging her belly. The cramp knotted her tight even as it rolled like an earthquake through her pelvis. A groan escaped her.

Meadows moved briskly. "Carpy."

They guided Pearl to her own room and put her to bed where the doctor set to work while Carpy retreated. Over the proceeding hours, Pearl had little choice but to attend to the task at hand, while her mind, which usually roamed so widely, was focused by the crashing waves of pain that left her ever more depleted with each succeeding assault. The only cogent thoughts that did manage to surface were awe that such pain was possible, respect for women who endured it over and over, and a vow never to let a man touch her again. Meadows guided her. Or tried. For his voice was small, distant, irrelevant, coming it seemed from the far end of the room, coming from a different world altogether. She felt as though she was in the depths of some cavern and the surface world of Meadows and Carpy impossibly remote, while she was immersed in forces tectonic in scale, lunar in reach, primal in thrust. With each successive surge the pain threatened to drown Pearl, who fought for some dry solid ground in her mind, a ground that continued to shrink as the agony increased.

At noon she delivered a boy. Meadows presented him to her and she wept and she laughed even as the infant, the creature that she had grown in her belly, her son, gazed up at her with enormous dark questioning eyes. Pearl held him, small and hot and squirming, smelling of blood and skin, both metallic and raw. She asked the doctor to send for Osmo and he said of course. Within the hour, Osmo appeared.

He arrived in a state of confusion and curiosity to find himself being ushered by Carpy into, of all places, Pearl's bedroom.

Exhausted and terrified and ecstatic, Pearl gazed at him with tears in her eyes.

"I'm sorry," stammered Beattie, "I don't understand . . ."

At which Pearl uncovered the face of the infant and Beattie saw the unmistakable resemblance in the eyes and brow. He looked from Pearl to the child and back to Pearl, expressions racing like swift sunlight over darkly churning water. He was shaking his head slowly, whether in wonder or denial Pearl couldn't say.

"The sphinx," she whispered.

His eyes widened then narrowed as he whispered, "Last summer . . . Craigdarroch . . ."

Was that horror in his expression? Pearl fought not to sob.

"And, that is to say, you are, you are certain . . ."

Pearl saw where he was headed with this line of enquiry and assured him, or rather delivered the dread verdict, that he was the only man she'd known.

"I see." How small the words sounded. A condemned man's final statement. He swallowed, frowned, turned his hat in his hands.

Not exactly the joyous response Pearl might have wished. She looked away. "You are under no obligation," she found herself saying. Did she sound convincing? Did her voice tremble? She continued to stare at the wall, at the beige wainscotting, the ledge with the knick-knacks, the wallpaper printed with maidens on swings and young swains presenting them bouquets. In the silence that followed the very bed in which she lay seemed to teeter upon a cliff edge. Would it tip over and plunge or would Osmo pull it back to safety? Then again, perhaps it was not up to him but to her; what with the fall she had survived this morning she reckoned she was capable of most anything.

"I cannot deny this is unexpected," he said.

She nodded quickly. She heard him inhale a long breath and exhale an even longer one. Pearl's pulse thumped thick in her ears and she felt ill. She wished he would leave and she wished she were dead. Why had she gone to his room? Why, for once, couldn't she have listened to her mother?

He sat on the side of the bed and took Pearl's hand.

"Look," he said. "He's sleeping."

"Well," said Pearl, keeping her face averted, "he's had quite a morning."

"As have you."

Pearl studied one of the swains in the wallpaper, kneeling there with his bouquet. Swain. Swine. "Yes, as have I."

"You should have told me." How sincere he sounded, almost injured.

"I should have done many things," she said, still unable to look at him. "And I suppose there was one I should not have done at all."

Osmo was silent.

Pearl studied the face of the maiden on the swing. Run, she advised her, run.

Osmo followed her gaze. "Romantic," he said.

"Delusion," she said.

The infant stirred.

"What a mad creature you are."

Was he referring to her or the baby? "A sphinx," said Pearl, turning now, at last, to face him. "And a cat and a cobra," she confessed.

His expression pinched into the gravest frown as if reaching a terrible resolve. "*You?*"

She lowered her gaze and nodded.

Osmo groaned as if this put things in a different light altogether. He put his hand to his face, covering his eyes, and shook his head slowly.

Pearl panicked. Could things possibly get worse? Look what she had done with her mad antics, for now Osmo must do his duty and arrest her for a double murder she'd not committed. Various scenes played out in her mind's eye, each more maudlin than the last: she found guilty, the baby taken off to an orphanage, or Osmo taking the baby and marrying some more suitable woman, while Pearl shuffled in leg irons to the scaffold.

Meadows joined them.

"How are we faring?"

Osmo stood and straightened his coat and cleared his throat and drew in a deep breath so as to face his unenviable task. "Doctor Meadows," he said.

"Inspector Beattie," said Meadows. His glance cut back and forth between Beattie and Pearl. "May I offer my congratulations."

"You may. And I thank you. However, I am afraid it is my sad duty to inform you that you are under arrest on the charge of double murder."

The doctor smiled, though only after his eyes first blackened with rage. "Who knew that the eminent inspector was such a wit?" He addressed this to Pearl and then plunged his hands into a basin of water and proceeded to vigorously wash, working up a good lather.

"This is no joke," said Osmo.

"You're exhausted, Beattie."

"You were at each crime scene."

"I was called. It's Charles Gloster you want."

"I thought so as well at first. I'm sorry, Doctor, but I am afraid we both know that it is you."

Meadows swallowed and frowned and finished washing and drying his hands. "I have to see my other patient."

"Of course, you must see to your patients," agreed Osmo.

"Congratulations again," the doctor said to Pearl.

Escorting Meadows out of the room, Osmo glanced back and nodded once to Pearl who could only stare, worshipful and grateful and yet bewildered and terrified. Doctor Meadows?

"You know you are mad," muttered Meadows as they went out.

"I was under the impression that if the mad knew they were mad then they were *ipso facto* not mad but sane."

The door to Florence's room was shut. With a show of irritation, Meadows gripped the doorknob and turned it. Locked. He glared at the inspector then rapped twice. Nothing.

"Carpy? Carpenter . . ." He waited.

Then the lock clicked. As the door swung slowly inward, Meadows demanded to know why Carpy had locked it. Except that it was not Carpy who stood there but Florence. Meadows was as shocked as he was joyful. She was pale and tremulous and yet she was smiling triumphantly, putting both men in mind of a wanderer who had staggered up out of the desert to a familiar oasis.

"Florence . . ."

"Doctor."

"Confound it, woman, will you not call me Giles!"

"I will call you whatever you please if you will be so kind as to fetch me a whiskey, a large whiskey." Then she nodded to Beattie. "Inspector."

"Ma'am. How are you feeling?"

"Better. And how is my daughter?"

"The mother of a son."

"And you are the father of a son."

This reality struck him with renewed force. "So it appears,

235

so it appears." Then, putting on a brave face, he added, "I am happy to say yes."

"Then I am happy as well. Though it must be a shock."

"Well..." He smiled and frowned then smiled again.

"Florence," repeated Meadows.

"Doctor—forgive me, Giles."

Then Meadows gazed past her to the bed where Carpy was lying stiff and white.

Seeing the direction of his gaze, Florence said, "I fear that Carpy has... has passed over."

"But—" Meadows rushed in and examined her, lifting her hand and seeking a pulse, thumbing up an eyelid, then looking toward Florence, bewildered beyond comprehension. He opened his mouth to speak but for once found no words. Finally, he said, "She was as healthy as a horse."

"She did often moan about her ticker," said Florence.

"I... I did not know that." Meadows looked down at Carpy pale and bloodless on the bed.

"She looks peaceful," said Osmo, peering from the doorway.

"Thank the Lord."

"The heart is a strange instrument," said Meadows. "Was she troubled of late? Had she been anxious?"

"I am afraid that Carpy talked a lot but at the same time kept her real thoughts to herself," said Florence. "She did not share the dirty, forgive me, the details of her health."

Osmo nodded slowly. "There were only the two of you?"

She looked at him, a flicker of suspicion in her eyes. "Of course."

Meadows folded the sheet up over Carpy's face and admitted that he was no stranger to sudden death but that this one was baffling.

"Strange," agreed Florence. "Most strange indeed."

"There is much that is strange under the sun," intoned a sombre and wondering voice.

"Ah," said Florence. "You got my note. Gentlemen, you know my fiancé."

And all turned to find Charles Gloster.

Uncharacteristically demonstrative, Florence went to him and gripped his hands and looked long into his eyes then gave him a full kiss on the mouth.

Chapter Twenty

FLORENCE AND CHARLES WERE MARRIED on the summer solstice. Bishop Hills performed the ceremony. It was a small but elegant affair and afterward they went to Gloster's house where they were serenaded by an earnest though not highly accomplished string quartet. If there were murmurs at Pearl having been maid of honour, they were subdued. She and Osmo had married a week before, with only her mother and Charles present. It had been far from joyous, but it was legal; Osmo had been adamant on that.

Pearl was relieved and her mother was happy—if somewhat changed. Florence seemed often wary and suspicious then loudly triumphant, very unlike her, after which her eyes would turn cold and hard, also unlike her. Pearl put it down to having so narrowly escaped death, the loss of Carpy, and adjusting to her new life after so many years a widow. Following the wedding, she and Gloster boarded a ship for Hong Kong and were gone for a year, visiting Siam, Ceylon, India, Egypt, and Portugal while Pearl, Osmo, and little Osmo settled for a honeymoon in Seattle. Gloster's house was shut up and Osmo relinquished his room at the Greers' and moved in with Pearl.

Even though she'd lived all her life in that house everything became new and odd. Her husband, all but a stranger, was a respected and dutiful man, but little by little Pearl realized, as she had so often feared, that she did not love him. And how could he love her? It was not as if he had courted her, not as if he had written her letters or sent her flowers, not as if he had wooed her like one of the young swains in her bedroom wallpaper. Yet he was a man of duty and he was fulfilling it, and for this she supposed she should be grateful, considering the grim alternatives she had so narrowly avoided.

Osmo had many strengths but conversation was not among them. There was no wit, no banter, no whimsical musings, nor did they lie in bed of a Sunday morning and analyze the criminal mind and all the nefarious characters he met. Most disappointing of all, Osmo was not intrigued by his young wife. Her escapade in disguising herself, infiltrating the Greers' establishment, and planting the three clues did not engage or entrance or intrigue him, in fact he was embarrassed by her shenanigans with the sphinx, snake, and cat, and certainly had no wish to hear any more about it.

"That wildness is behind us now. You are a wife and a mother and will please do me the courtesy of behaving appropriately."

That she had given birth before they married had incited the inevitable gossip. In doing the right thing, Osmo bore an air of martyrdom; he was a man who faced the consequences for his actions. When Pearl had slid the ring onto his finger, she thought of a noose going around his neck and wondered if he was thinking the same. Still, she thought of their future, certain that in spite of a turbulent and unorthodox start things would improve. They did not. He was a regular if not overly imaginative lover, going through the motions as if performing his nightly calisthenics. During these exercises Pearl found herself fantasizing, transforming Osmo and their bedroom to Ottoman decadence, a tropical isle, a far desert, or a palace of ice and bear skins. While these were diverting, she feared that she would soon be pregnant again, which would see her dug ever deeper into their life, such as it was. It seemed she had sorted one crisis only to have it replaced by another. She studied the faces of other women with children, seeking clues as to what they were really thinking. How did they look at their husbands, what was in their eyes in unguarded moments? And the men, were they equally entrapped?

Osmo at least got to escape into the world each day, while she, afternoon walks aside, felt housebound. She wondered if she'd have not been happier with Desmond.

But there was no denying that Osmo was a devoted father. He took genuine delight in little Osmo's accomplishments, such as his first tottering steps, though was less delighted at his first words: "I'll be buggered!" Later he took Pearl aside, demanding to know where she was taking him during the day that he heard such talk. Pearl, indignant, could only stare in disbelief, though might well have pointed the finger at Lewis, the new maid.

When Osmo had hired Lewis, Pearl had felt betrayed and naïve and even more alone. It was less than a fortnight after they were married when he brought her home. So, Pearl had thought, it is now two against one. Standing in the den holding little Osmo, facing her husband and Lewis, Pearl had hugged the baby so tightly that he'd cried out and Lewis, sly, clever Lewis, promptly stepped forward and took him and made soothing sounds implying that she was the source of solace and all that was good and Pearl the stranger.

Lewis was a young woman barely older than Pearl and was a perfect package, small and neat, everything just the right size, pretty in an elfin way—high cheekbones, eyes long and slightly pointed like her chin, her teeth short and white and even, her dark blond hair woven in a French braid around her head.

"Welcome, Lewis," Pearl had said, and for some reason at that moment recalled the clipping she'd found in Osmo's journal describing the murders committed by Sinead Molloy. Taking some strength from this Pearl smiled and commended Lewis's way with children.

"I'm one of eight," she said.

Little Osmo gripped her finger and gurgled in joy.

Pearl thought, then perhaps you won't be missed. "However did you find her, Osmo?"

"Ah, my dear, you forget that I am a detective. I think you'll find that Lewis has everything necessary for the job."

Little Osmo—sweet endearing little Osmo—began to cry and Pearl took him from Lewis's arms—a faint resistance to overcome—and, laughing, excused herself and went into the bedroom, for if there was one thing that Lewis lacked and Pearl had in abundance, it was milk.

✛

MIRANDA VISITED AND THEY HAD many afternoons together. Her father the admiral was planning to take her off to London for "the season" by which it was understood that Miranda was expected to meet some fellow of appropriate status and perhaps stay in England.

"You will become a lady of even higher rank," said Pearl, modulating her envy.

"Mrs. Beattie, you are already a lady of rank," Miranda fibbed graciously.

Pearl smiled and endured the humiliation tainting the room. "It's good of you to visit."

Miranda gazed at her with all the grave sincerity of which she was capable. "You're a strange one, G-Smith."

Pearl considered telling her everything then rejected the notion, for despite Miranda's best intentions and solemn vows, it could not fail to be shared with her other acquaintances and played like a conversational ace. Pearl did not blame her, knowing that she herself would inevitably, somewhere, sometime, do the same.

Lewis came in with coffee and cake.

"Thank you, Lewis."

"Ma'am." Lewis was not up to Carpy's standard in cookery—the coffee bitter, the cake dry, the bread raw in the middle—though was certainly her equal in sullen and sarcastic attitude.

When Lewis was gone, Miranda suggested that Pearl beat her.

"I consider it every day."

"Not on the face, though," cautioned Miranda. "On the buttocks. It is one of the last bits of wisdom given me by my dear *ma-ma* before she died."

Pearl agreed that this was certainly wise counsel.

Then Miranda said, "Dear Mrs. Beattie, forgive me for saying, but you look unhappy."

Pearl shrugged and, for a moment, as the tea grew cold and one of Mr. Livingstone's ale bottles burst next door, she was silent, not at the passing of an angel but at a boat—the last boat—departing the dock without her.

"He is a dutiful man respected by all," said Miranda with every ounce of sincerity of which she was capable.

Pearl knew this. She had sucked all the solace and strength and reassurance to be had from it and now, like the rind of a spent orange, only bitterness remained. Her husband was indeed dutiful as well as respected, and he himself respected nothing with greater veneration than hierarchy. There should be those above and those below, superiors and inferiors, all interconnected like the links in a chain, and this included the roles and duties of husband and wife. Work weighed upon him and when Pearl tried diverting him with such things as theosophy or Egypt or Angel Glow he dismissed it as trivial, and yet when she spoke of world events such as Lizzie Borden's gruesome murder of her parents, he shook his head and shut his eyes as if in agony and reminded her that he got enough of such business at work; at home he wished peace and it was the role of his wife to ensure that he got it.

Perhaps the worst discovery of all was that Osmo believed Pearl had lured him into the sphinx and not the other way around. Yes, he had convinced himself that he was a victim. They had just finished choking down one of Lewis's shoe-leather chops in salty gravy when Osmo, who had looked into the eyes of murderers, outwitted confidence men and thieves of every stripe, stared off out the window through the leaves of the enormous old philodendron, Balthazar, and said that she had entrapped him.

Pearl thought she had misheard. "I?"

His admirable chin trembled. "You."

"I," she repeated, "I entrapped you..."

He nodded, once, with adamance.

"Sir, if that was not so pathetic, I would laugh."

He turned his head and regarded her with eyes like rivets, hard and yet beaten flat. Pearl understood that he saw a con-niving female while she saw a child in a man's body.

"Do tell me," she asked, "how many other girls you've had in that sphinx."

"None."

"You certainly knew your way about it."

"You did not seem terribly reluctant."

She felt the air hard in her nostrils as she clenched her jaw to retain control of her tongue. "I was drunk."

He smiled. "Ah. One of the least imaginative of excuses. In my profession I hear it rather a lot. I'd have thought you might do better."

"And I'd have thought you might do better than take advan-tage of a girl ten years your junior." She left the table, gathered up little Osmo, and slept that night in her old room. Lying in bed she wept, worse she feared that he was probably using her absence to take solace in the arms of Lewis. Pearl often retreated to her old bedroom during the day and recalled those torturous nights of her pregnancy when all seemed lost. Again and again, she wondered if she had made the right choice in going to the Greers'. Should she have simply gone east with her mother? She did not doubt that Osmo would be happier on his own; certainly, Pearl could be no more miserable.

One evening Osmo chipped a tooth on a stone in a plum pudding. He winced and cried out and clutched his mouth then spat a shard of enamel into his napkin. Pearl called Lewis to account.

"Look at this!"

"I'm so sorry, ma'am, I thought I'd destoned them all," she mumbled.

"Take it away," said Pearl. "Go."

To her amazement, Osmo chastised Pearl for being too hard on Lewis, reminding her that she was young.

"And may I remind you that she's six months older than I."

"It was an accident."

"It was laziness. If it's not stones in the pudding, it's burnt biscuits."

"A burnt biscuit is hardly a crime."

"She's been with us almost a year and still turns everything to charcoal."

In a rare moment of dour wit, Osmo—still tonguing his chipped molar—observed that doctors were now professing the health benefits of charcoal.

"Charcoal," repeated Pearl, that Osmo might hear the absurdity.

He nodded.

She stared.

"Quite the champion of Lewis, aren't you."

✦

WHEN MEADOWS WENT ON TRIAL for double murder, Pearl was questioned in court. Her mother would have been called as well but was still abroad. All Pearl could say was that Doctor Meadows had been an attentive physician, though admitted that he had developed a more than professional attachment to her mother. How Meadows learned of the two women, Brennan and Curtin, she did not know.

Judge Begbie sentenced Meadows to hang and Harry Hearne took up the flaming sword of his pen, discoursing widely, ranging from the decadence of the age to the tragedy of the times before planting his blade, like a sword in a stone, into the plinth of Empire.

> *The story of Dr. Giles Meadows is as sad as it is*
> *stunning, that of a fine man falling victim to*
> *his baser self, letting his body triumph over his*
> *mind. That a man who had done so much for*
> *so many for so long should succumb to such an*
> *end must be a cautionary tale else it be wasted,*
> *making it a double tragedy. We must therefore*
> *ask who and what drove him to these deeds,*
> *who and what infected him, just as we must be*
> *vigilant as to who and what threatens to infect*
> *this most august British Empire. Is Meadows*
> *the canary in the coal mine? What foul and*
> *seeping vapour does his demise signal? Did he,*
> *we must ask, do us a service in ridding us of the*
> *two women who were by some accounts bent on*
> *undermining the pillars of the community?*

While Pearl was relieved that the family name was not mentioned, Hearne did go on to congratulate the inestimable Inspector Osmo Beattie for having solved the crime.

Lewis burned him a cake in honour of his celebrity. Pearl did not critique it, nor did she taste the slice Lewis served her, merely tapped it with her fork, thinking, but not saying, that it sounded like a hard-boiled egg, and then watched Osmo make appreciative sounds as he ate not one but two pieces. Finally, Pearl could not resist cautioning him to take care of his teeth, reminding him of the agonies he'd endured at the dentist after his last incident. He ignored her.

Lewis asked if they would like tea or coffee.

The one tasted of boiled laundry and the other boiled asphalt. Again, Pearl withheld comment. "Perhaps a bottle of Mr. Livingstone's ale," she said, judging it safer even if occasionally explosive.

She noted Osmo's gaze follow Lewis down the corridor to the kitchen, her small round rump rolling under her skirts, and the slow manner in which he licked the cake icing from his lips.

✦

A WEEK AFTER THE HANGING of Giles Meadows, Florence and Gloster returned. Pearl immediately sussed that something was off. Her mother was not her mother; certainly she looked the same on the surface, if somewhat gaunt and sun-browned, yet it was more than that, much more, her facial expressions were odd, and she carried herself differently. It was elusive but unmistakable. At times it was there in her voice and grammar and at others in a glance or the set of her shoulders. Pearl assumed it must be the effect of their time abroad, and while she detected no such changes in Mr. Gloster, she reminded herself that he was a seasoned traveller. The most obvious change was that her mother had taken to smoking cheroots. She did not puff decorously but in the manner of an old hand, even turning to spit bits of tobacco that clung to her lip.

On a walk one afternoon, Pearl asked if everything was fine.

Florence deflected. This was not unusual, she being a master of the art, but Pearl persisted, citing all the little changes she had noticed, from the expression in her eyes to the manner of her speech. Pearl laughed and said that she had returned a different person. "Even your walk is different."

Her mother made a little performance of gaping at her feet as if she might not recognize them. This too was out of character.

They were on Beacon Hill. Lewis was up ahead, pushing little Osmo in his perambulator.

"Well, one thing has not changed," said Pearl. "You are hiding things as per usual. What an ever-expanding store of secrets you must have locked away."

"My dear, are you so very unhappy in marriage?"

Pearl understood that this, too, was a deflection, and while it was insightful it was also a question her mother asked every time they were alone. Pearl halted and glared off at the arbutus trees and Garry oaks, at the other families, the shouting children, and the sea in the distance with the August sunlight glancing glassily off the waves. "We have already discussed this. I want to know what is wrong. Something's odd. You are not you," said Pearl, turning at last and facing her. "Even before you left you were not you."

Now Florence halted and did something else that was uncharacteristic, she crossed her arms over her chest and bunched her lips as if she might spit—the very idea that her mother would spit was utterly absurd—then sucked her teeth the way Carpy used to.

"There's something you need to know."

The grave tone of her voice alarmed Pearl.

"You remember the bottles and tubes in my...in Carpy's room off the pantry."

"The ones you asked me to leave in place when you went off for your honeymoon? Carpy's spirit bottles."

"Yes, Carpy's spirit bottles."

"The ones she claimed to catch souls in?" Pearl could not keep a note of mockery from her voice, thinking it might lighten the mood and draw them together.

Her mother, however, did not fall in with the humour. In fact, her eyes darkened and she bunched her lips as if she might spit again. "The same. But not so much catch as rescue, or house."

"House? I had not realized that you'd paid such close attention to the finer points of Carpy's spiritual malarkey. I thought that you, more than anyone, rated it nonsense."

Her mother regarded her in that odd way she now had. Then she went through her bag—purchased in Rangoon, blue and red wool with a geometric pattern and tassels, utterly out of character—found her tin of Sultans, a box of matches, and striking one lighted up and sent out a long dark cloud of smoke.

A slowly mounting horror filled Pearl's mind like some ghoulish scene from Mr. Poe. Sultan was the brand that Carpy had smoked. Pearl narrowed her eyes and peered into her mother's. It was not unlike looking into a cave, seeking some lurking minotaur within. Pearl's imagination, always erratic, ever spiralling, was one thing that had not been subdued by marriage or motherhood. She said, slowly, fearfully, "No . . ."

"I'm afraid so, miss."

Pearl stared. Then grinned. "Mother, along with everything else, you have returned from abroad with a new sense of the absurd. I don't quite know that it becomes you."

But her mother saw no absurdity. She inhaled on her cheroot and sent two plumes of smoke from her nostrils, the way a dragon might exhale.

Pearl glanced around. Lewis had halted up ahead, one hand on the perambulator while looking back questioningly. How hot it suddenly was, the heat somehow all that much more intense for the sun hidden behind a high haze. "Carpy . . . You?"

"Yes, miss."

Thinking she might be sick, Pearl rode out a heave of dizziness. She shut her eyes, opened them, found her mother gazing frankly at her. Then Pearl understood: her mother had suffered a brain injury with her stroke or spell or whatever it was that had happened when Carpy had died, with the result that she was under the mad delusion that she was, of all people, Carpy. It was mad but it made more sense than what her mother was claiming. But then what had happened to Carpy? An even worse thought now struck: her mother, who had killed before, had done Carpy in as well.

"Carpy," she said, strategically, "what do you think about seeing a doctor?"

Carpy smiled as if she'd expected as much. "And say what?"

"Try to see it from my perspective," pleaded Pearl.

"Yes, I understand it is difficult."

"So you'll go?"

"And what, tell some quack that I took your mother's body and he thinks right, Florence is off her nut, so chucks me in the bin. Is that what you want? Is that what Charles wants? Is that what's best all round?"

Pearl understood that regardless of the truth, she, they, all of them, were stuck with the story.

In a grave and sober tone, she, *Carpy*, said, "I assure you it is the truth, miss."

"Truth," echoed Pearl, as if it were a novel concept. Certainly, her mother, if it was her mother, had Carpy's manner and delivery down to a T. "Explain."

"She was ready."

"What are you talking about? Ready? Ready for what?"

"To move on. She did not love Charley."

"And so you . . ." Pearl could scarcely speak, could scarcely think. "You exited your body and, and *entered* hers?"

"In part, yes."

"In part? In what part? And what of her, is she in there with you?" Pearl envisioned a body with two souls, two beings in one. "Mother," she whispered, urgent, pleading, desperate. "Are you there?"

"Listen," said Carpy, "listen, miss, and I will explain. I siphoned her off out of her body and into a bottle."

This was even more mad. "Wait. What?"

"I mean that I did exactly what I said."

"But why? Why trap her in a bottle?" hissed Pearl. "Why punish her?"

"Punish? No. Not at all. To have allowed her soul to disperse into the—" she gestured with her cheroot—"into the air, that would have been punishment. That would have been cruel, like condemning a weak swimmer to the middle of the ocean, whereas in the bottle she is a weak swimmer in a small pond."

"But she is in a bottle!"

"She is safe."

"Safe? How? Where? What will become of her?"

"A reasonable question, miss, a reasonable question indeed, one I've been mulling. I think I see a way through. Or saw," she added, her brow darkening. And she went on to explain that Florence could move on to a different body, that she, Carpy, could do this. She'd done it once, she could do it again. She blew smoke and, pointing to it, said, "Breath. Life. Prana."

Pearl watched the smoke disperse. "And you simply exhaled your own soul into my mother's vacated body? Like filling a balloon?"

Carpy stood taller. She appeared to be gazing from a high tower. "You breathe out, then you must breathe in."

But Pearl shook her head. "This is mad. You're mad."

"This is theosophy. This is yoga. You see, I've not been as idle or gormless as you have always assumed. Indeed, there is more to the world than you have always assumed."

Pearl let this pass. "What, all we have to do is find her a body? We are now to become Burke and Hare?"

"No," cautioned Carpy. "We need a live one."

"Then we are kidnappers."

Carpy leaned closer and whispered, "Lewis."

"Lewis?" Pearl again glanced toward the maid who, seeing that there was intense discussion underway, was keeping a discreet distance.

"She's a right little cunt," said Carpy, nodding at an inarguable fact. "But she's young and healthy and has a fine bit of a figure as I'm sure you'll agree, as I'm sure your Osmo agrees as well, unfortunately. He fancies her. It don't take no genius to suss that."

Pearl could not argue.

"It's a dilemma," conceded Carpy. "For you wouldn't want your mum taking up residence in Lewis only to be ogled by Mr. Beattie now would you? No, that wouldn't do at all. So, we'll leave Lewis be. But don't fret. We'll find someone else. There's time. There's plenty of time. Your mum's not going anywhere."

"Which bottle is she in?"

"The one in the parlour, with the ship."

Pearl went home and found the ship-in-a-bottle. A bark or ketch or sloop, she did not know exactly what style of ship it was. Certainly, it was finely crafted, right down to the rigging and the sails and even the tiny painted figure of the woman on deck with windblown hair.

"Mother..." She held the bottle close and whispered, "Mummy..."

✦

FLORENCE REACHED OUT WITH PHANTOM hands to touch her daughter but met only the sheer, hard, light-refracting surface of the glass. It had taken months to make sense of what had happened to her. At first, she'd put it down to an ongoing nightmare, or some delusion brought on by the heart spasm, or the laudanum. Perhaps I am deranged, she'd thought. Before departing on her honeymoon with Gloster, Carpy had done her best to explain things to Florence but it had been too soon to grasp it.

Fortunately, there was sunlight whose radiance filled her and surrounded her so that it was as though she *was* sunlight. And, strangely, free. Unfettered by a body, she could go anywhere after a fashion. Australia? She was there. Limerick, the house in which she had grown up? She was there. The rolling pin with which she'd coshed Davis Milton who had been molesting her, plus that shrew of a wife who stood by and watched? She held it in her hand, knew again its heft and shape, the cloud pattern of flour clinging to it, the dead grey light of the scullery with its odour of coal smoke and bacon fat, the sensation of that hardwood rod striking bony skull. It was all there like the sets for a theatre production, whether in her memory alone or in some other dimension she had no idea. And yet at the same time she could not escape the bottle, at the same time she was there and yet not there. She was a creature of mind, of essence without substance. Her consolation was the sunlight, the radiance—she fairly groaned aloud it was so satisfying. And if it was only a manner of speaking, for she had no body, no lungs, no tongue or lips with which to taste or kiss or sing, it seemed no less tangible. She would press her phantom palms to the glass walls, she would scream to be heard, or she would laugh or she would sing and hear her own high, hard voice, but there was nothing that anyone else detected. As for the one whom she so dearly wished to contact, he had yet to respond.

Doctor Meadows paid her a visit. Or that is to say his spirit, his presence, his essence. He did not dwell upon the experience of being hung by the neck until dead, recounting instead how he had murdered the two women out of love for Florence. Florence felt stricken. Meadows, however, was philosophical. He was also bemused, speaking of himself in the third person, with a new perspective, one he had never known while alive, and which offered him solace. Florence felt sympathy and she was grateful for the companionship, finding him much more palatable dead than alive. To her surprise and relief, he did not linger overly long, for in death he had discovered tact. He had a journey to make, his own path to follow, and was soon gone. She almost missed him.

The winter months of overcast and rain were difficult. She found herself curling inward, drifting and somnolent, fogged and grey, and then with spring and the return of the longer days and brighter sunlight she unfurled. She had watched the flowers in the garden and the trees in the yard do the same, drift into slumber and then stir to wakefulness with their bright, innocent, incomparable optimism.

✦

WHAT PEARL DID NOT UNDERSTAND was why Carpy had taken her mother's body. To rescue a dying woman's soul was noble, yet to take possession of her body—a body that was ill—was strange indeed. Carpy anticipated these questions and one afternoon, arriving in Gloster's gig to take tea, clarified the fundamental misconception.

"It was not your mother's body that was dying, but her spirit that had had enough. When you did not come home that night, she thought you'd gone and topped yourself."

Yes, Pearl knew how foolish she'd been. "But," she said, "is not the spirit eternal?"

"I did not say it wasn't. I said that it had had enough of things as they were." Seeing Pearl's confusion, she said, "She wanted to move on."

"But she was getting married," cried Pearl.

"She was fond of Charley but she didn't love him. There's the man she loves." And she pointed to the picture of the hussar.

"I don't even know if he is my father."

"Not the point then, is it? Your mum'd hardly be the first person to love a fantasy."

"I thought I killed her," said Pearl.

"I thought so too, at first."

"But how can you know, how can you be sure about any of this?" insisted Pearl, suspicious, desperate.

Carpy's eyes softened and widened and her tone of voice took on a rare note of wonder. "She knew—she knows—that I love Charley. I'd been seeing him for years at the meetings of the Theosophical Society, he gave me rides home during which we talked, but we were from opposite ends of the hierarchy, weren't we, him at the top and me at the bottom. She asked me to make him happy. It only made sense that I take her body. I had to take her body, otherwise he'd never look at me. And why should Charley, why should *Charles*, be made to suffer?"

+

GLOSTER WAS TROUBLED BY THE fact that Florence seemed distant with Pearl and oblivious of her grandson. She'd changed, she was different, but he asked himself what he knew about mothers and daughters much less grandchildren. Give him a cobra or a glowing corpse. One morning he saw Pearl pushing the perambulator along one of the Beacon Hill paths, just her and little Osmo. They exchanged formalities and he dutifully tickled Osmo Junior who gurgled and waved his arms. Then, before Pearl could go on her way, he confessed that he was worried.

"No, not exactly worried," he clarified, though his frowning expression said otherwise.

Pearl guessed what was coming and felt both eager and ill.

"I was wondering if you have noticed any . . ." He hesitated. "Changes in your mother since our return."

Before Pearl could respond, he said that he understood that travel affected people in different ways, some people bowled over by it and others scarcely touched. He'd known men to yawn with boredom on the banks of the Ganges at dawn or be unmoved by the Taj on the full moon.

"What sort of changes?" she asked, feeling like a fraud.

He winced and sucked air through his teeth.

Again, she waited.

"In many ways I am relieved, I am happy," he said.

To her confusion, Pearl was disappointed to hear this. Could he actually prefer Carpy?

"Her interests have broadened," he explained. "It might have been the temples of Kyoto or Ayutthaya. They are most impressive."

Pearl nodded as if she understood.

"And certain priests with whom we had interviews. And, of course, Madame B. in Madras."

"You find her more spiritually inclined," offered Pearl.

"Much. Much." .

It was September and hot. He was wearing a cream linen suit and perspiring. Pearl recalled the beard she had worn as part of her disguise. She did not envy men beards. In the distance some lads were running. Small marauders, she thought. Would young Osmo be joining them one day, would he defy her and run off to sea or to join the army or perhaps be a policeman like his father who might take him aside and caution him regarding the duplicity of women?

"But there are other things," Gloster admitted. "I don't know. Small things, odd things." He paused and regarded Pearl, who understood this as an invitation to enlighten him and hopefully ease his concern.

What could she say? "I'm not sure. She has always been . . . been a bit of an enigma. What do you think has happened, what is going on with her?"

He stood away, stretching his shoulders back and looking up as if to consult the sky. "I know she has a history," he said, still gazing upward.

"Then you know more than I."

"Ha." He lowered his gaze then shrugged.

Again Pearl wondered what she could possibly say. Surely he, with all his Angel Glow and theosophy, must be knowledgeable regarding souls and the Bardo and reincarnation. But what would he think of his being married to Carpy? Or was she doing him a disservice? "What, sir, if I may be blunt, what drew you to my mother? I mean to say, you knew she was not in the least mystical." She almost added: or was he merely desperate and his options few?

"I do not honestly know. A certain sadness?"

"And is that gone?"

"Something is gone, but something else is there in its place." He shrugged.

"How is Dot faring?" asked Pearl.

"Dot," said Gloster. He frowned then smiled then frowned again. "Very kind of your mother to take her in on Carpenter's behalf," he said ambiguously.

"It was. I hope she is not proving burdensome."

"Well, I must say that your mother is very patient with her. And Dot is diverting after a fashion. Rather like a large hound forever knocking things over. Bit of a bull in a china cabinet."

"Oh dear."

They mused upon Dot.

"Mother has evolved an interest in theosophy, that . . . that is good, is it not?"

"At first I thought she was merely indulging her silly old husband," he said. "But it seems deep and sincere."

"You are surrounded by singular females."

"Indeed, I am."

Pearl wondered if he included her.

✦

PEARL ALSO WONDERED IF SHE herself was mad to believe that Carpy was inhabiting her mother's body. Did it not make more sense that her mother was simply deluded? She wrote to Edwin Simon Dale of the Provincial Lunatic Asylum in New

Westminster, on the mainland. He replied promptly, saying that it was an intriguing case and must be handled with care or risk driving the patient deeper into her delusion. They were, however, in luck, for Doctor Dale was coming to Victoria on business. And yet how to bring him and her mother together without her suspecting he was a doctor? Pearl thought of engaging Mr. Gloster but that would mean revealing the delusion of being Carpy and Pearl feared the consequences, her mother thinking Pearl had betrayed her on the one hand and on the other that Mr. Gloster might actually believe that he had in fact married Carpy. Could she say that Doctor Dale was a colleague of Osmo's? That too would require revealing more than was prudent. A chance encounter at the Tipperary Tea Room? But how would that work? Oh, Mother, here is a strange man who wishes to take tea with us? Or could he be Miranda's father the admiral? Yet what if he could not pass for a seafaring man? And it would mean involving Miranda in the ruse. No, she revisited the idea of being direct. Under the circumstances, Doctor Dale agreed, and so Pearl invited her mother to tea and was forthright enough to say that there was someone she'd very much like her to meet. To her relief, and at the same time suspicion, her mother did not ask for details, and so on the appointed hour she arrived in Gloster's gig.

It was an icy November afternoon and she was dressed in a fur collar and matching hat. They went into the parlour.

"I see that Lewis has yet to learn the art of laying a proper fire," she said, noting the black scorch marks on the hardwood beyond the tilework fronting the fireplace. "Is Osmo in love with her?" She gazed at Pearl, eyebrows up and expression blunt.

Pearl's eyes filled with tears of indignation. There was no doubt the remark was more suited to Carpy than her mother. Or had her mother sunk so deeply into this other persona?

"And where is our mystery guest?" She sniffed and looked around as if he might be in a corner.

A moment later the gate clapped and Pearl met him at the door. He was younger than expected, perhaps thirty-five, slim, tall, clean shaven, dressed snugly in dark grey wool. She ushered him into the parlour and made introductions and soon they were seated before the fire. Lewis entered with tea and scones.

"Where do you practice?" asked Florence.

"New Westminster."

"Ah." Florence nodded and pursed her lips and smiled a little. Her sliding glance touched Pearl then caromed away and she busied herself with a scone and observed that it was the work of a mason. "And what brings you to Victoria, Doctor?" She stirred sugar into her tea then tinged the spoon once on the rim of the cup. "Not me, I hope," she added, levelling her amused gaze at the young man.

Doctor Dale maintained an easy manner, not too casual and not too official. He praised Florence's powers of perception.

Florence waved this off. "My daughter thinks I am quite mad."

"And are you?"

This earned a loud laugh. It was not a laugh Pearl recognized, belonging neither to her mother nor Carpy. Had the two merged to create a third person, an altogether different person? Or was the more accurate term persona? She looked her mother in the eyes and her mother looked back and for a moment there was something unexpected: understanding, sympathy. This passed, however, and a door shut and Pearl saw anger.

"Mad?" Florence laughed that strange laugh, mocking and indulgent and somewhat fatigued as if she'd heard it before.

"Your daughter is concerned," said Doctor Dale quietly.

"My daughter."

"Yes, Mother," said Pearl, "your daughter, remember me?"

"My dear, you are rather difficult to forget."

Pearl heard the implications, that she was as demanding and bothersome as ever. She also knew that this was not her mother speaking. No. This was her mother as Carpy, angry that even after having explained everything Pearl would persist in rejecting it.

"It is," suggested Doctor Dale, "extraordinary, wouldn't you agree?"

"This tea is extraordinary," said Florence, wincing and setting her cup down then pushing it to the far side of the brass table. "Really, that girl." She found her Sultans.

"You never used to smoke," said Pearl.

"And this signifies to you that I am a madwoman." She sent a plume of smoke toward the ceiling where she discovered cobwebs. Indicating the corner above and to the left of the fireplace, she asked what it was that Lewis occupied herself with all day.

They all considered the wobbly grey mesh pulsing in the rising heat.

Doctor Dale asked Florence if she dreamed.

Pearl's mother, or Carpy in Florence's body, either way this persona Pearl did not recognize, regarded the doctor with indulgence. "Often."

"And are they ... pleasant dreams?"

"I dream dreams of dreams," she said as if quoting poetry. "Are yours?"

Doctor Dale smiled and tipped his head side to side meaning sometimes yes, sometimes no. "Occasionally I dream of falling."

"Occasionally I dream of soaring. Does that signify that I am an optimist whereas you are a pessimist?"

"It is not as easy as that."

"No?" She pouted and considered the glowing tip of her cheroot. "I suppose the lunatics in your asylum exhibit a fascinating array of behaviours. I should think it dizzying, or tedious. I mean, really, what would be more tiresome than listening to another fellow's dreams day in, day out? Rather like listening to them bang on about their aches and pains."

"Is that the bottle into which you siphoned the soul of Florence Greyland-Smith?" He was pointing to the ship-in-a-bottle on the table before the window.

"Now who is being mad, Doctor? Did Pearl tell you that?"

"So it is not?"

"Ask her."

Both Florence and Doctor Dale looked at Pearl, who could only gaze back helplessly.

"Why is Pearl so concerned, then? Do you have any theories?"

"Theories? We live in an age of theories, medical and metaphysical. Some theorize that there are men on the moon. But you know, her father was whimsical. That is he in the photo."

The doctor considered the hussar. "He appears a feet-on-the-ground sort of fellow."

"Well, if you ever met him I assure you that you would think otherwise."

Doctor Dale asked Florence if she considered herself a feet-on-the-ground sort.

She smoked and frowned and reflected. "Parenthood forces one to be. Especially being a woman alone. Do you have children, Doctor?"

He grew fond. "Three daughters."

"Oh my. Look out." She ground her cheroot against the scone then left the butt.

Pearl stared in disbelief. Her mother was deranged and sly. Had she not always been sly when it came to her origins? But sly was too strong, too defamatory. Clever? Or merely prudent? Why, though? Was she really the woman in the newspaper clipping who had killed her employer? Pearl looked to Doctor Dale and shrugged.

Florence too shrugged and then spoke of how rare it was that things were simply light and dark, that they were rather more often mid-tones and shades, fogs and mists.

When the doctor had gone and Pearl and Florence were alone, Florence, in the cold tones of Carpy, said, "Ah, miss, clearly I misjudged you."

✦

OSMO ASKED PEARL IF ANYTHING was amiss between her and her mother. Pearl admitted that her mother had returned somewhat altered by her travels and Osmo expressed his hope that his mother-in-law might pay a bit more attention to her grandson.

This was awkward, for Pearl found her mother's company stressful. Whether it was her mad mother or whether this was indeed Carpy in her mother's body no longer was the issue, Pearl could bear neither of them. This aversion made her feel guilty for she feared she was abandoning her mother to her madness. What to do? She told her mother Osmo's concern that she was not paying enough attention to her grandson.

"I never much liked rug rats," Carpy admitted.

"For the sake of appearances," said Pearl.

"Of course. Understood," said Carpy. "By all means, the veil of appearances." She passed her hand before her face as though a master of metamorphosis.

Pearl saw that they shared the bond of wishing to avoid each other and at the same time had no choice but to accept their entwined destinies.

Inevitably she thought of the novel *The Strange Case of Dr. Jekyll and Mr. Hyde.* This offered little solace or understanding, in fact it made it worse because perhaps it was based on reality, meaning such things did occur. She had little choice but to plod onward. Perhaps things would work out, perhaps her mother would come round. Time, the great healer.

And yet while time did not heal it did effect change. There was some small relief in the fact that the more Pearl saw Carpy, the less she saw her mother. For all that it was her mother's body, the animating spirit was someone else. The eyes were different, the manner was different, the way she moved, the way she ate, the way she laughed, sighed, and spoke was different; everything in fact that really mattered was different. Of course, Carpy did her best to be Florence when circumstances demanded but the effort was often too much, and she occasionally let slip a *fecking* this and *fecking* that. Certainly, the extended honeymoon had given Carpy a more worldly and sophisticated polish. She had explored the night market of Kowloon, the floating market of Bangkok, sipped gin-and-tonics at Raffles, talked theosophy with Madame Blavatsky in Madras, bathed in the Ganges at Benares, meditated in Bodh Gaya, even visited Longwood House, Napoleon's residence-in-exile, on St. Helena. At times Carpy paraded these experiences as war medals, as heroic accomplishments, at others she seemed genuinely matured by them and a dusk-like calm inhabited her eyes. Occasionally, she even dandled Osmo Junior on her lap.

Osmo Senior dandled his son as well. If he did not love Pearl any more than she loved him, he was a devoted father. He tossed him in the air and played peekaboo, which reassured Pearl.

Less reassuring was her husband's attitude toward Lewis. She was a fine one, Lewis, knowing just the line to walk, and all too aware of her own beauty compared to Pearl who by contrast felt like an ox. There might be no love between Pearl and Osmo, but it still hurt to see him looking so longingly at Lewis. Did his hand ever stray to her shapely arm or rest reassuringly upon her shoulder? And as for Lewis, did the trollop brush against him? Pearl considered dismissing her and hiring an old woman but could imagine Osmo's outrage.

"I had stomach pains all day yet again from Lewis's so-called cuisine."

"I felt fine."

"She's sullen."

"So are you."

Just what had happened to the man once so besotted with finding the mystery killer? Pearl vividly recalled watching Osmo confess to her mother how distraught he was. She could still see him sprawled exhausted in the chair in the parlour, his normally impeccable hair a mess, his tie, his shirt, everything awry, his entire manner bespeaking devastation. He was a lover who had lost his woman. He was at the edge of the world, looking into the abyss. Where was that man? Where was that passion? Or was it merely an obsession with control, merely an issue of alignment that had to be corrected so that everything was in its proper place and performing its proper function, like the cogs in an engine, like her, his wife? Is this what a family was, is this what the Victorian family had become, some sort of device whose component parts must mesh and whirr? How romantic. Apparently matters of the heart had been reduced to mechanics. It seemed to be how the dominant powers of the day approached their goals: with increasingly efficient machines to cut and build and subdue.

Pearl found herself resorting to brandy in the evenings and was relieved when Osmo turned his back to her in bed, for she had begun to think that, with only one child, she retained a small measure of mobility and she might yet, as her mother had done, make an escape. It even occurred to her—mad notion but nonetheless there it was—to kill Osmo and then enjoy a dignified widowhood at the age of twenty. Of course, to deprive little Osmo Junior of the protection, guidance, and love of a father was not right, no, not right at all. She gazed into the wet little nuggets of her son's eyes and wondered if he divined her thoughts? Could infants—souls newly coalesced from out of the aether—do that? Pearl cradled him in her arms and looked out the window at the stony sky. She felt even more trapped, encircled by guilt in the form of her son, obligation in the form of her husband, and competition in the form of Lewis. She looked to the bottle with the ship and her mother's spirit and was about to remark to her that they were both of them in bottles, but that would be maudlin and, whether true or not, hardly a fair comparison. Then again, if she were to take up her pen and transform it all into a novel or anonymous memoir that might offer Pearl a means of escape even if only imaginary. It occurred to her to resume stealing as a means of generating material. She might plan and commit a most outrageous theft and then write about it under an alias. She might resurrect Alexander Nyle.

✦

POSITIONED OPPOSITE THE PHOTOGRAPH OF the one and only man whom she'd ever truly loved, Florence recalled how she had often given up hope, warning herself that it had not been love at all but a passing infatuation and nothing more, and hence she must forget him and move on. At times she'd been successful and had got on with her life, devoting her attentions to her house and her daughter. Nonetheless, she had followed the exploits of the overseas forces in the newspapers, telling herself that she was merely staying informed as any good citizen should, but in fact scouring for mention of a Greyland-Smith. The challenge was that as years had passed, she lost track of where fantasy ended and fact began. Did she believe that he was alive and had forgotten her, or that he was dead and his spirit hadn't been able to find her? Could spirits lose their way and go adrift? Or perhaps he was fated to be somewhere else? Not for the first time she decided that she was a madwoman who had spun out a story and fallen in love with it. And the truth was that she had been strategic. Only when Pearl had reached the age of three and begun asking questions did Florence have the photograph enlarged and framed and hung it on the wall so that there would be an answer to the inevitable questions and some tangible figure for her to look at. And then she had written all the letters.

Gazing at his picture, Florence had little else to do but indulge her nostalgia, and recalled her first impression of him in the train station, which, above all else, was that his uniform was pompous. What a lot of unnecessary flash, standing there with his silk and braid and sword, or was it—oh do excuse me—a sabre. And then, to her alarm, he discovered her looking at him, worse he smiled and nodded and then, her alarm rising to horror, he'd approached and offered her a good morning and asked if he could carry her bag, which caused her to clutch it more tightly given that it was stuffed taut with the jewellery she'd taken—taken, not stolen—taken as her due from the Miltons. Still, she supposed that he was doing his bit as a well-bred fellow, even if she was not a well-bred lady, though how could he know that, unless of course he knew exactly that, that he saw right through her and was counting upon it for his own nefarious ends? Such had been her thinking and the reason she had thanked him and said no, he need not carry her bag, she could carry her own bag. To her surprise and irritation and, admit it, intrigue, he'd laughed as if delighted, as if that was the best response she could have given, certainly better than: Oh, yes, thank you ever so much, kind sir.

And there he was the next morning on the platform, offering her that cup of tea. The evil glint, she noted, was gone from his eyes, quelled perhaps by the cold and sobering dawn. Or maybe that was just it, he was sober. Not that she couldn't have done with a large hot whiskey herself that frozen morning. If the weather hadn't chilled her the sight of the Pinkertons had.

"By dint of dire circumstance, we find ourselves flung together," he'd said once they were safe in his compartment and the train had reached speed.

Sometime later, quite out of the blue, as the train was rhythmically lolloping across the plains, he'd turned from the window and asked, "Is ballast a burden? Even if it enables you to ride low and steady in the water?" She had no idea what to say. She wasn't sure he expected an answer. He'd resumed his brooding, shoulder against the wall of the compartment, looking out the window at all that land sliding past.

But years had slid past as well, and he had not found her and she'd felt betrayed then ridiculous and, as a result, closed herself off and put all of that behind her until, for her own sake as well as Pearl's, she let herself be swayed by sweet Mr. Charles Gloster.

✦

WHEN THE PHOSPHORESCENCE WAS AT its peak, they planned a pilgrimage to the beach. Gloster and Carpy—Pearl had finally accepted that it was she—and Dot came to the house for a late meal beforehand hosted by Pearl and Osmo. Dot had adapted well to life at Gloster's. She was fascinated by all his antiquities though deeply disappointed that Cleopatra, the cobra, had died and the glass tank was empty. At the phosphorescence party at Pearl's, Dot discovered the ship-in-a-bottle in the parlour, exclaiming that it matched the other ship-in-a-bottle at Gloster's. She was intrigued to see two the same, and she sat a long time studying it and concluded that the woman in this bottle must be the twin sister to the woman in the other bottle.

"Like me," she said, "Desiree and I were twins."

"Come outside and join us, Dot," urged Carpy.

Dot nodded though stayed where she was.

Carpy regarded her then went out, leaving her to come in her own time. In the yard incense sticks burned to keep off the mosquitos. The setting sun cast long shadows and fiery red light upon the ceiling of clouds. "It's perfect," said Carpy who had consulted the almanac. "No moon."

"The ancient Hellenes believed that the moon affects the blood," observed Gloster.

"Selene," said Carpy.

"Yes." For all his concerns, Gloster was pleased with his wife's evolving interest in natural phenomena. He had been delighted when she began accompanying him to the meetings of the Theosophical Society.

At midnight the party travelled in two carriages to the beach.

"Thank you for indulging me," Pearl said to Osmo.

He smiled thinly and gave her hand a bit of a pat, or was it a swat?

Pearl knew he thought it a load of bunk and was only going along because Lewis was enthused and it placated his burdensome wife. But Pearl was determined to enjoy the phosphorescence. She would take pleasure when and where she could. Bottles for collecting the water were passed around, trouser cuffs rolled, the hems of skirts gathered and pinned, and off they marched barefoot down the cool and gritty sand. The tide was high and the water mild as it washed luminous about their legs. It was as though fireworks were going off in the sea, as if aquatic fireflies were dancing. Soon Gloster and Carpy, Pearl and Lewis, and even Osmo were dipping their bottles and then holding them up and shaking them to admire the small miracle of liquid white fire.

Dot had waded out farther than anyone else, until the water was up to her waist. "Goodbye and farewell," she called. "Safe voyage," she added and waved her arm.

"Dot," said Carpy, "whatever are you doing?"

"I have launched the ship in the bottle."

No one understood.

Then Pearl and Carpy, who had both seen Dot admiring the ship-in-a-bottle in the parlour, suffered a stab of panic. "Dot!" cried Carpy. "What have you done?"

Dot laughed. "Yes. She's off. She's away. She's free!"

Pearl and Carpy both waded in farther and then began to flail. Gloster and Osmo went in after them and, battling the strength of the tide, pulled their wives back out onto the dry sand.

"She told me," said Dot, ploughing her way back to shore. "I talked to her."

"Who?"

"The lady in the bottle. She wanted to go. She said so."

Pearl put her hands to her face and sobbed in horror.

"Dot!"

Seeing their disapproval, Dot began to pout. She stared down and crossed her arms over her chest and grew sullen. "She asked me. She said please."

They all strained their eyes to spot some glint of the glass in the waves, but there was so much glitter and froth that it was impossible to tell bottle from sea from light.

"Good God," said Osmo, as if this was yet one more in an interminable list of aggravations, "is it that important? I'll buy you another."

"It was an elegant ship," ventured Lewis with uncharacteristic sensitivity, "and the figure of the lady so lifelike. I often talked to her."

With a groan, Osmo stripped off his vest and shirt and plunged into the water and swam out then went back and forth, side to side, searching with his hands outstretched, but the bottle was gone.

✦

FLORENCE HAD BEEN MORE THAN a little fearful of Dot's intense interest in the bottle. It was as if a bear had sniffed something too intriguing to ignore. Dot had talked to her, saying how much she missed her sister Des. Florence had found herself cringing with foreboding.

"Des said she'd always be here. One way or another. Des knew things, big things. But me I've got a small brain. Everyone says so. And you, miss," Dot asked, "where are you off to in your ship? Are you trapped in there? Would you like me to set you free? I think you do," concluded Dot, wise and magnanimous. "A boat should float," she said, pleased with the rhyme.

When Dot had hidden the bottle under her jumper and packed it down to the beach Florence panicked. But what could she do? And then she found herself sailing end-over-end through the air and plopping *kerplunk* into the sea and then bobbing and rolling and the phosphorescence wrapping itself all around her like a whirling robe of fireflies. This was followed by all the hullabaloo from the shore. How close Osmo had come to retrieving her, his fingers missing her by mere inches.

Now the tide was taking her out through the luminescence. It was as if she were journeying through meteor showers. She and her hussar had watched meteors from the train, a fireworks display celebrating them which had made him laugh while she'd only smiled.

"You're a tough nut," he'd said.

"I could be bounded in a nutshell," she'd responded.

"I would very much like to crack that nut," he'd said. "If you were willing."

"Why?"

"So that the seed can sprout and the tree grow and I can sit in its shade."

"I think I've had enough shade for one life," she said.

"Then step into the sun."

"It's midnight," she said. "Or had you not noticed the moon?"

He'd shrugged. "Sun, moon, they both glow."

The bottle rolled in the waves and continued away from the shore. By the time dawn had drowned the stars in light, Florence had had many visitors who'd told her many stories and assured her that in the fullness of time's eternity she would meet everyone she was meant to meet with perhaps a few extra thrown in for good measure, and that after its fashion all would be well, for it was the nature of fate, that oblique, remorseless, and whimsical force, that it did not recognize any distinction between stories and facts, the quick and the dead, but travelled its own course, blind even unto itself, but forever drawn toward life.

✦

PEARL WAS SHOWN HER FIRST-CLASS compartment; she thanked the porter and tipped him a nickel for carrying her trunk, then settled little Osmo. Moments later the train lurched, shunted, and with a slow squeal of wheels began drawing away from the station. She'd been in Vancouver one night and already she was leaving but what choice did she have? She felt trapped in her marriage and knew that Osmo felt the same and, worse, that he blamed her. She could not live this way. Better to start over, to remake herself. True, she was taking little Osmo from his father, an act many would rate utterly selfish. Should she remain then, sacrifice the next twenty years of her life, until her son was on his own, enduring her husband's scarcely suppressed rage? She'd tried but could not do it. What she might be able to do is pass herself off as a widow. That had been her mother's plan, albeit in different circumstances. Of course, there were public records and Osmo would initiate a search, meaning that she had to get far away as soon as possible. She would go to the United States and from there perhaps England or France or Argentina or Australia. This meant procuring a passport, which would require money. It had occurred to her to beg Miranda for help but pride had prevented her. In the end she'd gone to her stepfather, Charles Gloster, visiting him when Carpy and Dot were on their afternoon walk, something Dot could not live without.

Gloster had listened with his characteristic patience and solemnity, frowning and nodding and making musing noises as she described her circumstances. They were in his library with its books and desk and artefacts, and the glass case that had once been home to his cobra, Cleopatra.

"Does your mother know?" he asked.

"You tell me," said Pearl with more edge to her voice than she'd intended.

Gloster's eyebrows rose. He cleared his throat and regarded her with his yellowed eyes. "She has not said anything. But I for one have noted a certain lack of," he paused, "amicability between you and Osmo."

"I just need a little money."

"More than a little," he said, as if he knew whereof he spoke.

"I'm sorry."

"This is a grave step. And I am an accomplice."

She repeated that she was sorry and hung her head, feeling both remorse and impatience. Help me, don't help me, she thought, but let us be done with this ordeal.

In the end he'd been more than generous and had promised discretion as well.

$$+$$

NOW, ON THE TRAIN DRAWING out of Vancouver, she watched the darkly glittering water of Burrard Inlet slide past. How close those mountains across the way were, and how high. *Looming*, that was the word. She settled deeper into the padded leather seat next to little Osmo. It was the first time she'd been to Vancouver and the first time she'd been on a train. What a lot of adventures you are having, she told herself. It occurred to her that this might well be the scene with which to open a novel, for she had resolved that this must be her path, she would write. She gazed around the compartment. What a snug affair. Everything so perfectly fitted in dark wood and burnished metal and oiled leather.

"What do you think, Osmo?" she asked her son, who blinked his wide, dark eyes.

First we need to give you a new name. She thought: John,

Robert, Daniel. No, no, and no. Something more distinctive. Alexander? Alex? She frowned out the window at the ships along the wharves and imagined them pitching and rolling in the middle of the ocean, and inevitably thought of her mother in the bottle, or the little wooden figure in the bottle who had come to represent her in Pearl's mind. She still did not know what was what, still could not wholly accept Carpy's—or was it her brain-damaged mother's—mad story. What a thing was the mind, as evanescent as mist and yet as adamant as iron. Was that not her in a nutshell?

The train began to slow down and came to a puffing halt at New Brighton. A grassy field sloped down past the post and telegraph office to a hotel and wharf. On the far shore a large ship appeared to be taking on lumber. What complex affairs were ships with all those masts and spars and booms and rigging. She imagined marine engineers bent over broad sheets of paper with their pencils and straightedges and compasses. Perhaps she should rename Osmo after a ship. Caravel? Galleon? Bark? Brig? Brig Beattie. Brig Greyland-Smith. Was a brig a ship or the gaol on a ship? She thought of Miranda who only days before had sailed with her father the admiral on a steamship for England. Ketch. Yawl. Schooner. A schooner was also a beer glass. Benjamin? That was not bad, it had weight. She unlatched the window and raised it and leaned out to inhale the morning air but even though they were at a halt in the station the air was tainted with smoke from the engine. She shut the window and sat back. It was mid-October and the leaves red and gold. She was heading into winter. She looked at her son. "We must go south. What do you think?" He blinked and yawned.

The whistle blew and once again the train lurched and shunted and began its slow, aching advance, the wheels ticking along the rails and the smoke rolling past. The rhythm soon lulled Osmo to sleep. Ulysses? Jack? Hieronymus? A hierophant was a keeper of secrets. In her books she would be a revealer of secrets. She thought of Carpy and Mr. Gloster, both secretive in their way. Charles. Yes. There was a name that was both kingly and regal. Now the trees blocked the view of the water as well as the sunlight and Pearl discovered her reflection looking back at her from the window. She reached out hesitantly with her forefinger, as did her reflection, and they, the two of them, strangers but identical, touched fingertips from either side of that wall of glass as the train picked up speed.

About the Author

GRANT BUDAY is the author of the novels *Dragonflies*, *White Lung*, *Sack of Teeth*, *Rootbound*, *The Delusionist*, *Atomic Road*, and *Orphans of Empire*, the memoir *Stranger on a Strange Island*, and the travel memoir *Golden Goa*. His novels have been nominated for the City of Vancouver book prize, the City of Victoria Book Prize, and the BC and Yukon Book Prizes. His articles and essays have been published in Canadian magazines, and his short fiction has appeared in *The Journey Prize Anthology* and *Best Canadian Short Stories*. He lives on Mayne Island, British Columbia.